CW00867579

The Easterling

The Easterling

Legends of Avalyne Book 2

Linda Thackeray

Contents

Yesterday

She was too far away from the river.

Ninuie knew this because she could barely feel the connection to Yantra-hai, the great river of Avalyne. If she were closer, she would be able to defend herself; but the enemy was wily, barring her from it. The river was her place of power, and as long as they remained separated she was diminished. Since the pursuit began, every effort to escape the forest and reach the shore had been in vain. The enemy was there at every turn.

With no choice but to retreat into the shadows of Iolan's ancient woods, Ninuie could feel her withering link to the river, and it made her heart sink with dismay. Like a thread being pulled tighter and tighter, she knew it would not be long before it snapped completely and she would be defenceless. It was a stark contrast to the growing menace overpowering her senses as the enemy closed in on her. Their paws thundered across the ground until she could feel the vibration against the soles of her bare feet.

They were experienced pack hunters and they outflanked her from the river and the forest, keeping her trapped between them. Helpless to escape, she knew with anguish they were converging on her position, and that when each group met there would be no place left to run. She would be helpless to stop them from taking her.

In a moment of desperation, she considered returning to the Man, but sense prevailed. She refused to let her fear endanger him or their child. The enemy would not hesitate to kill them both to gain her subservience. She would not risk them for anything. The Man was an able warrior but he was no match for the servants of the Aeth, and she no longer possessed the ability to protect him.

Near her breaking point, Ninuie continued her desperate flight across the woods while the midnight moon gazed upon her aloofly, indifferent to her plight. Branches clawed at her as she ran past the thick trees and tall shrubs. Around her, the pounding footsteps of the enemy were like a drumbeat in her ears, growing louder with their relentless persistence. Her terror was almost complete now, just like the screaming danger she could feel in every part of her soul.

They were almost upon her, sooner, if her strength gave out first.

Please help me, Water Wife! I am sorry for abandoning you and my sisters! For turning away from the river!

The Celestial goddess chose not to answer. Ninuie uttered a frustrated cry of misery, but desperation made fools of everyone. For the love of the Man, she abandoned everything she knew—her goddess, her sisters and her covenant with Yantrahai. They did not forget nor forgive the slight.

Ironically, she left home this night to go to the river. Ninuie intended to find her sisters and put her affairs in order. She was going to tell them she was leaving with the Man and the Child. She was travelling with him to his land in the east to become his wife and to die a mortal, surrendering her place among their pantheon. It was the proper form so the goddess could appoint another in her place.

The Aeth Lord's servants put an end to her good intentions.

She knew of him of course, the seraf of the dark Celestial Mael, who broke the rules of the Five Realms by entering the Aeth where only the dead resided for all time. Straddling that terrible afterlife and the living world, Balfure harnessed the dark energies of one to become a god in the other. Why he wanted her, she did not know, but fear of his evil kept her from returning home to the Man and Child.

She would risk no harm to them, whatever the cost to herself. She could no longer feel the river or its life pulsing through her and Ninuie knew that Yantra-hai had abandoned her at last. The void it left behind was so absolute that her fear of capture paled in comparison. She wept openly at the loss.

Slowing down, she trudged across the blanket of rotting leaves, surrounded by thick, ancient trees, their branches reaching towards the sky in silent worship. Their leaves created a shroud of darkness Ninuie took comfort in, hoping it would keep her concealed. At least long enough for her to catch her breath.

Despair and exhaustion broke her will to evade and when she reached a clearing, she raised her eyes to the moon and sank to her knees. She shuddered a little when her skin made contact with the damp foliage and the tears on her cheeks glistened beneath the moonlight. She could hear the Enemy closing in on her, hear their paws crush the leaves underfoot as they circled.

Let them come, she thought to herself, *let them take me.*

The Man and the Child are safe. Nothing else mattered.

Chapter One

Chains of Duty

The message came to him on the day of the elven new year.

Nothing in it should have surprised him, but Prince Aeron of Eden Halas was nonetheless affected by its contents. He didn't realise until he read the message how much he dreaded what it would say, and he wished very much for a stay of execution. Reading it over and over again did nothing to lessen its impact and, finally, like a man beaten into exhaustion, he surrendered to his fate.

It was time for him to go home.

In truth, Aeron was surprised the demand to return took as long as it did to come. He expected its arrival following Balfure's defeat and the delay allowed him to become complacent. Of course, it was always inevitable he would have to return home. His father saw no reason for his continued absence from Halas now that the war was done and Aeron had no excuse to remain.

Despite missing his mother and the woods he grew up in, Aeron never felt as bound to Eden Halas as his father or his brothers. Eighteen years ago, he was more than happy to leave his home to help Dare vanquish Balfure from Avalyne. He was closer to Dare than he was to his own brothers and travelling with the exiled heir of Carleon seemed like fate. Once away from the woods, Aeron discovered he enjoyed travelling to new lands and meeting its people, something his brothers and father would never understand.

After the Aeth War, he remained with Dare, making only the occasional visit home to see his mother. Using the excuse he was needed to help Dare with hunting the remnants of Balfure's forces, Aeron was able to avoid his father's request to return permanently. It was always going to be a temporary salve and now it seemed his time in Carleon was done. Aeron knew if he returned to Eden Halas, as requested, it would be to stay.

While he would be happy for a time, reunited with his family, Aeron knew it would not last. After eighteen years away from Eden Halas, he no longer fit in with life there. Isolation was not for him and he would be trapped by the Veil and his father's insistence on keeping the world away from Eden Halas. Everything he had experienced these past years proved he enjoyed being in the world instead of being sequestered from it.

From the first, there was no denying Aeron was cut from a different cloth than his father and sibling. When Dare was brought to Eden Halas, Aeron accepted him with little difficulty, while his older brothers, Hadros and Syannon, took time to warm to the child. His father remained aloof until the day Dare left Halas, and never understood Aeron's decision to accompany him. Being away from home blunted the differences between father and son, but if Aeron remained in Halas permanently, they would become acute. Aeron had no wish to see his mother in pain because of their conflict.

Still, it was more than just the demand to return home that bothered Aeron.

Dare was now a king with a wife and an heir. He had a kingdom to consolidate and strengthen. Kyou, head of Clan Atrayo, had recently wedded his long-time love Hanae in the Jagged Mountains. When the Master Builder completed his work fortifying Sandrine, he would return home to Iridia to begin his life with his bride. Celene was now the Lady of Gislaine and, as wife to Ronen, would be expected to bear him children for their own house. The mage Tamsyn was travelling Avalyne, seeking out acolytes to restore the Order of Enphilim.

And what was he doing? Nothing.

He was doing nothing, and if he returned to Eden Halas he would continue to do nothing. As Aeron walked the sculpted gardens of Sandrine Keep, this bothered him a great deal. Adventuring and fighting Balfure had given Aeron purpose, but those days were now past. His friends were settling down, preparing to live the rest of their lives. Aeron had no such plans. Being immortal, he had no need of them and, until now, did not realise how hollow that felt.

There had to be some purpose to immortality beyond growing stagnant with time.

"Aeron," Dare's sudden call broke him free of his thoughts. "There you are."

The prince glanced briefly at the sky above and was somewhat surprised to see the sun had crested overhead and was beginning its evening descent. It was early afternoon when the message from his father had arrived and he had retreated into the gardens to read it. Now he realised the day had slipped by him without notice.

"I am sorry. I did not mean to be away for so long."

"There is nothing to be sorry for. I merely wondered where you were. I was told that there was a message from your father." Dare stood beside Aeron before one of the ornate fountains in the garden. This one was constructed from blue marble with the likeness of the Water Wife perched up high in the centre.

"Yes," Aeron frowned, clearly implying it was not good news.

"Is it what you feared?"

Although Aeron never spoke to Dare of his anxieties regarding his father, the king suspected Aeron feared that his responsibilities at home would soon draw him back to Eden Halas.

"More or less," Aeron shrugged, not bothering to hide his discontent from his old friend. "My father would like me home as soon as possible."

"And you mean to go," Dare was unable to hide the disappointment from his voice because he could not imagine Aeron being absent from his life. Not only was Aeron family, but they had been constant companions for almost two decades. Dare did not relish the thought of losing his best friend even though it had always been inevitable that they would someday have to part company.

"I do not see that I have any other choice; he is the king after all," Aeron reminded.

"And you are his son, not his possession," Dare pointed out.

"I have responsibilities at home," Aeron countered, but he knew argument was weak. His older brothers Hadros and Syannon were of more use to his father than he. The only reason Halion wished Aeron at home was because he disapproved of his son living a life beyond the Veil. During Balfure's reign it was a necessary evil, but now the Aeth Lord was no more, there was no longer any reason for his continued absence from home.

"You have responsibilities to yourself first," Dare stated firmly, conscious of the fact that while Aeron was more than 950 years older than him, the elf spent very little of that time actually living. As much as Dare loved the elves, he felt their immortality was more a burden than it was a gift from the Celestial Gods. Time was no one's friend when you had too much of it.

"Do you know what your trouble is, elf?"

Aeron stiffened, for Dare did not refer to him that way unless he was about to impart some uncomfortable insight Aeron probably would not wish to hear. Even if he needed to.

"You are more like us that you care to admit. You want more from life than just hiding behind the Veil. You want to experience life, not hide from it."

Aeron flinched uncomfortably because, as always, Dare's observations were not only astute but utterly correct. He was a different elf than the one who left Eden Halas so many years ago. Like the rest of his friends in the Circle, he wanted to accomplish something. It was probably the first time he actually admitted to himself he wanted more out of life than what was expected of him by his father and by his people.

"Even if you are right," the prince conceded, "one does not simply go and tell the king of Eden Halas his son wishes to abandon the kingdom for a different life."

"Life is what you will it to be, not what someone else decides for you. If you feel chained by it then defy the conventions keeping you captive. Do not be chained to duty, Aeron. It will break the spirit far quicker than time."

As much as Dare loathed the idea of Aeron returning to Eden Halas, he would like it even less if the elf resigned himself to an unhappy fate when it could be avoided.

"I do not know what to do," Aeron sighed heavily. "I know you are right, but if I do not return to Eden Halas then what awaits me? You have your own life to live now and I cannot remain here indefinitely. Since leaving Eden Halas, you and I have journeyed from one place or another to rid the world of Balfure. You have stopped running because you have a place to stop. I do not."

Dare would have begged to differ but there was some truth to Aeron's words. Dare would have him remain at Carleon for good but it was not the purpose the elf sought.

"Only because you never considered your existence beyond Halas," Dare countered. "Take some time, Aeron. Think about what you *really* want. You took the first step by leaving Halas with me, and look at what we accomplished together. While I may have my responsibilities to Carleon, there is much you and I can still do together and you will always have a home here."

"Thank you," Aeron replied, touched by the king's offer. They were more than friends and, while not bound in blood, they were still family. Perhaps it was such an in-between that made their bond so strong. "I will do as you suggest; I will give this matter some thought."

"Good," Dare grinned and gestured Aeron to follow him out of the garden, "now come on, we should join the others."

"Yes," Aeron replied, still surprised the time slipped by him so completely.

With Kyou continuing the work on Sandrine's fortifications and both Ronen and Celene in the city for a time, Arianne showed her delight at having so many of their friends present by insisting they shared dinner every night. The nightly meals had become an intimate gathering of friends whose time together was growing shorter and shorter as their lives diverged on different paths. These occasions would become rarer as time went on, and Arianne wanted to savour as much of them as possible.

"I must confess, Aeron, I did have another reason for seeking you," Dare revealed as they took the familiar path back to the Keep. A barely concealed smile of mischief crossed the king's face as he spoke.

"Really?" Aeron threw Dare a sidelong glance as they reached the doors leading into the castle.

"I thought you would be interested in knowing that Melia has just arrived."

Dare's tone was nonchalant even though he was burning with curiosity to see Aeron's reaction.

After their adventure in Sanhael defeating Syphia, while the king and Arianne returned to Carleon, Aeron, Kyou and Melia travelled together towards the Jagged Mountains. Kyou's account of the journey, particularly Aeron's interaction with the lovely watch guard, was a source of great amusement. Their bickering obviously masked an attraction which interested the Circle to no end, since the elf so rarely expressed an attraction for any member of the opposite sex.

Aeron received the news with an expression of stone.

"Melia is here?"

"Yes, Arianne invited her to Carleon for a visit," Dare explained, delighted by Aeron's feigned indifferent to the news. "They became good friends during the quest to defeat Syphia."

"I suppose a watch guard has little choice but to accept an invitation given by the queen," Aeron remarked, trying to hide from Dare this was the best news he could have received after the summons by his father.

Still, he bore no desire to share with anyone how he felt about Melia. In fact, how the prince of Eden Halas felt towards any lady was his own business. Some things were private, not to be confided to even a trusted friend such as Dare. After all, he did not recall the king being any more forthcoming about Arianne before their wedding. If anything, Dare was quite close-mouthed about Arianne, for fear that daring to hope for such a union was foolish.

"She looks well," Dare continued to speak. "Though one wonders why a woman would choose such a life for herself."

"I'm certain she has her reasons," Aeron said quickly, instinctively rising to the lady's defence without a second thought.

"I suppose she must," Dare agreed, hiding his smirk. Dare did not get a chance to know Melia before she left their company all those months ago. Still, she seemed to him a strong woman with deep thoughts she kept to herself. Whether he knew her or not mattered little; she would always have an ally in her king for helping Arianne to save their child.

"She must have travelled a long way to be here," Dare added. "We know almost nothing about the eastern lands from which she originates, beyond the fact that its people were allied to Balfure and our peace with them is a fragile one."

"They considered him their god and we struck him down," Aeron reminded. "Right or wrong, it's a poor foundation to begin any sort of alliance."

"Agreed," Dare sighed with resignation. He wanted time to rebuild Carleon, to restore the wounded spirit of his people before he inflicted another war on them. Though he had been reluctant to extend the friendship across the Burning Plains to the very people who warred against them, Dare knew Carleon could ill afford another conflict after three decades of Occupation. They needed recovery more than vengeance. He only hoped diplomacy would be enough to heal the rift between the east and west, because the alternative was war.

* * *

Melia stared at herself in the mirror of the room she was provided in the Keep and tried to remember how long it had been since she was last required to dress for a dinner. With sadness, she realised it was well before her father's death. Those days seemed so far away now and there were times Melia wondered if that other life was just a dream and this had always been her reality.

Staring at her reflection in the mirror and not seeing the watch guard but the woman in the one dress she owned, Melia could not help think it was a stranger gazing back at her.

The dress was simple, a blue shift clinging tightly at the bodice with flowing sleeves cut in elvish fashion. She had bought the gown from a peddler in Cereine, who made his mark selling dresses sewn in the fashion of highborn ladies. It was such a frivolous purchase, but the colour of the fabric made the decision for her, impractical as it was. It remained in her saddlebag, forgotten until the invitation from the queen gave her an occasion to wear it.

The summons to Carleon itself had rather astonished her. While she and Arianne had shared an extraordinary adventure together during the quest to save the royal heir, still it was a watch guard's duty to aid her queen. While friendship had come,

Melia never expected the relationship to survive beyond the completion of the quest.

In all honesty, when Melia left Arianne and Celene at the Frozen Mountains, she never expected to hear from either again. But when the Captain of the Watch in Baffin sought her out to present her with the invitation to visit Sandrine Keep, Melia realised she was mistaken. It was not an invitation she could refuse so she set out, convinced when she reached the palace she would be told it was all a terrible mistake.

Of course nothing of the sort happened. When Melia arrived and was presented to the queen, she was greeted with open arms. Arianne embraced her like a friend and proved her regard was no aberration.

After donning the gown, Melia pinned back her dark hair and hoped she was suitable for the company she would be keeping tonight. Her reflection still jarred her each time she glanced at the mirror, startled by the person she saw there. The woman in the mirror did not look like a watch guard. After one wore breeches and spent most of the time riding through the wilderness, where neither identity nor gender mattered, it was easy to forget she was once a child of nobility.

The reflection in the mirror reminded her she was once Melia, daughter of Hezare, a general of Nadira.

It was almost to her relief when she heard the door behind her. The sound of knuckles rapping against the thick wooden door snatched her away from her anxious thoughts and sent her hurrying to answer it. With no idea of any customs or protocols to be followed in the royal court, Melia did not wish to be perceived as discourteous by leaving her visitor to languish outside her door.

"Melia!" Celene burst into the room as soon as Melia opened the door wide enough. She greeted the startled watch guard with another enthusiastic hug of friendship and joy.

"Celene," Melia stuttered a response, still rather overwhelmed by the reception she was receiving from the lady of Gislaine and the queen, respectively.

"My goodness," Celene exclaimed, sweeping her gaze over Melia in the blue dress. "Now I can see why so many were shocked when I discarded my breeches for a dress. You look beautiful."

"I feel as if I should be better armed," Melia retorted, remembering that Celene's dry wit would appreciate the comment.

Celene laughed and took her hand, leading her to the wing chairs in the room so they could talk. Like Arianne, Celene did not forget how Melia risked her life to aid them in the quest to Sanhael. Though she claimed she was duty-bound to aid the queen, Celene and Arianne knew better. Besides, it was rare for Celene to find other women who shared her common interests, who did not think battle and swordplay were wholly inappropriate subjects of conversation.

"How have you been?" Celene inquired earnestly when they were nestled comfortably in the chairs.

"I have been well, though life does not vary much for a watch guard. We ride, we watch and we report what is important to those in authority," Melia explained.

"And how goes your search for your mother?" Celene inquired, remembering Melia had set aside her own quest in order to help them.

Melia let out a disappointed sigh. "I am afraid I have found little evidence of her. Wherever she and her people disappeared, they hid well, for I have spoken to no one who has even heard of her."

"You will find her," Celene patted her on the arm in support, showing more confidence than Melia herself felt at this moment.

"I hope so," Melia smiled, grateful for the gesture. "Now, how about yourself? How have you and your husband been?"

"Ronen and I fare well. We have spent much of the past months in Gislaine trying to rebuild the outer settlements there, but I fear that our resources only stretch so far. Many fled to the coast during the Occupation, and until we prove that the south is free of Balfure's forces we will not bring them back. I know the king would like the Southern Provinces peopled, but it is going to take a long time for that to happen."

"I understand that land east of Gislaine is quite beautiful and the woods of Eden Ardhen are quite magnificent," Melia remarked, knowing something about the local geography.

"It is," Celene confirmed. "Unfortunately many of Balfure's forces have taken refuge there. Tor Ardhen still stands, even though the Disciples are gone. It's a pity, because it was the centre of elvendom until Lylea was driven out."

"I suppose they are retreating behind the Veil again now that Balfure is gone. It is a pity they chose not to reclaim Eden Ardhen. That might solve your problem."

"It might," Celene nodded in agreement and then added rather coyly, "Speaking of elves, Aeron is here."

Melia received the news with an expression of stone.

"Is he?" She feigned nonchalance, unaware this was not entirely unique behaviour in the keep today.

"Yes," Celene remarked, betraying none of the amusement she was presently experiencing at Melia's supposed indifference to the news. "Though I fear not for long. I am told he has been summoned home to Eden Halas by his father King Halion."

"Well that is hardly surprising," Melia snorted. "If he were my son I would try to keep a tight rein on him as well."

Celene chuckled, "I see you remember him well then."

"And trying to forget him just as well," Melia replied sarcastically, recalling how she had almost taken her knife to him when they travelled together. He took the idea of chivalry beyond the boundaries of its intended use. She could not understand how she could have fought Syphia at his side only to have him treat her like some fragile damsel who needed protection at the very next opportunity.

"Are we speaking of the same polite elf?" Celene teased.

"Are we speaking of *a* polite elf?" Melia cocked a brow at her.

Celene laughed and Melia joined her before the conversation regarding the prince of Eden Halas deteriorated even further.

"It is time we join the others for dinner," Celene prompted their departure. "Arianne thought you might prefer a friendly face to accompany you to the hall instead of a serving girl. We will talk more tonight."

"I am grateful for your company," Melia said, because Arianne was correct about that assertion. She made a mental note to thank the queen for the consideration when they had a moment alone. Hopefully the rest of the night would transpire as smoothly.

* * *

"Did you miss me?"

A familiar voice spoke so closely to Melia's ear she felt the hairs on the back of her neck stand on end. They were walking down the corridor leading to the great hall when they were intercepted from behind by someone who knew how to approach without giving himself away.

Melia sucked in her breath, perfectly aware who was asking the question and replied sweetly without turning around. "Like the pox."

"Are you saying you're afflicted with me?" Aeron quipped as he rounded the two women and stood next to Melia, smirking.

Celene rolled her eyes, realising Kyou did not exaggerate.

"*Prince* Aeron, I take it you remember Melia?"

"Vaguely," Aeron shrugged, a little smile crossing lips as his eyes continued to stare at Melia. "Though I am certain I travelled with a scruffy watch guard, not this, this woman," his gaze raked over her in approval.

"I remember you," Melia retorted, feeling uncomfortable enough in these clothes without this elven aristocrat making her feel even more self-conscious about it. "You were that annoying little puppy tugging at my heels. I thought I succeeded in losing you in the woods so you would not find your way home."

Celene laughed softly, shaking her head as she drew away from them both to avoid being caught in their sparring. "I leave you to your verbal jousting. If you can rest your bladed tongues long enough, do join us in the hall. I believe the queen is waiting."

Neither spoke until Celene was gone, and despite his efforts to keep from falling into old patterns around her, Aeron's resolve crumbled the instant he saw her again. Seeing her in the dress simply took his breath away.

At Sanhael, he was impressed by her courage and her skill. Later on, as they travelled together, he enjoyed immensely their witty banter; but now as he saw her again, he realised there was a beautiful woman beneath all that leather and dust.

"Would you let me escort you?" He offered her his arm.

"Now you behave like a prince?" She stared at him, wondering what was to be done with this impossible elf.

"A moment ago I was pox," he pointed out. "It requires time to rise above that distinction."

"You are quite impossible," she stated before breaking into a smile. Taking his arm, they resumed walking towards the hall and Melia couldn't deny he was good company when he wasn't being quite so infuriating.

"I can assure you, I am not the only one," he countered before his tone turned a little more serious. "So how have you been?"

"I've been well," Melia replied, always finding his ability to switch from teasing to sincere difficult to keep up with. "I hear you are bound for home."

His shoulders stiffened only slightly but enough for Melia to immediately guess he was not happy about it. She wondered why a prince would dislike returning to his realm but decided against questioning him about it.

"Yes, my father requires me home and I've been away for far too long. It is time."

"Does that not make you happy?" She found herself asking, even if a moment ago she was trying not to. Subtlety was something neither seemed to have cultivated with each other. In moments like this, it had its advantages because it disturbed Melia how clearly unhappy he was. Despite herself and for reasons she did not want to delve deeply into at this time, she hated to see him this way.

"Not as much as I should be."

An awkward silence followed and Melia debated if she should prompt him into speaking further. Their relationship was far simpler to deal with when they were trading barbs and insults. Seeing him in the midst of an obvious personal crisis made her forget all that and surfaced the feelings about him she knew better than to indulge.

"Perhaps you should go home only to visit," Melia suggested although she suspected this was not an option.

"That will not satisfy my father. I do not wish to disappear behind the Veil like the rest of my people and forget everyone I care for. I enjoy being in the world too much."

"Good," she was genuinely pleased to hear he was not conflicted on this point. Even with a short time in their company, Melia saw the bond of friendship shared by those in the king's Circle. In her youth, she would have given anything to have that kind of love and support from the people in her life.

"What of you, Melia?" Aeron looked at her, realising he didn't wish to linger on a problem that had no easy solutions and took the opportunity to learn a little about her. Obviously she had come from the lands of the east, but they were not known to depart their borders unless it was to join Balfure in his conquests. "How does an Easterling find her way so far from the lands of her birth?"

"When she has even less choices than you," Melia replied without thinking.

His brow knotted, not at all liking the sound of that. Was she driven from her home for some reason? "What do you mean?"

Melia frowned, rebuking herself for revealing something so personal, and knew he would continue to ask if she did not explain in some way. "In Nadira, a woman's family decides who she is to wed. After my father died, his family believed it was time I was married. I was given no choice in who my husband was to be, and since I had no wish to be dragged to the altar, I fled."

"You couldn't refuse?" Aeron found the idea of forcing a woman into marriage to some man she could not endure to be rather barbaric. He knew the marriages were arranged by the noble houses of men for political reasons but elves found the whole thing rather odious. Kingdoms came and went but marriage among elves lasted forever. Eternity could last a very long time, if love was not part of that equation.

"In Nadira, a woman may not refuse a proposal of marriage arranged by her family. It is dishonourable," Melia recited the words as it was explained to her at the time. "My father spared me from such traditions because he didn't wish me loveless marriage. Unfortunately, once he died there was no stopping such an arrangement from being made by my well-meaning relatives. Leaving was the only course left to me."

"That is a sad tale," Aeron frowned, disliking any institution that made running away the only path for a young woman to escape her fate. "But I supposed you ought to be grateful," he cast a sidelong glance at her.

"Grateful?" she stared at him in puzzlement.

"If you did not find this suitor so terribly unacceptable, you would never have left to meet me and where would we be then?" He winked at her, wearing that damnable smile she found so hard to resist.

"Deluded apparently," but Melia was smiling when she said it.

"Admit it, my lady," he refused to yield, "I know you like me."

"I admit nothing," Melia snorted, but did not resist when he pulled her arm closer to him.

Chapter Two

Inquiries

Although the dinner took place in the great hall of the Keep, the proceedings were surprisingly informal, with only the handful of people Arianne and Dare considered their extended family in attendance.

Aside from the king and queen, also present were Ronen, Celene, Kyou, herself and her escort. Until she was seated at their table, Melia did not appreciate how much of an honour it was to be considered a part of their circle, for she was in select company. It was the first time in too long she was a part of a celebration where she was welcomed at the table.

"Melia, are your accommodations suitable?" Arianne, queen of Carleon asked as they were waiting for the food to be served. She had recovered her bloom after the exhaustion of birth and now radiated with the glow of new motherhood. It was no wonder to anyone the king could only look upon his wife with adoration.

"Luxurious in comparison to what I am accustomed to," Melia confessed.

"Come now, Arianne," Dare joined them. "Melia is a watch guard. Like any able adventurer, we spend most of our time in the wilderness. As long as it is dry and safe, we can sleep anywhere."

"And yet she manages to look less bedraggled than you," Arianne reminded him teasingly. "I remember your state when you returned to Eden Taryn from the wilderness."

Dare gave his wife a wounded look. "It was because I was making haste to return to you, Rian. If I stopped for even one moment to groom myself, it was one moment longer I was kept away from you. I could not endure even that slightest delay." Dare flashed his wife a grin that drew laughter from everyone present.

"Nicely evaded," Arianne laughed, not believing him for a second but nonetheless impressed by his sly weaving of words.

Appearing completely unrepentant, the king smiled proudly at his wife. "Diplomacy has taught me much."

"In any case I thank you for your hospitality," Melia remarked once husband and wife finishing sharing their private joke. "My room is a luxury I shall relish until I have to return to the Range."

"How goes it there?" Dare asked, always interested in how things were transpiring in the rest of his kingdom. As one who once travelled Carleon quite extensively, he knew the observations of the watch guards were the most accurate intelligence he could receive about the state of Avalyne.

"It goes well. The Berserkers have decreased in numbers and their raiding parties are sporadic," she answered, remembering now that he was not Dare but her king, and gave her report accordingly. "They are being driven further north by the soldiers of Cereine with help from the watch guards. I do not think it will be that long before we are no longer troubled by them at all."

"That is good to know," Dare said. "Avalyne was blighted by their evil long enough during the Occupation. I think there will always be pockets of them emerging from time to time but it pleases me that we are making some headway."

"Which is more than I can say of the south," Ronen spoke up. "There are Berserkers there in greater numbers."

"As long as Tor Ardhen stands, they will consider it theirs to occupy, even with the death of Balfure. Those woods are formidable and they know you do not have the resources to drive them out," Aeron pointed out. "It is a shame that Lylea's former home is despoiled in this way. I am told those forests are vast and ancient. They deserve better."

"What is needed there is settlement," Dare declared. "If more people were willing to dwell there, the Berserkers could be driven away. Unfortunately, they cannot do that until we empty Tor Ardhen."

"It is a difficult situation," Celene sighed, having ridden out with Ronen during the expeditions to clean out the territory.

"I doubt there is anything left after we were done with it," Kyou said enthusiastically. "The war decided Balfure's fate once and for all."

"I would not be so quick to dismiss the dark powers that were once of *that* land," Arianne replied. "Evil of such power is extremely hard to kill. For all we know, our future progeny may suffer for something we did not finish."

No one could argue with her on that point after what they had experienced with Syphia. If anything reminded them that not all evil was vanquished with Balfure, it was the reminder of the Primordial, who caused so much mischief with her deception. No doubt there were other threats lying hidden, waiting for the right moment to wreak havoc upon them as Syphia had done. Still, Arianne did not wish to dampen the evening with such talk.

Aeron lapsed into silent contemplation regarding the subject of Tor Ardhen and the woods surrounding it. An idea formed in his head and the more he thought of it, the more inspired it seemed to be. *This needs further thought*, he told himself silently. To his chagrin, the elf was forced to admit Dare was right. He needed to be the master of his own fate.

* * *

The evening transpired with much merriment by the time the meal was served.

It was the first opportunity for Melia to observe the people she had met only briefly during their adventure in Sanhael. While she had gotten to know Arianne and Celene closely during the quest and travelled with Kyou and the prince on their return, this was the first time Melia really got to know the king and Celene's husband, Ronen.

It was easy to forget that Dare was the leader of Carleon when he had such a dry wit, a love of life and more intelligence than was customary for a man of his station. It also warmed her heart to see how much the couple adored each other, if was not already apparent by how far he travelled to find Arianne in Sanhael.

Ronen was no different in his love for Celene, though his manner was quite different than Dare's. A captain of Sandrine during the Occupation, he appeared to have as much difficulty becoming accustomed to his station as the Bân of Carleon as Dare did to being king. He would always be a soldier at heart, even if he was now a lord with his own city to rule. Though not as charismatic as Dare, Ronen possessed a quiet strength. In comparison to Celene's headstrong and often fiery personality, he was the perfect foil to her heated disposition. They suited each other well.

Of the men, it was perhaps Kyou she knew the best. He was the first dwarf she had ever met. During the journey to the Baffin, when the urge to strangle Aeron became so intense she needed to stay well away from the elf, she distracted herself by getting to know the head of Clan Atrayo.

She found that she liked Kyou a great deal. He was astonishingly practical. When he examined her crossbow, he suggested all sorts of interesting ideas on how she might hone the shape of its bolts to perfect her accuracy. He spoke of Iridia and the hopes of rebuilding the dwarf kingdom after its rule by Balfure. He told her about Hanae, his childhood love who had waited for him for years at the Jagged Teeth while he travelled the length of Avalyne with Dare. Melia was pleased to hear they were finally married after he parted company with her and Aeron while they continued the journey south.

She learned something of the Prince as well.

She knew from experience elves did not like to leave the Veil. They preferred to remain in seclusion within their forests, leaving the world to the younger races. Aeron's emergence from Eden Halas to travel with Dare and the Circle was unusual. Aeron, it appeared, was something of an aberration when it came to elves. He enjoyed travelling with his companions and was loyal beyond all measure to them. He considered Dare his family and Kyou believed Aeron to be a remnant of the elves who used to explore Avalyne extensively before the Primordial Wars had changed them so.

* * *

When the party had disbanded, Melia found that she could not sleep.

Being a watch guard enabled her to exist on little sleep and, so far, the day had not been so taxing that she was exhausted. The business of dining with friends in the great hall was far less work than roaming the wilderness. As a result, she was restless and took herself to the gardens, where she wandered aimlessly, enjoying the sight of greenery beneath the pale moonlight of the twilight sky. She was so accustomed to sleeping under the stars that being surrounded by walls made her uncomfortable. Hopefully, the walk outdoors would settle her.

Her mood was good because, for the first time in too long, she had friends who were noble and kind, who knew what she was and did not reproach her manner. Not since her father's passing had she felt such acceptance. Even though she would soon have to return to the wilderness, it was good to know that, for awhile at least, she would have these people in her life.

Following the path of blue stones, she soon reached the marble fountain where the Water Wife stood in sculpted splendour over the shimmering water. Melia had become lost in the reflection of the full moon upon the surface when a voice slipped out of the darkness and brushed her ear.

"You should not be wandering the grounds alone," Aeron declared behind her.

Melia let out an exasperated sigh, folding her arms in impatience as she turned around to see him standing up from a stone bench next to a tall hedge. It appeared as if he had been there for some time and Melia wondered for what reason was he sitting here in the darkness like this. During the night, he showed none of the melancholy she saw when he confessed his reluctance to return home. In fact, the seating arrangements at the king's table placed them side by side and he was surprisingly pleasant company.

"Please tell me you have not followed me," she teased, knowing full well he had not, but insults were the way they greeted each other and provided a good segue into why he was out here alone.

"Oh yes, I sat here in the vain hopes that you would happen to walk this way instead of a dozen different paths that crisscross these gardens," he retorted with exaggerated dramatics as he reached her.

He stood at arm's length from her, aware they were far too familiar with each other. This chance meeting might be considered improper. There were some lines of propriety Aeron would not cross out of respect for her, even when they were alone, enjoying each other's company in the moonlight.

"Well then, you are fortunate," she rewarded him with a laugh before looking at him with affection. "Really, why are you out here?"

There was real concern in her voice, Aeron noticed.

"I could not sleep and I think better with the stars above me," he glanced briefly at the canvas above them before meeting her gaze again. "But always in my heart was the thought maybe you would be here as well," he teased.

"I'm sure," Melia rolled her eyes. "How fortunate you are that I chose this path and decided to end your misery."

Aeron uttered a short laugh and stared at her. "What is it about you that brings a lilt to my heart?"

"Your enjoyment of rejection and your misguided belief that I am swayed by your charms."

"Well, it is hard for me not to try when I see you wearing a dress. I do not know what shocks me more, that you look lovely wearing a dress or that you have one at all," he winked.

Melia glared at him through narrowed eyes. "Tell me Prince, were you always so blessed with a silver tongue?"

"A thousand years of practice, actually," he responded, enjoying their verbal sparring intensely. He really had not expected to find her out here when he wandered into the garden this evening. He wasn't lying that his future would come easier to him if he had the cloak of the stars above his head. Still, her arrival was an unexpected boon, and he thoroughly enjoyed the fencing match they seemed to engage in whenever they wandered into each other's orbit. "Am I not sweeping you off your feet?"

"You could not sweep me off my feet even if you had a broom."

He pretended to suck in his breath as if wounded mortally. "You are harsh with me, lady. Did I tell you that I enjoy that?"

"You have no shame," Melia retorted and steered the conversation away from its flirtatious slant. "Are you alright?" she asked, not bothering to hide her concern.

"I am." He found it was easy to talk to her. "I have been at a loss for some time, but today the king challenged me to answer a question I never thought to entertain in a thousand years. Duty and tradition have bound me for so long that it is difficult to imagine any other way of being."

"I understand," she brushed his shoulder gently. "Before I fled Nadira, I grappled with such questions. I have always tried to be the good daughter because my father went against so many traditions to see me happy. I thought I would be dishonouring him by fleeing, but then I knew he would not wish me miserable for the sake of tradition. It is why I took charge of my life and ran. Perhaps I live less comfortably than what I was accustomed to, but I am happy, especially when I am surrounded by people who have come to mean much to me."

"I am glad," Aeron was sincerely pleased to hear her say that. "Unfortunately, my father is nowhere near that understanding."

"Do you not get on with him, then?"

"I love him," he admitted without hesitation. "But I do not think I have been the son he wished. Perhaps I am too much like my mother. I cannot harden my heart when I see someone in difficulty, no matter what race they are. My father lost everyone he loved during the Primordial Wars and he has never forgiven the Celestials for using our people to cleanse the world, when they were in fact preparing it for Creator Cera's other races."

"Really?" Melia said with surprise. "That is a shame. I imagined Cera always planned for the elves to guide the younger races, not hide away from them."

"My mother thinks that, but my father disagrees. In fact, I was sitting out here contemplating how many of my people may feel the same way. Perhaps it is time for our isolation to end and return to the world. Even if my father chooses to retreat behind the Veil forever, I cannot imagine all our people wanting to do the same."

"I think that there is much your people can teach the rest of us," Melia stated in earnest. "I think that if you choose to join the rest of us in the world, it can only be a good thing. Look at what you have done as a part of the king's Circle."

"I know," Aeron agreed on that point. "I have found more fulfilment in the last eighteen years than I have in the previous nine hundred and eighty. During those years, I have seen great and terrible things, felt despair and elation. I fought a war and helped restore a kingdom. That by my reckoning is living, not trapped in amber where nothing changes except my growing boredom."

Melia reached for his cheek without even realising she had done it. "Then live, Prince. Live the way you wish. Be free to run, because existing is not enough. You yourself know this."

Her hand on his cheeks was soft and warm. He covered her hand in his and held it in place, liking the sensation of her flesh against his. For a moment, they did not speak, because staring into each other's eyes was a language in itself.

It was Melia who broke away first, realising they had crossed a line, invisible to all but lovers. With the stars above their heads, the beautiful scenery before them and only each other for company, Melia imagined anything that transpired now would only deepen this thing between them, and so she withdrew. She knew better than to encourage this attraction, even if he did not.

"It is late," she said, stepping back, grateful her dark colouring did not reveal the blush across her cheeks. Her pulse was racing and she felt breathless. "I will leave you to your thoughts. Good night, Prince."

"A lady should never wander about without an escort," he called out to her, trying to steady his own reaction as she moved towards the Keep once more.

"And when I find a suitable one, I will be sure to ask for him his assistance," she returned sweetly before disappearing into the darkness, leaving Aeron with a corresponding smile on his face.

* * *

When Melia returned to her room, she was surprised to find that Arianne was awaiting her. The queen was seated on the same chair occupied by Celene earlier that day.

"My queen, is there something wrong?" Melia wondered what could warrant Arianne's presence in her room at so late an hour.

"Nothing is wrong," Arianne quickly assured her, aware of how self-conscious Melia felt at being in the Keep. In the woods it was simple; she, Celene and Melia were on a quest, equal parts of an important triad. Here in Sandrine, the dynamic was no more. She was the queen, and no matter how much Melia or Celene tried, they would never be able to forget it. "I came to your door and entered when I realized that you were not in your room."

"I am sorry. I have difficulty sleeping indoors and thought a walk might help my slumber this evening."

"As is your right as my guest," Arianne beckoned her to sit down so that they could talk. "I did not mean to impose upon you, Melia, but I did invite you to Sandrine for a reason."

"I am at your service as always, my queen." Melia meant it sincerely. Arianne had extended a hand of friendship that Melia would never have dreamed possible, and whatever the queen asked of her, it could never be enough.

"Then call me Arianne, as you did when we were fellow travellers," Arianne implored.

"As you wish," Melia nodded, trying to rise to the friendship this noble woman was offering her. "Arianne."

"Good," Arianne was glad that bit of nonsense was dispensed with. "Melia, as I said, I had reason for inviting you here to Sandrine Keep. I hope you do not think me presumptuous when you hear why."

Melia's brow arched, intrigued. "Please continue, Arianne."

"Yes," Arianne nodded. "For your consideration and your invaluable assistance to me and my son, I wanted to do something for you when I returned home."

"I did not require a reward," Melia started to say when Arianne cut her off.

"I know that but I thought I might aid you in your own quest, since you were gracious enough to ensure I survived mine."

"How so?" Melia was intrigued by the queen making overtures on her behalf.

"Let me ask you one thing first," Arianne returned. "Who exactly was your mother?"

Melia swallowed, not expecting to have this conversation today, especially with the queen of Carleon, but she suspected Arianne had purpose for asking.

After a lengthy pause, Melia finally spoke.

"I am not sure. I know her name but little else. My father claimed she called herself a river daughter, but since I have begun my search, I have made little headway in finding out what that means."

"I have heard of the river daughters before," Arianne stated.

"You have?" Melia's jaw dropped in shock. Finally, after all these years of searching, someone who had the answer she sought! It was almost too good to be true! "You know them?"

"No," Arianne shook her head, hating to dash the hope she saw in Melia's eyes, and quickly added, "I know *of* them. They were supposedly servants who served Dalcine, the Water Wife."

"River daughter?" Melia's shock continued to grow. Was *she* some kind of an immortal hybrid? "My mother was not human?"

"It has never been truly discovered what they are, though they are known to take mortal lovers for a time. Men seem to suit their purposes best and are somewhat disposable," Arianne tried to explain it as kindly as possible but there were some truths that were simply unavoidable. "I asked my mother, when she last journeyed here to see my son, what she knew of the river daughters along the Yantra, particularly of one named Ninuie."

"And?" Melia asked, her voice hushed as is she dared not speak too loudly for fear of ruining the revelation.

"Lylea knew nothing of Ninuie," Arianne replied and saw Melia's crestfallen expression before continuing. "However, prior to the Aeth War, Tor Iolan was occupied by the Disciples and they used that terrible place to commit all manner of atrocities against Eden Halas. It is believed that the Disciples may have captured and killed river daughters in their dungeons."

Melia said nothing for a moment because her heart was turning into stone and threatening to shatter. She would have wept at the unfairness of it, the cruel trickery of fate that would allow her to come so far and search so long only, to be met by this unhappy conclusion, but she could not deny the possibility. She could not because she knew that Arianne was wrong. Perhaps only some of the river daughters were killed in Tor Iolan. She could not deny the source of the intelligence but she knew her mother was not among the dead.

"Not my mother," Melia whispered after a while. Her eyes closed when she answered, "my mother is not dead."

Arianne took her denial to be borne of frustration and grief and sought the right words to not cause Melia any more sorrow than she already felt. "Melia, you must face the possibility. I encountered some of Balfure's Disciples. They were beyond darkness. They existed in evil and every waking thought of their existence was to serve Balfure in any way possible. The river daughters, if they were indeed servants of a Celestial, would have compelled the Disciples to destroy them, to ensure they did not ally themselves with Dare."

"I do not doubt your words," Melia answered after composing herself. "I believe that many of the river daughters were killed but my mother is *not* one of the dead."

"How can you be so certain of this?" Arianne asked, starting to understand that her denial of what was almost certainly the truth may have some foundation other than her stubborn refusal to believe. ,

"I simply know," Melia replied, reaching for Arianne's hands and holding them entwined in hers. For the first time, she really did feel like Arianne's friend and she loved Arianne dearly for the inquiries made on her behalf. But she could not believe that Ninuie was dead.

"You must trust me in this. I know that she lives, and thanks to you, I now have a place to begin my search, a place that is more than just unsubstantiated rumours. I must go to Tor Iolan and see for myself."

"Tor Iolan!" Arianne exclaimed, never expecting her words to send Melia to that dark place when she had sought this audience. "There is nothing there! It has been cleansed of all evil since the death of Balfure and the end of the war."

"If the river daughters were there once, then that is where I must go," Melia said firmly. "It is a place to start."

"How can you be so sure that she still lives?"

Because every night when I sleep, Melia thought, *I hear her screaming.*

Chapter Three

Travelling Companions

Arianne should have anticipated this.

The queen of Carleon cursed herself for a fool at not foreseeing Melia's reaction when she delivered the news that Ninuie might have perished at Tor Iolan. Men could be notoriously stubborn when their mind was set, and Melia appeared to be no exception to the rule.

Why should she? The woman had spent years searching for her mother, *years*! Of course she would persist in the hope her mother still lived. After all, the alternative was to face the possibility that the years of searching were for nothing. Arianne could not begin to imagine what it must feel like to face the disintegration of one's purpose in life because of a queen's good intentions. Everything Melia had become since arriving in the Western Sphere was defined by her quest to find her mother.

If that search was over, what else was left for her?

Such considerations aside, it did not alter the fact that one way or another Melia was determined to go to Tor Iolan.

While considered the realm of King Halion, the woods of Iolan were separated from Eden Halas by a tributary of the great Yantra River. While the forest of Halas was renowned not only as the home of the elves but also for its resplendent beauty, Iolan's reputation was far more sinister. Home to the remnants

33

of Mael's army at the end of the Primordial wars, the creatures within it were ancient even by elvish standards. While some effort was made by Halion to cleanse the woods of their menace, it was far from successful, and too many travellers had fallen prey to them over the years.

When Balfure had decided to build Tor Iolan to house the Disciples overseeing the Northern Provinces during the Occupation, he had done so to take advantage of the wood's notorious reputation.

Arianne was led to believe that Melia knew nothing of Tor Iolan other than of its existence. It was sheer recklessness for the watch guard to attempt a journey through its forests without any knowledge of what awaited her there. Despite Arianne labouring this point strenuously to Melia, she remained adamant in her decision to go there nevertheless. Short of ordering her against it, Arianne could do nothing to prevent Melia's eventual departure.

That night, the queen lay awake, unable to sleep as she pondered what to do. Arianne was all too aware she needed an answer quickly. Now that Melia was in possession of this information, she would not linger in Sandrine. If she was not already of the mind to leave the very next day, she soon would be.

The solution, when it finally came to Arianne, was painfully obvious.

* * *

Rising early the next morning, Arianne set out immediately to do what necessary to save Melia from herself. While she was unable to persuade Melia from her dangerous journey, she did manage to convince the watch guard not to leave Sandrine without saying goodbye first. Leaving Dare in their chambers, Arianne went to the stables, where she hoped to intercept Aeron before he embarked on his morning ride.

Unlike the rest of their Circle, Arianne did not make light of Aeron's obvious attraction to the lovely watch guard. As much as their banter might be amusing to those who witnessed it, only Arianne knew of the delicacy of the situation. Aeron was not prone to making attachments lightly. While she knew he had shared company with elven ladies in the past, what she saw of his affection for Melia was of an entirely different order.

And only she understood how tragic it could be for both of them.

Whether or not he knew it, the greatest gift Arianne's father gave her had been the gift of mortality. By being his daughter, Arianne could choose whether or not she lived as an elf or died as a human. The choice allowed Arianne to live a mortal existence with Dare, and it was not a decision she regretted, even with the knowledge she would someday watch him die and follow him soon after.

Aeron did not have that choice.

He was a full-blooded elf, the son of elven aristocracy. There was no choice for him, and like all elves, once he mated the bond was forever. Not even death could break it. In the light of such finality, it was no wonder he had yet to form any serious attachment. Furthermore, she knew the union of his parents warned him against choosing unwisely. Such a mistake could have lasting repercussions. If Aeron cared for Melia or any human, Arianne knew his ultimate fate would be to watch that lover grow old and die.

As much as she wished the best for Aeron and Melia, she knew any relationship between them could only end in pain. Yet now she had no choice but to ask his help, aware that it could only make things worse.

* * *

Ever since he began his stay at Sandrine, it was Aeron's habit to ride out of the city for a few hours in the morning. He was, by his very nature, an elf of the wood. This urban living was unnatural to him – unlike Arianne, who was now accustomed to it. He still needed to feel the forest air around him as frequently as possible. The few hours he was allowed to explore the wilds around Sandrine Keep was more than enough to satisfy the need, for now, though he suspected eventually this would not be enough.

Sooner or later, he would leave simply to get out of the city.

Arianne entered the stable and found him saddling his steed Idris, the horse presented to him by Yalen, king of Angarad, during the first days of the Aeth War. Since then, Idris had travelled with him everywhere.

"Aeron," Arianne called out to the prince in elvish. When they were alone, they often spoke to each other in their native tongue.

"You awaken early my lady," Aeron stopped what he was doing and bowed at her in greeting. "I thought I was the only one who chooses to ride at this hour."

It was early, but like him, Arianne woke with the dawn. It was a habit she was unable to shirk since leaving Eden Taryn, where everyone began the day at the sunrise. Since becoming queen, Arianne found it was similarly beneficial to continue the practice, since it allowed her to gain more from her day. More so, now that she had a baby to attend to as well.

"It serves me to have more hours in my day," she responded with a smile.

"Will you join me this morning for a ride?" In their youth, they had ridden a great deal together and he knew her to be an even better rider than Dare.

"I wish that I could," Arianne sighed, thinking there was nothing better than a morning ride. "Unfortunately, I must be close by for the little prince's feeding. He makes demand of me already."

"He is his father's son," Aeron laughed, thinking how well motherhood suited her.

"True," Arianne agreed, giving him no argument because it was the truth. "I do have an ulterior motive for seeking you out this morning, Aeron. I require your aid."

"Indeed?" The archer's brow crooked upwards. "I am at your service as always, my queen."

"You are a good friend," she reached for his hand and gave it a gentle squeeze. "I fear I have done something foolish and now I have set events into motion I cannot stop."

"What do you mean?" His tone became serious and one could very well believe he had once led many of the elves into battle at Astaroth.

"I have given Melia intelligence that will send her riding towards Tor Iolan," Arianne confessed, still chagrined at not foreseeing Melia's reaction to the news.

"Tor Iolan?" Aeron exclaimed, his surprise as evident as his horror. "Why in the name of Cera would she wish to go there?"

Arianne hesitated. She debated whether or not she should break Melia's confidence by telling Aeron the truth, but even as the thought crossed her mind, she knew she would not, "I cannot tell you, Aeron. I promised her I would not but she has good reason to go there."

Aeron started to protest but Arianne silenced him by continuing to speak.

"All you need know is nothing will keep her from going. I doubt even an order from Dare will succeed in dissuading her. I know her determination in this. She will go there or die trying."

Aeron could not imagine any reason justifying a journey to Tor Iolan, and Arianne's reluctance to tell him only served to remind him how little he really knew about Melia. Was fleeing from Nadira to escape a marriage only a small part of Melia's tale?

"Arianne," he said firmly, "The woods of Eden Iolan are not to be travelled lightly, especially by those who have never wandered those paths. I know what roams those forests and how many have died because of their ignorance."

"That is why I have come to you," Arianne countered. "You intend on returning home to Eden Halas, do you not?"

"Yes?" he answered suspiciously and began to understand why Arianne sought him out this morning. While her idea might have some merit, Aeron knew Melia would not consider it a good idea in any shape or form. At the very least, she would consider Arianne's solution a violation of her privacy.

"Could you not travel with her to Tor Iolan?" Arianne implored, unaware Aeron already guessed her plan. "If you went with her, you could see to it that she is safe. You could be her guide through those woods."

"Arianne," he interrupted before her idea took further root in her head. "Even if I agree to what you ask, and I do not say I do, there is no way you will be able to convince Melia to accept my aide as her guide."

Even if he knew little about Melia's past, Aeron was astute enough to grasp that Melia would refuse this offer outright. Despite their playful banter, there was no denying the undercurrents of attraction between them. Aeron could not deny it any more than Melia herself. Last night proved how necessary it was to keep each other at arm's length. For them to embark on this journey together would be tempting fate, with only tragedy as its outcome, no matter how much he wished otherwise.

Arianne stared at him pointedly, refusing to abandon the suggestion because there was no other way to keep Melia safe.

"Aeron, I have known you all my life and I have never seen you look at anyone the way you look at her. You are like my brother, prince of Halas, and I know your heart. If you care about this woman as much as I think you do, you will find a way to convince her. Short of issuing her an order as her queen, I have been unable to dissuade her from going to Tor Iolan. This matter for her is too personal for her to abandon, and if she goes alone, she will come to harm. Could you live with that consequence?"

Aeron turned away, uncomfortable with Arianne's ability to see through him. He could not deny what he felt for Melia, but its intensity frightened him. While they had only dabbled with harmless flirtation thus far, Aeron knew if he surrendered to his passion for Melia, it would consume them both. Still, he could not deny that Arianne's words struck a nerve inside of him. He could not stand by and let Melia attempt to enter Tor Iolan alone.

"Alright," he conceded defeat, his eyes staring at the stable floor, for it was better than allowing Arianne a glimpse into his soul. "I will do as you ask. I will go with her, but I tell you now that facing a nest of wyrms will be easier than going to her door with *this* request."

"You can do it," Arianne smiled encouragingly. "I know you can."

"Well," Aeron frowned, not at all sharing her confidence at his ability to convince Melia to accept his help. "You had better let me tell her. She's accustomed to being angry at me."

* * *

Melia slept poorly.

Her thoughts were too filled with Arianne's news to be able to close her eyes and drift into slumber. She thought of all the years spent searching, following clues leading nowhere, the embers of hope ending with ashes of disappointment. Now here was tangible proof of who her mother might be, beyond her father's hazy recollections of the wife he never stopped loving. There were times she feared the goal she'd set herself was unattainable, that this quest was an empty one.

All that changed with Arianne's report that the high queen of the elves, Lylea, knew of river daughters. Even if Lylea did not know her mother in particular, Melia felt vindicated. Despite her fear of admitting it, she secretly harboured doubts regarding her father's account of Ninuie, fearing his memories to be little more than fanciful tales to make bearable the truth of abandonment. In adulthood, Melia came to realise Hezare's explanations were scant because he, too, knew little of his wife's origins.

With sleep eluding her, Melia sought out the Athenaeum, the library established by the first kings of House Icara when Carleon was still young. Kept within its walls was the history of the kingdom, recorded in ancient texts, royal journals and old maps charted by travellers throughout the ages. Arianne's point that Melia knew little of Tor Iolan and its dangers was well made. If she intended to traverse its treacherous woods, it would be prudent to learn all she could of the place first.

After perusing the old maps, she decided following the Yantra River was the best route to Tor Iolan. Upon reaching the Falls of Iolan, she would take the eastern fork and head towards the woods. The fortress was located deep within its borders and, no matter how she approached it, there was no avoiding the route through the forest. Even if Arianne had not warned her of its peril, Melia was familiar with Tor Iolan's infamous reputation.

Yet she had no choice in the matter. The answers she sought were there. She could feel it.

* * *

The next morning Melia was grateful to see the familiar reflection of the watch guard in the mirror instead of that woman in the blue dress. Here was someone she was comfortable with. The watch guard feared little, was capable of handling herself in most situations and never felt an ounce of self-doubt. In this guise, she could face whatever terrible price her journey to Tor Iolan might exact, far better than the woman in the dress could ever manage.

Being the watch guard was far safer than being Melia.

Packing away the last of her belongings, Melia intended to thank Arianne for her kindnesses and take her leave as soon as possible. Fastening the clasp on one of her saddlebags, she was startled by the loud knock on the door. Perhaps it was Arianne, Melia thought as she walked towards it. If she could make farewells in private without fanfare, Melia would prefer it. A long and involved farewell with the others would simply make her uncomfortable, and Melia was eager to begin her journey.

The persistent rapping against the wood became quite irritating by the time she reached the door knob. When she opened the door and saw who was on the other side, she should not have been surprised.

"Leaving so soon?" Aeron asked.

"Yes," Melia's answer was short and her annoyance at his presence was growing. Had Arianne told him that she was leaving? Of all the people at her door this morning, it was he she wished to see least. Not after their exchange the night before. "A matter of some urgency has arisen. I must leave immediately."

"What could possibly be important enough for a watch guard to deny the hospitality of the Queen?"

"I do not have time to spar with you elf," she turned on her heels, retreating into the room so she could retrieve her belongings and be on her way.

"It would seem so," Aeron remarked, looking over her shoulder to see how prepared she was for departure. Without being invited, he followed her into the room, much to Melia's chagrin.

Melia paused, uncomfortable by his presence and puzzled as to why he was here. Turning around after retrieving her saddlebags, she faced him once more. "Are you here to say goodbye, Prince?" Her instincts told her otherwise.

"Why do you not call me Aeron?" he took her by surprise with the question.

"Because I would rather call you vexing!" she cried out in exasperation. "What is it you want?"

He straightened up and fixed his eye upon her as if he were bracing for a blow. His determined expression signalled to Melia she was not going to like what he had to say.

"I know you're going to Tor Iolan," he stated.

Melia let out a groan of frustration, bristling with annoyance at the queen's betrayal of her confidence. What was Arianne playing at? Did she think this elf was going to convince Melia not to go when she had failed to do the same?

"Yes I am," she replied stiffly, convinced he would not leave unless she gave him his answers. "Not that it is any of *your* concern."

"If you are going to Tor Iolan then it becomes very much a matter for my concern," Aeron declared firmly, taking an air that was far different that the bantering tone they'd exchanged with each other. Whether she knew it or not, at this moment, he was addressing her as a representative of King Halion's rule. "The Tor and its woods are part of my father's lands. He does not take lightly to trespassers ignorant of its dangers. The evil there is ancient and not to be trifled with."

"It is my choice whether I trifle with it or not," she returned just as determinedly. "Not yours."

"I am a prince of Eden Halas and the territory of Iolan is part of my father's realm. You will not get within a league of the Tor without encountering Lord Gavril and his men. Furthermore, once they discover you, you will not be able to continue further."

"I will take my chances." Melia tried to brush past him, hiding the fact that his words struck home and succeeded in unsettling her. Damn him!

What in Cera's name was so important to her in those woods? Aeron wondered silently at the obstinacy she was displaying. She was an experienced woodsman. Surely she knew of Tor Iolan's reputation, as any member of the Watch Guard should.

What reason could she have to ignore all infamy? He knew his words had effect but not enough to shake her resolve to go. Why?

As she attempted to slip past him, Aeron caught her arm and stayed her beside him so he could make one further comment.

"If you must go, then let me go with you." He hoped the urgency of her need would make the suggestion palatable.

Her eyes flashed and she pulled away from him fiercely. "Absolutely not!"

Her vehement response stung and forced him to conclude there would be no middle ground upon which they might meet on this matter.

"Melia, if you must go to Tor Iolan, I can get you there. You need me."

"I need nothing from you! This is not your concern. Arianne had no right to bring you into this!"

Travelling with him, alone. It was folly. Did he not see it? She cared for him, far more than she ought to ever care for any immortal but anything between could only end in tragedy. Worse than that, he was a distraction and, now more than ever, she needed focus.

"She brought me into this because she cares about you," Aeron retaliated, rising to Arianne's defence. "The queen fears for your life although, quite honestly, I cannot imagine why since you are so determined to squander it by ignoring common sense! I have appealed to you as a friend, and as a prince of the realm; you're so determined that you will not see reason. Are you so determined to rush to your death? Because that is exactly what will happen if you ignore what I am trying to say!"

He had no wish to be harsh but blind stubbornness would not save her if she entered Iolan without any idea of its dangers. Arianne was right. He did care for her, too much to spare her feelings by not speaking bluntly.

Melia stared back at him. Her eyes revealed the internal battle she was waging with herself. After a long pause, Aeron guessed she might be seeing sense, but the person she was made it difficult for her to admit it.

"Melia you are no fool, and I will not treat you as one. Despite how I may jest at your inability to fend for yourself, we both know I do not believe such a thing for an instant. So believe me when I say to you the woods of Iolan are dangerous. I have lived with its dangers all my life and I still use caution when I must walk those paths. You need a guide or you will never reach Tor Iolan alive."

Melia blinked, wanting to refute every word he uttered. Still, she wished he grasped the reason for her strenuous objection had little to do with her quest and everything to do with *him*. For reasons she could not name, this elf touched her heart. She could not deny it to herself any more than she could ignore his affections. Yet any attachment between the two of them was dangerous and she knew it, even if he was too stubborn to see the tragedy of it.

On this occasion, it seemed as if fate was against her. Protestations aside, he was right. Even she knew the woods of Iolan were dangerous. Lord Gavril was a former captain of King Halion's Forest Guard, charged with establishing a small settlement on the outskirts of the woods to ensure its evil remained within its borders. His elves would halt any attempt she made to enter the forest, let alone reach Tor Iolan. Unless she had a guide of impeccable credentials, like a prince of the realm.

As much as she loathed admitting it, Melia needed him.

"Alright!" She broke down in exasperation. "We will travel together but you will not get in my way! I mean to go to Tor Iolan one way or another! I would prefer it without you, but since that is not meant to be, I will accept that I must have your assistance!"

"You are welcome," Aeron retorted sarcastically. "Thank you for your gracious acceptance."

"You are impossible!" she shouted before storming out of the room.

"I assure you," he countered, following her out, "I am not the only one."

Chapter Four

Departures

Since becoming High King, the most difficult thing Dare faced was the realisation that, as time passed, he would be saying goodbye to more and more of his friends.

The most recent of these farewells were not a farewells at all but the loss of Tully Furnsby in the Frozen Mountains, and to a lesser extent, his wife Keira. Dare still carried the guilt of their tragic ends, wishing on more than one occasion he'd never found their small house in the Green. Their act of kindness in sheltering him had only brought them disaster.

The others in his circle would leave under better circumstances but, still, their departures stung. Kyou would eventually return home to Iridia once the fortifications to Sandrine were complete. While Celene and Ronen still spent the summer months in the Keep, there would come a time when children would keep Celene home in Gislaine. Tamsyn was already gone. The mage was now wandering the Western Sphere in search of acolytes to rebuild his order and today he was saying goodbye to Aeron, whose parting was the hardest of all to bear.

Even when Aeron returned to Sandrine, it would not be the same as before. The days when Aeron was a constant at his side were nearing an end. Even for an immortal, life changed, and while Dare was glad the elf would be travelling in Melia's com-

46

pany, the king was still saddened at the departure of his best friend.

"You take leave of me far sooner than I would have liked," Dare said to Aeron as he stood on the dock with the rest of the party seeing the prince and Melia off on their journey down river.

"The sooner I begin, the sooner I will be able to return," Aeron reminded, but it was little consolation and they both knew it. He too could feel the sand shifting beneath them and knew their lives were finally at a fork.

"Not in the same way," Dare said quietly. Emotion welled up inside of him but he maintained his composure.

"No," Aeron agreed with the same sadness. "Not in the same way."

The two men embraced warmly as brothers might do but knew that their friendship was closer than blood. When they parted, both tried to dismiss the emotions churning within them, but it was hard to do. Aeron was grateful to turn away so he could make his farewell to the others present. He could not endure the heartache of any more tearful goodbyes.

Fortunately, Aeron knew what to expect when confronted with Kyou of Iridia. Kyou stood beside Dare and did not show his upset at seeing Aeron leave. They had said their goodbyes on numerous occasions before this and always found occasion to see each other again. Kyou simply accepted, as Aeron did, that each had responsibilities to their own people and sometimes simply needed to go their separate ways to attend them.

"I wish you could come with me on this journey, Kyou," Aeron admitted with sincere affection. Throughout the Aeth War, they'd been constant companions and it would've been odd to look over his shoulder and not see the dwarf there. For this journey, however, Kyou would have been an effective buffer between him and Melia.

"Surely you jest," Kyou retorted, raising a brow as he gazed past the elf at Melia, who was speaking with Arianne. "Even I am not so foolish to be caught between the two of you," he teased, knowing perfectly what Aeron was thinking. "Astaroth was less bloody than this is likely to be."

"You are a *true* friend," Aeron grumbled.

Kyou laughed and then patted the elf on the arm and said in a more serious voice, "Be careful, Aeron. You are still my favourite elf."

"Why, thank you, Master Kyou," Arianne remarked sarcastically as she and Melia joined them. "I will not take offence at that."

As Kyou stammered to respond, Arianne turned to Aeron. She embraced him warmly, grateful he was accompanying Melia on her quest but guilty at hastening his departure from Sandrine. It was obvious Dare needed more time to prepare for Aeron's eventual departure, but she supposed no amount of time would ever make their farewell less difficult. "Safe journey, Aeron," she smiled at him.

"Take care of yourself and your babe, Arianne," he replied with just as much sentiment as he leaned forward and delivered a gentle kiss against her forehead. "I hope to see you both when I return."

Melia's guilt at watching the sad farewells taking place before her made her regret allowing Aeron to accompany her to Tor Iolan. The sorrow etched on his handsome face as he prepared to leave his friends for some time was obvious and she wished she was not the cause of it.

"Be safe, Melia," Dare's voice brought Melia's thoughts away from the Prince. "Tor Iolan is a dangerous place even with Aeron for company."

Although he did not know her as well as Arianne or Celene, Dare did not forget how she came to help his queen during their confrontation with Syphia. For that, she would always have his regard.

"Thank you," she replied, touched by the sincerity of his wishes for her well-being. "I will rely on the Prince to see me out of trouble."

"He is good for that," Dare grinned, sensing more than a little mischief in her tone.

"Try not to kill him," Kyou added as he joined them, wearing an equally mischievous smile after she hugged him goodbye. "Though sometimes that princely arrogance warrants it."

"I am perfectly aware of that and I will try to heed your advice," Melia winked, more than accustomed to Aeron as a travelling companion after their last journey together.

Kyou laughed, allowing Melia a moment alone with Arianne as the hour of their parting was finally upon them. The watch guard and the queen exchanged a long stare until Melia broke the silence between them.

"I know you did what you thought was best, so do not fear that I am angry with you. You thought of my safety and no one has done that for a very long time. Thank you."

"I hope you find what you seek, Melia," Arianne's eyes softened with emotion and she took Melia's hand in hers. "But if you do not find it, I hope you will try to find happiness at least."

"I will try to do both," Melia replied, hugging the queen once more. "You are a good friend, Queen of Carleon," she whispered. "Please take care of Serinda and give your son a kiss for me."

"I will be happy to do both," Arianne answered and watched as Melia and Aeron turned to leave Sandrine at last.

* * *

Neither had a great deal to say to each other once the boat left the dock and took them down the Yantra River.

Melia seemed deep in thought but made no attempt to reveal why they were journeying to Tor Iolan. Although Aeron was burning with curiosity at why she was so determined to visit that terrible place, he did not press the matter. Nevertheless, while he respected her need for privacy, he also wanted to help her. The urgency he saw in her eyes was nothing to dismiss lightly.

Unfortunately, trust was still a thing forming between them.

"Am I to assume, you intend to remain silent throughout our entire journey to Tor Iolan?" Aeron asked an hour after leaving Sandrine behind them.

Melia relaxed visibly, aware she was probably being a little unreasonable, not to mention hostile, by her silence. She was behaving like a wilful child throwing a tantrum and was somewhat embarrassed at being called out on it. He was only here because he was worried about her safety and could have very easily left her to stumble about in Tor Iolan, possibly to fatal consequences.

Letting out a heavy sigh dispelling not only her petulance but also her lingering resistance to his presence, she decided if this was how things had to be then she ought to try and make the best of it.

"Of course not," she answered, staring at his back while he rowed down the river.

Aeron had expected her silence to last a few more hours but was pleasantly surprised to hear her relenting before that. Besides, a thousand years of living had taught him women could not be deprived of speech for too long.

"Will wonders never cease," he teased when he paused his rowing to glance back at her.

"Do not make me regret speaking to you, elf," Melia warned, her eyes narrowing in mock anger.

"I doubt you would have been able to resist my charming conversation for very long," he smirked, glad that things were back to normal between them. Well, as normal as it could be, Aeron supposed.

Melia rolled her eyes but she too was pleased that they were on more familiar ground. "If I can resist the Berserkers, I can resist you," she said sweetly.

"You never did tell how us how you and Celene escaped from their hands in Sanhael," Aeron reminded, recalling how closed mouth she and Celene were about that part of their liberation.

"It is not important," Melia grumbled, still wincing at what she'd been forced to do in order to escape the Berserker captain.

"Oh, come now," he balked at her attempt to deter him. "It is a long journey to Tor Iolan. I must be entertained."

"If you want entertainment, you should have stayed in Sandrine," Melia retorted tartly. "I am not your court jester."

Aeron was not about to let the matter rest since her reluctance to tell him convinced the prince the tale must indeed be an interesting one. "It will pass the time," he insisted. "Besides, how awful could it be?"

"You have no idea," Melia muttered under her breath.

"I promise you," he replied, looking over his shoulder again so that she would see that he was completely sincere in his next statement. "No I give you my word, as a prince of Eden Halas that if you tell me I will not breathe a word of it to anyone."

Melia let out a groan, wishing that she could throttle him except, if she did, it would most likely capsize the boat and that was probably not the best thing to have happen in the middle of the Yantra River. Still, the word of a prince was not something to be refused when offered so earnestly.

As much as they enjoyed trading insults, she knew it would be a real offence if she did not believe him. Even if he was not offended, which she very much doubted, Melia could foresee being asked this same question continuously throughout their entire journey. Since killing him was out of the question, because it was *wrong*, she reminded herself, Melia supposed how bad could it be to tell him?

"Why is it?" Melia asked no one in particular, exasperation oozing from every word, "of all the elves in Avalyne I could possibly find as a travelling companion, I have to be with the one who is the most infuriating?"

"Luck?" Aeron quipped, with a grin on his face she could not see because he had faced front again.

"Oh, alright!" she exclaimed, conceding defeat. "I will tell you only to have you stop asking me."

"Finally," he exclaimed with more than a hint of triumph in his voice. "You have my undivided attention. How did you manage to free yourself from a room full of the Berserkers? I have faced them in battle; that you escaped unscathed while in their power, unarmed, astonishes me."

"Well it is not that difficult to escape when one is a woman," she said, clearing her throat. "All I had to do was pretend to seduce him and he became so eager to accede to my every request, he sent his men away. Once alone, I caught him in a vulnerable position and freed myself."

She noticed he stopped rowing and had turned around so he could look at her, a dark frown on his face.

"Pray tell what do you call a *vulnerable* position?"

"Not *that* vulnerable!" she slapped him across the arm, her jaw dropping open in outrage. "Do you think me capable of bedding a Berserker? Even to escape! Are you completely without wits? What do you take me for?"

"I was mistaken!" Aeron started to recant, realising his mistake. "You said vulnerable position! What was I supposed to think?"

"I meant vulnerable as in *alone* with me, distracted by the thought of pleasure with a human female, not the actual pleasure! You know, this is why I did not wish to answer this question or wish the details known! Small minds like yours instantly think the worst!" she ranted furiously.

"I am sorry!" he apologized, properly chastised, though not enough to keep the smirk from stealing across his face. Despite himself, he could not help feeling some measure of pity for the poor deluded Berserker who actually believed a woman like Melia would couple with him for any reason. "I must confess it is a very different way of securing your release. Certainly Dare and I never considered using that tactic."

"Well you are very pretty," Melia returned with an equally wicked smile. "It might have worked."

Aeron bristled at the suggestion. "That is *not* funny."

"I think it is," Melia chuckled, seeing the distaste on his face. "In any case, I was never so terrified in my entire life. If I had failed in freeing myself, the consequences..." she shuddered visibly at what she could not say and he was able to guess well enough to spare her the indignity.

"Well you were fortunate indeed that it went as well as it did," Aeron agreed with her. "Still, in the event that we do encounter a similar sort of peril, I would request you do not resort to that same plan to secure our freedom."

Melia almost cast him into the river.

Chapter Five

Night Attack

They travelled the entire day, until the sun began to set in the western horizon, turning the blue sky into a vibrant shade of amber. Deciding it would not be long before a blanket of stars drew over them, they steered the canoe towards the embankment of the river.

Their limbs ached from their cramped confinement in the narrow boat and Melia, in particular, needed to feel the land beneath her feet. Of course she would not admit such vulnerability to Aeron and wondered what it was about him that made her so determined not to show weakness?

They made camp along the Eastern Shore, which was supposedly free of Berserkers activity now that Balfure was no more. While there were still many of the creatures in the Northern Province – or the Northlands as it was known to the locals – they were far enough away to be able to let down their guard for the evening. Nevertheless, Aeron insisted on keeping their boats within easy reach should trouble arise. Melia was in agreement with this because she was just as aware of the dangers as he. Even if she did not know this region as well as the prince, the end of Abraxes left many of its denizens scattered and wandering the wilderness looking for easy prey.

When he returned to their encampment after scouting the area to ensure nothing stirred except them, he was glad to see a fire burning. Although elves were able to endure the harshness of weather far better than men, he was still chilled by the night air. Furthermore, the aroma of roasting fish rattled a growl of hunger from his stomach. They had not discussed the cooking duties, though he guessed accurately it would be unwise to assume it was her place to do it.

Still it did *not* mean he could not amuse himself.

"Now there is a sight to put order to my world," Aeron stated playfully when he returned to her and saw her hunched over the fire.

"What?" Melia mused, more focused on the sprinkling of a little spice over the fish to give it flavour than giving Aeron her full attention.

"Seeing you waiting for me with a meal cooked," Aeron smiled at her teasingly.

At that, she shot him a glare of annoyance. "Do not get too accustomed to it. Tomorrow it will be your turn, and I hope your skills involve more than just carrying cured meat in your pouch."

"Lady," he said with proud dignity as he sat down next to her. "A prince of Eden Halas does *not* cook."

"Then the prince is going to go hungry," she returned just as swiftly.

"You are a hard woman," he pointed out as she removed the fish from its skewer over the fire.

"You have no idea," she arched one brow playfully as she handed him his meal on a plate. He was teasing her, Melia realised. "Be careful: it is hot," she instructed dutifully.

"Thank you," he said graciously and they both relaxed away from the flames so that they could dine in comfort.

"You saw nothing out there?" Melia asked as they ate.

This part of Avalyne was unfamiliar to her. During her searches for her mother, she had mostly explored the lands nearest the Baffin. She did not wish to reveal to him that she was a little anxious by this unfamiliarity because, as a watch guard, she relied on knowing the land intimately and being able to anticipate all its dangers. This part of the Northlands was still a mystery to her.

"Nothing," he shook his head in answer. "This area is not known to be plagued by Berserkers but I cannot say for certain that nothing will wander into our path. It is difficult to predict the behaviour of Balfure's minions now the Iron Citadel has fallen. Before he was destroyed, we knew his minions would be found at his places of power. Since he is no more, they are scattered and hiding. Thus I do not know if we are any more protected than if we had camped on the Western Shore."

"You fear they are moving into lands that are not common for them," Melia said in understanding, having encountered something of the same problem in the Baffin.

The pattern of these foul creatures was no longer a constant, now that they were leaderless and without direction. Their power in Avalyne was done but, like wounded animal about to die, they were perhaps even more dangerous in these final hours than when Balfure guided their every move.

"Fortunately, if danger nears, I should be able to sense it before it arrives," Aeron offered.

"That is good to know," Melia replied. "I do not wish to awaken with one of their poisoned blades to my throat."

"Fear not, I shall protect you from harm," he teased.

"On the contrary, I shall protect you," Melia did not look up from her plate when she responded just as smoothly. "If they mean to harm us, I will simply have to seduce their Captain to secure our freedom."

The remark drew such a sharp glare from him Melia almost laughed.

"Do not even joke about such things," he said tersely.

"Who was joking?" she winked at him.

"I would kill anything that attempted to take advantage of you in that way. After all, I have staked a claim upon you. If you seduce anyone it will shall be me," he retaliated with a smug smile.

This time, Melia did laugh out loud. "Only in your dreams."

"Not in yours too?" He gasped in mock hurt. "I thought that you would dream nothing else."

"Perhaps in your dreams, not in mine," she laughed, enjoying their bantering as much as he.

Suddenly, the boyish smile melted from his face and his blue eyes became hard like flint. His gaze shot past her shoulder and he set down his plate immediately so he could stand up, his expression was one of grave concern. Melia might not have known him well enough to read all his moods but she recognised the look he wore now. It spoke volumes. She reached for her own weapon before rising up to take her place at his side.

"What is it?" she whispered.

"Something approaches," he said quietly, arming the bow he'd picked up when he stood, arming it to fire.

"Can you tell what?" Her eyes swept the bushes framing the tree line past the shore and saw nothing. What did his eyes see?

"I am not certain," he answered but she noticed that he threaded his bow with two arrows instead of one.

"I do not hear anything," she remarked and knew immediately she was talking too much.

Aeron frowned and silenced her with a sharp look. His elven hearing could sense the approach of two, their heavy feet pressing into the soft ground as they neared. He was impressed by their ability to move so silently, for the space between each footstep indicated that the enemies were large in stature. Yet, it required the heightened sense of the fair folk to detect their approach. He doubted a human would have heard them until it was too late. He had a fair idea of what was coming at them.

"Take this," he ordered as he handed to her the long dagger he wore on his back just as they began to hear branches being bent and leaves rustling nearer and nearer to them.

"I have my own weapon," she insisted, wondering why he required her to use a dagger instead of her crossbow.

"Your bolts will not penetrate their hides," he said hastily. The ground started to rumble now. "This requires weapons crafted by dwarf skill," Aaron stated, prepared to use his sword if the arrows were not enough to put down their enemy.

"What are they?" she demanded, her heart starting to pound because they were terribly close now, enough to hear everything being said.

He looked at her briefly and answered, "ogres."

Melia gaped at him but had little time to comment because the creatures chose that moment to launch themselves through the shrubbery, drawn to the light of the campfire. She had never seen ogres in the flesh before, but knew of them and their fearsome reputations.

Not quite as big as cave trolls, they were twice the size of normal men and craved human flesh for their sustenance. Their skins were scales of thick hide and they clutched large hammers with clawed hands. Their teeth were distinct by the two tusk-like canines that could rib apart bone with ease. Since Balfure's fall, the few remaining creatures not killed at Astaroth now wandered the hills aimlessly, scavenging for prey.

Aeron let both arrows fly when they revealed themselves. Slicing through the night air, the sharpened points pierced the hide and then flesh of their targets. The ogres bellowed out in outrage, the arrows giving them only a slight pause before they resumed their advance towards the archer. Aeron stood his ground undaunted, continuing to fire arrow upon arrow with deadly accuracy.

In an effort to stop the barrage, one of the ogres flung their large hammers at the prince, forcing him to move. He did so, avoiding the weapon with effortless grace while they continued their charge. Melia had yet to draw their attention. As a result, she shrank back into the darkness, allowing them to run past her so that she could approach them from behind. Once they were past, she ran to the fire and picked up a burning log. Melia flung it against one of the beasts, hoping to draw the ogre away so the prince need only deal with one.

In hindsight, perhaps it was not the wisest plan.

When the creature turned its yellow eyes upon her and his mouth pulled back to reveal jagged teeth, Melia wondered what in the name of Spit was she thinking, provoking a creature she never before combated. Reminding herself this was no different and certainly less perilous than shooting bolts at a Primordial, she had little time to debate the matter before the beast was coming straight at her.

The ogre moved surprisingly fast for a creature of such bulk, and when he swung his hammer, she could hear the rush of air as she ducked to avoid it. The wideness of the swing unbalanced him and he stumbled a little, letting the hammer drag him when it thudded against the ground.

Taking advantage of his lapse, Melia used the dagger Aeron had given her and slashed at the ogre's shin. Even though he was wearing leather guards, the dwarf dagger cut through the armour and met flesh with ease. She saw dark blood running down the blade and over her gauntlets. Screaming in fury, the ogre lashed out at her suddenly, his meaty fist connecting with her chin and swatting her away like a fly.

"MELIA!" She heard Aeron's anxious cry echo distantly through her ears.

All sound seemed to be muffled around her when she hit the dirt. Her fierce desire for self-preservation did not leave her disorientated very long because she saw the approach of the hammer once again. Still held firmly in the grip of its master, the ogre raised it in readiness to hurl it at her. Eyes widening in fright, she rolled as it slammed into the dirt where she had been lying. Forcing back her terror, she remembered the dagger still in her hand.

The ogre, already bleeding from the wounds on his legs and from the arrows protruding from his body, bellowed once more as another struck him, causing him to spasm. The beast convulsed, his hand clawing behind him in an effort to dislodge the painful object impaled in his back.

Aeron's gaze touched hers briefly and she saw the relief in his eyes until her notice fell to something even more pressing.

"Prince! Behind you!" she warned in horror as the second ogre he had been fighting swung its shield against the prince. The sound of metal made a terrible crack against bone and there and then, she knew his ribs were broken. She saw him crumple to the ground as the ogre closed in to finish him off.

Blind rage filled her and without thinking Melia flung the dagger through the air, praying her aim was as good as she believed. With typical elven agility, Aeron darted from under the path of the enemy's weapon and stumbled to his feet. Even though he was hurt, he still managed to unsheathe his sword and ready himself for a fight.

The dagger she had flung struck the ogre in the chest, distracting the foul creature long enough for Aeron to finish it off. Wielding a broadsword with far more skill and ability than anyone as injured as he should be capable, Aeron lunged forward with a powerful thrust. He drove the sword through flesh and bone, finding little resistance in the thick hide. Melia flinched as she saw the spray of dark blood.

The ogre uttered a guttural sound of agony before it tumbled forward, landing on the ground with a heavy thud as Aeron staggered out of its path. Upon collapsing, the creature sent a cloud of dust up in the air while its blood created a pool of slick darkness beneath it. Face down, against the dirt, it moved no more, but its companion still breathed.

Melia watched as Aeron strode purposefully towards the second ogre who was still occupied with removing the arrow from its back. The prince's eyes were no longer blue but almost black, like the blood dripping from his sword. Melia followed him, picking up his long bow because her own crossbow would do little against the ogre's hide. She ripped an arrow from the creature's dead comrade and shadowed Aeron, in case he needed the help.

She did not think he would need it.

After their playful flirtations, it was difficult to believe this handsome prince was a thousand years old and had fought more battles than she could possibly imagine. In Eden Halas, he hunted spiders. During the Aeth War, he'd led the elves to Astaroth. As she saw the glare in his eyes as he stalked his enemy, she could well imagine him as the battle-hardened warrior. Especially after he delivered the killing blow.

The ogre's head came away from its body, spinning in midair before landing in the fire, trailing embers as it rolled over the charred wood and across the ground. Melia turned away from the grisly scene because, no matter how much she thought she was inured to such things, carnage still had the power to make her queasy. Aeron exhaled deeply after the ogre fell, displacing leaves and dirt upon landing. The strength carrying him this far faltered at last and Aeron sank to his knees again, the sword falling from his hand.

Melia was stumbling towards him before he collapsed. She hobbled a little, not realizing until now that her hard landing earlier had twisted her ankle badly. It ached as she tried to walk, but it was pain she could endure. The side of her face burned and she imagined she was bruised but it seemed incidental next to her fears for his injuries. The sound of bone breaking under the shield was branded into her psyche and it was possible he was seriously hurt. His display of pain certainly implied it.

"You're hurt," she lowered herself next to him, clutching his arm to keep him from landing on his face.

"Not badly," he lied.

"Fool!" she snapped at him. "You are in agony! I see can see it in that face of yours. Now move your arm and let me look."

Aeron reluctantly allowed her to pull open his tunic and hissed in discomfort when the cold night made contact with his sensitive skin. He did not think he was severely injured, but he was in considerable pain. The ogre's shield was made to break bones, and bearing the brunt of it had certainly earned him a few cracked ribs. He cursed his carelessness in letting the creature come so close but, at the time, all he could think about was Melia.

All rational thought had fled his mind when he had seen her in peril. How could he think about his life when hers might be lost? He had lived a thousand years, long enough to experience life with its infinite possibilities. In comparison, hers had barely begun, and he could not endure the thought of it ending before he had a chance to know her.

Or more correctly, before *they had a chance to know each other.*

"You have broken bones," Melia announced unhappily as she examined his side and saw the discoloration of his pale skin. She had never seen an elf so exposed before and had to marvel at the softness of their skin to the touch. Her fingertips grazed the swelling and felt the heat of inflammation radiating from his bruises. He would need at least a full day of rest before they could even think of resuming their journey to Tor Iolan. Not even the speed of elven recovery could overcome the injury he had sustained this night.

While she should have been annoyed by this delay, Melia found she was simply grateful he still lived. When she had seen him battered by the ogre, the despair she felt at his possible loss stabbed at her more than she could possibly imagine. Furthermore, she knew exactly why he allowed himself to be harmed this way. He was trying to protect her and while she did not know what to do with that yet, she did know she felt just as strongly about preserving his life.

"I will manage," he replied bravely.

"You will manage nothing if you do not rest," she snapped in annoyance at his stubbornness when she lowered the tunic down once more. "We will move camp a little further downstream where it's safer. All this blood is going to bring wolves or something worse upon us."

"Perhaps I should have let you seduce them after all," he grimaced when he tried to move.

Melia laughed softly and smiled at him warmly, taking his arm in hers to help him to his feet. "Perhaps you should have. You would have been better for it."

"Well, never let it be said that a prince of Halas would not suffer for a lady's virtue," Aeron grunted as Melia helped him to his feet.

"I am not a lady," Melia reminded as she led him toward the boat whose spine was pressed into the shale embankment. "I am just a watch guard."

"You are a watch guard for certain," Aeron insisted, wondering why she found it so necessary to hide behind the title, "But you are also a lady."

"Well, this lady will have you remain here," she said firmly as she made him sit down next to the boat so she could pack up their campsite. "Remain still please, while I gather our things?"

"I did not know that you cared so much," Aeron teased, needing to regain his wounded dignity by placing them on familiar ground again. Better to flirt with her than tolerate this wholly unacceptable situation where she needed to attend to him like a little boy.

"I do not care at all." She pretended to turn up her nose at him, but a sly glance and little smile told him that she was indulging in the play for his benefit. "I just need you to guide me to Tor

Iolan, so I should at least ensure that you are well enough to make the journey."

"And here I thought I was starting to melt your heart," he winked at her, though it was difficult to remain quite so charming when the pain in his side ached so much. "Have I not suffered enough to prove myself?"

"Just stay where you are," she ordered with more than a hint of exasperation creeping into her voice as she walked back to the camp site. "I shall be back soon."

Aeron watched her go and was unable to resist calling out after her. "No farewell kiss?"

Chapter Six

Nightmares

Melia did not sleep well.

This much Aeron had learned about the watch guard by the second night of their journey.

After their encounter with the ogres, Melia rowed them further down river and, upon finding a safe place to camp, moored their vessel so she could tend to his wounds. She was no healer the way Arianne was, but she knew enough to relieve some of the pain he was experiencing. Once she ensured he was comfortable for the night and he was done crowing over how much he enjoyed her fussing over him, she took some rest herself.

He woke to the scraping friction of fabric against the ground. By their nature, elves did not require as much sleep as men. They were able to endure long periods of wakefulness, but this was a practice used only when necessary and certainly not when injured. Melia insisted he sleep when they settled at their new campsite and, despite offering protest, Aeron eventually succumbed to exhaustion and caught a few of hours of complete slumber.

The sound that brought him out of his sleep had an urgency to it that forced his unconscious immediately awake. It did not take him long to discern the cause. Melia was tossing restlessly under her blanket. She rolled onto her side towards him where a gleam of moonlight illuminated her face and revealed genuine fear in her expression. Whatever she was witnessing in her dreams was clearly disturbing and he debated whether or not he ought to intrude upon her slumber by rousing her from its unpleasantness.

Fortunately, he had only a brief moment to debate this when suddenly she sat upright with a small gasp. For a few seconds, she sat in place, panting hard as her mind came to grips with the realisation that she was free of the nightmare. It took her even longer than that to realise she was not alone and Aeron had witnessed the whole event.

If this thing between them wasn't so new, Aeron would have gone to her and offered his shoulder in comfort. However, they were far from that point in their relationship. It alarmed him to see the fear in her eyes, because he could not imagine what she saw in her dreams to inspire such vivid nightmares. She was not a woman who scared easily and yet, as he watched her, wide-eyed and on the verge of tears, he wished she would confide in him.

"Melia, are you alright?"

Melia jumped at the sound of his voice and she stared at him as if she had forgotten he was there at all before she wiped the tears, from her damp cheeks. It broke Aeron's heart to see her tears but his inability to comfort her was not as worrying as seeing one of the strongest people he knew reduced to this state. For an instant, he saw the vulnerable woman beneath the watch guard. The one who felt things more profoundly than most would believe.

"Yes," she answered slowly, wishing he had not seen her so exposed and feeling a flush of embarrassment at being caught in such state. "I am fine."

"You do not sound it," he stated, genuinely concerned. "That must have been a terrible nightmare," he remarked tentatively, hoping it would lead her to tell him what was plagued her.

"It is nothing I have not dealt with before," she replied, her voice almost a whisper.

"Do you often have such fearful dreams?" he prodded gently, though he suspected she would be reluctant to speak of them.

"Of course not," she shrugged. "Everyone has nightmares. Do elves not have such dreams?"

Aeron knew she was lying, but let it pass because she had a right to her privacy. Besides, despite their obvious attraction, they had not known each other long enough for her to trust him with something so personal.

"Yes, we do," Aeron answered recalling a few terrors in the dark that had awakened him the way she had a short time ago. "There are times when I dream of the demon we encountered in the catacombs of Iridia," he confessed.

"Demon?" Melia looked at him, her eyes round with wonder.

"During our attempt to free Iridia," Aeron explained, telling her the tale of the Nameless.

They called it the Nameless because none of them had seen its kind before. Tamsyn believed it was a creature of the Primordial Wars, birthed by the unholy union of Syphia and Mael. They encountered it while journeying through a secret pass in the Starfall Mountains of Iridia. They had been on their way to a gathering of dwarf clans to discuss their participation in the alliance against Balfure.

Its savagery was such it was hard to believe such a thing could live outside of nightmares. The beast had lain in wait in the bottom of a fissure the dwarves called Unending Well, gaining sustenance from victims using the steps carved into its wall to travel to other parts of the mountain.

Far larger than a dragon, it possessed four serpent necks as thick as columns and that, when raised to their full height, almost touched the roof of the cavern. Each of those sightless heads were little more than large mouths filled with teeth. They waited in silence and darkness, snatching their prey from the path with the speed of a cracking whip. More often than not, only an abrupt scream was all anyone could make, before being crushed by powerful jaws.

It had taken everything they had to kill it, until Tamsyn was forced to bring down the cavern walls to bury it under tonnes of rock. To this day, Aeron did not know if it still lived, trapped beneath the earth, waiting for someone to release it and, on occasion, he dreamed of it and those terrible snapping jaws.

Aeron's voice was soft as his mind drifted back to days when their purpose was clear and the enemy so well defined. There was something freeing about knowing one's course with such certainty that nothing else seemed to matter, except the fate of his friends in the Circle. Until they scattered to the winds, each to follow their own destiny, Aeron did not realise how dearly he missed the camaraderie they afforded each other.

Melia saw the longing in his eyes and felt sad for him. For the first time, she wondered if elves kept to themselves because it was too hard to be friends with races they would almost certainly outlive. How hard was it to be the one always left behind to mourn? Seeing his pain and hearing of his nightmares made hers seem less terrible.

"Arianne told us of how Dare was almost lost at Iridia. Was this when?" she asked, having heard something of the tale during the quest to Sanhael.

Even now, the moment made Aeron shudder. When the enormous neck of the Nameless had struck the steps they were using to cross the Unending Well, great chunks of rock had broken off and rained down upon them. Dare was knocked off his perch and only Aeron's quick reflexes kept him from plunging to his death.

"Yes. He almost fell to his death, but I caught him in time. Until that moment, I do not believe any of us knew how much we needed him to hold us together. If he had died, the alliance would have gone with him."

Melia could well believe that. King Dare had a way about him, a sincerity and unwavering belief in people that transcended race, colour and even belief. He saw the races of Avalyne as a whole, not separate parts limited by their own selfish boundaries. He showed the Western Sphere how strong they could be together and, if he had died then, the fragile alliance would have shattered.

"I was ready to tie him up and send him to the safety of Halas after that," Aeron uttered a short, humourless laugh. "Anything to keep him safe. After losing Braedan, I did not wish to bury another friend."

"Braedan?"

"Before Celene and Kyou joined our circle, it was Braedan and I that followed Dare when he began visiting the people of Avalyne to rally them against Balfure. Braedan was the son of Braelan who ruled Sandrine for Balfure. His father was a brute, but Braedan had a good heart and he believed Dare could save us. When the Disciples chased us down seven years ago, I sent Dare into Barrenjuck Green while Braedan and I led them away. Braedan pretended to be Dare and the ruse worked. They were led enough astray to allow Dare's escape. Unfortunately, Braedan and I were separated and they were able to capture him."

Melia did not need to hear the rest of this tale, for she knew it already. Braedan had no more survived the interrogation by the Disciples than Keira Furnsby. How sad it was they lost two friends that night. The only difference being that, at least with Braedan, there was a body to bury. They still had not found where Syphia left Keira in the old wood.

"I like to think my father died in the same manner, fighting to the last to defend the people he cared for," she said quietly, not looking at him. "I was so accustomed to him going off to fight one battle after another that it never occurred to me that one day he would not return. He was the only one who loved me for what I was and, once he was gone, everything in my world changed."

Neither spoke for a few minutes as they thought of the loved ones gone from this world and shared in silence the sadness that only strengthened the bond between them. Since her father had died, Melia shared nothing about him with anyone, because no one cared enough to ask. After being alone for so long, it was difficult to reach into one's soul and find again the things she buried so deeply. She had not spoken of her father since his death, and the years of loneliness following it made her forget just how much she truly missed him.

"How are you feeling?" she asked, wishing to dispel the melancholy settling over them.

"As if I have battled ogres," he answered through a groan when he made an attempt to ease back into his sleeping place.

"We will rest tomorrow." She spoke gently but there was force enough in her words to indicate she would broke no argument on this matter.

"I am hardly in the position to say otherwise," he conceded as he saw her nestle into her bedroll as well.

"Good," Melia said with a little smile as she closed her eyes to sleep, "perhaps there is some use for the ogres *after* all."

* * *

It was not long before she was tossing and turning again, the demons plaguing her resuming their torment in her slumber. Aeron rose from his sleeping place and crossed the circle of campfire light between them. Stretching out next to her, he brushed his hand against her dark hair and began to sing an elven song his mother Syanne used to lull him to sleep as a child. He continued to sing softly into her ear as he stroked the strands of jet against his palm.

When he saw she no longer struggled and drifted off into a peaceful sleep, he smiled.

* * *

Melia appeared to remember nothing of his efforts on her behalf the next morning, but her spirits were bright and cheerful, and she attributed her mood to a good night's sleep. The day of rest aided Aeron's recovery from his wounds and, though he still ached, he was well enough for them to resume their journey the following morning.

In truth, he did not wish to linger out in the open indefinitely. After battling ogres, Aeron could not be certain what other remnants of Balfure's army were at large on the banks of the Yantra River. While he was recovered enough to be on the move, if something more formidable than ogres appeared out of the darkness, he was not confident of his ability to defend them against it. The only safe place at present seemed to be on the river.

Of course, he kept this to himself because Melia would have taken exception to knowing he felt it his duty to protect them both. She would have argued she was perfectly capable of taking care of herself.

They travelled for five days up the Yantra River, and it was five days Aeron found extremely enlightening.

He learned Melia's father was a distinguished commander of the Nadiran army and she left behind a large family to journey west. Despite their demand she marry, they were not a cruel people, simply rigid in their ways. While he could understand why she fled, he also suspected she missed the aunts and cousins left behind. Aeron laughed when she revealed how she pretended to be male during her first years in the west, until unwittingly revealing her gender during the battle of Cereine. The captain who accepted her as one of his own soldiers, cared little for her sex, only that she could fight.

He in turn, told Melia of his family, of his mother Syanne, to whom he was closest. While he cared for his brothers Syannon and Hadros, they had little in common. More complicated was the relationship with his father Halion, who did not hold with his liking of the outside world and his consorting with other races. While Dare was an inconvenience he tolerated for the sake of his queen, Halion could not understand why Aeron chose to spend time away from Eden Halas now that the war with Balfure was done.

Ironically, despite being worlds apart in race and culture, both Aeron and Melia appeared to be fleeing from their families for the same reason.

* * *

While the woods of Iolan were considered part of Halas, its distance from the court of King Halion necessitated the establishment of a smaller colony by one of his vassals, a former Forest Guard Captain called Gavril.

Lord Gavril was a friend to Aeron since childhood. The former Captain fought with his father during the Primordial Wars and was one of the oldest elves in Avalyne. Both grew up together in Sanhael before Mael destroyed the city and claimed it for his own.

The settlement established by Lord Gavril was called Eden Iolan and, despite the ancient terrors living there, the elves of Eden Iolan had learnt enough about its many paths to avoid falling prey to its dangers. Despite his friendship with the King, Gavril was a different sort of elf. While Halion had little time for mortals, Gavril ensured his own Forest Guard kept watch over the woods to ensure travellers were guided away from danger.

It was Gavril who taught Aeron all he knew about the bow, and his archers were known to be the finest in elvendom.

While most would think otherwise, elves preferred using the sword instead of the bow. Unless an archer possessed exceptional skill, as did Gavril's archers and now Aeron himself, the density of trees and branches made it problematic for an arrow to find its mark. Archers with moderate skill found it extremely difficult to use a bow properly in the woods, and most opted for the blade instead.

The forest was thick and, as soon as they crossed the tree line away from the river bank, the sunlight which had warmed their backs all morning vanished beneath the canopy of leaves overhead. The trees of the Eden Iolan were old: many of them had stood for hundreds if not thousands of years. They reached into the sky and their barks were sheathed in moss and lichens, making them appear likes giant blades of grass.

Melia tried to see the path Aeron navigated so effortlessly and found herself lost amongst the waist high shrubs and plants. The terrain was uneven, with boulders and gnarled roots protruding from rich loamy soil similarly covered with moss. Younger saplings grew next to the older trees, with streams of light crisscrossing the place through the thick roof of leaves above.

"What are these ancient evils?" Melia asked once they left the boat behind to continue the rest of their journey on foot. "Arianne spoke of their menace but did not say what they were."

"Well," Aeron's eyes were fixed ahead as he read the landscape and followed the unseen path through the forest, "there are many that reside here. You know of the spiders we drove out some time ago, or rather we thought we did before Caras Anara."

It still stung Aeron to think that the creatures that decimated the small coastal town and nearly killed Celene and Arianne were the same swarm he thought he'd vanquished from Eden Halas.

Without blinking, Melia spoke immediately, "I have been instructed by Kyou to tell you that it was not your fault if you bring up Caras Anara." She finished her recital by smiling sweetly at him.

Aeron made a face. "That dwarf thinks he is so smart. Put him on a horse and let us see how smart he is," he grumbled, before resuming his answer to her question about the creatures roaming these woods.

"It is believed a plant Primordial called Viridae in the service of Mael was pursued here by the Celestial Atae and, upon her death at his hands, scattered her seed across these woods. Much of these ancient evils I speak of are her progeny, not all of which I am certain we have seen yet. We know of the Night Hunters, creatures who emerge only during the dark but remain harmless shrubs during the day. At night, they take on the shape of a creature moving on four legs and hunt their prey in packs. Anything they find, they kill and devour."

Instinctively, Melia's hand went to her sword, since they were in fact surrounded by shrubs.

"Then there are the Asanek, spirits who dwell in tree stumps and can turn themselves into the form of small children. They wander the woods until some well-meaning person encounters them, believing they are giving aid to a lost child but unaware that at the first opportunity they will be eaten. After feeding, these children return to their original forms. Of course the worst of these are the Mother Trees."

"Mother trees?" Melia asked warily, certain by the time he was done, she was never entering any forest ever again.

"Yes, we have no other way to describe them. These are the ones that are most concerning. A mother tree does not move but she can spawn creatures that scour the woods in search of food to be brought back to her. Over the years, Gavril and his guard have patrolled the forests of Iolan to ensure any mortal passing through stays well away from the places these creatures are known to exist."

"Well, Prince," Melia said, giving him a look, "you have succeeded in seeing to it I am utterly terrified now."

Aeron paused and looked over his shoulder at her. "Do not worry. I will protect you, fair maiden."

Melia snorted.

Despite the tales he was telling her, Aeron could feel his spirits rising as he took a deep breath of the forest scent. In his youth, he'd visited these woods often and, later on, when Dare was old enough to leave Eden Halas, Aeron had brought him to visit with Gavril, who was kinder than his own severe father. It almost felt like he was a boy again, thrilling in the simple joy of who he was and being happily content by that alone.

Melia did nothing to dampen his mood because she was rather amused by his boyish demeanour, even though everything he described about these woods made her wish to run out of it. Still, it was difficult not to be swept up by his cheerful spirits, and it surprised her how much she enjoyed seeing him happy. He seemed familiar with every tree, every path where there might be danger and which way was safest to travel. Melia supposed she could have found her way through this maze had she attempted this journey alone but, after hearing what lived here, she was grateful for his company.

It was with a sudden start Melia realised that she'd been enjoying his company so much that she had forgotten why she was going to Tor Iolan. Damn him, she fumed inwardly, this was exactly what she feared. He was distracting her!

"How far away are we from Tor Iolan?" Melia asked suddenly, her tone turning hard.

"Two days from here," Aeron replied, noticing a sudden change in her manner. He wondered what caused it and wished he could be assured of an answer instead of a sharp rebuke if he asked. "We will go tomorrow at first light. Tonight we must stop at Eden Iolan."

"Must we go there?" she asked, a little more acerbically than she had intended.

She knew it was wrong to be so abrasive with him, but she could not help feeling a little resentment at his being able to make her forget her goal. For so long she had searched for her mother, driven forward when most would have faltered, and then finding nothing for her efforts.

Now that she was in reach of an answer, she was allowing herself to be distracted by a handsome prince of all things! It was the sort of nonsense little girls dreamed of when they were still playing with their dolls. The absurdity of it made Melia angry at herself for even indulging the thought. What fool chose to become lost in the eyes of an elf? There was no future with one, nothing but years where he remained beautiful while her body disintegrated before his eyes. It was folly!

And yet each moment she spent with him, she found herself pulled towards a catastrophe she was powerless to avoid because her heart was betraying her.

Aeron stared at her, unable to fathom why her mood had become so dark. They had been together for almost a week and in that time their arguments, though frequent, were laced with good humour and gentle mischief, not this cold edge he could feel piercing his skin.

"We have been travelling in Iolan for almost a day, and night will be here soon. I do not plan to sleep in the open, Melia. We will not see the morning. Furthermore, it is extremely discourteous to enter his realm and not pay our respects to Lord Gavril." His tone was equally sharp but she had given him just cause.

"I suppose," she muttered sourly realising, perhaps she was being somewhat unreasonable. "I have delayed enough in my journey: I wish only to get to Tor Iolan so that I can have my answers."

"What answers would those be?" he demanded. Until now he had not asked why she was so determined to reach this misbegotten place because he respected her need for privacy. Yet her manner provoked his own frustration and it frothed to the surface when she spoke so coldly to him.

"I told you," she paused in her step and stared at him. "That is none of your concern."

"Lady," Aeron started to say but paused and reined in his anger before it overwhelmed him. "I told you before, if you desire passage through here, you will observe the proper customs!"

"I am not an elf," she bit back. "I do not have to observe anything!" With that she stormed past him.

"Melia!" Aeron called after her.

Melia ignored him, having every intention of continuing doing so until they reached their destination, wherever it was. She had taken no more than a few steps away from him when suddenly, stepping out of the trees like phantoms in the dark was an entire contingent of elven warriors. As a watch guard, she knew how to move stealthily but even she was startled by how flawlessly they stepped out of their hiding places without warning. It was as if they slipped through a tear in the fabric of the forest.

She and Aeron were surrounded.

The leader, a dark-haired elf bearing more than a passing resemblance to Aeron, stared at her as if she was something of an oddity.

"I am surprised at you, Aeron," he said as Aeron came up alongside of her. "You are now travelling with the enemy?"

"Melia is not the enemy," Aeron retorted impatiently.

"My apologies," the elf returned. "The way you both were arguing, you can understand my mistake."

Despite his sarcasm, Aeron broke into a smile at the sight of his older brother. "Hadros, what are you doing in Eden Iolan?"

"We chased a band of Berserkers into these woods," Hadros answered, staring at him with that haughty expression Aeron knew so well growing up. "What are *you* doing here? And why are you travelling with this... woman." He made no effort to hide the contempt on his face.

Before Melia could respond, Aeron silence her with a gesture and shot her a look that demanded she give him lead to speak for them both. "Hadros, mind your manners. This is the Lady Melia."

"Lady?" Hadros' brow pressed into his forehead as he regarded Melia with disbelief at her being described as such. "She hardly looks like a lady to me." His eyes travelled up and down her form critically, "In those clothes, I would say she looks like a man."

"At least one of us does," Melia responded icily, eliciting stifled sniggers among the other elves present.

"Melia!" Aeron ordered, wishing her to remember Hadros was a prince of Eden Halas and commanded respect even if he was poor at showing it. Still, Aeron did not deny enjoying seeing his brother put in his place for his discourteous behaviour. "Hadros, the lady is a watch guard and we are travelling companions," Aeron explained while he felt Melia's glare burning into his back.

"Really?" Hadros turned his eyes upon her and seemed to study her in a new light. A little smile curled his lips and at first Melia did not understand why he looked at her that way. The other elves too seemed to study her with renewed interest and Melia began to feel a little self-conscious by their scrutiny.

"I would have thought that you would have selected an elven woman to be your 'travelling companion,' not a barbarian whose people were known allies of Abraxes. Is she a souvenir from Astaroth?" Hadros sneered.

"Enough brother!" Aeron said sharply and gripped Melia's elbow to keep her from reacting to Hadros' insult she was his whore. "Hadros, Melia is my guest and I will have you treat her accordingly. She is a friend to Arianne and helped with the defeat of Syphia. Arianne has asked I guide her to Tor Iolan. I should not like Arianne to hear we could not afford her friend simple courtesy."

Hadros stiffened because, if Arianne was displeased by his conduct, that report would find its way to Lylea and Halion would be furious if it resulted in censure from the High Queen.

Surprised and somewhat touched by his defence of her honour, Melia calmed down somewhat and decided her own behaviour bore scrutiny. Aeron was absolutely right of course. Hadros was the heir apparent of Eden Halas and he deserved her respect even if he was a dolt.

"Prince Hadros," she spoke in a calm and conciliatory tone, "I beg your forgiveness for my rudeness. I wish no disrespect to you, nor do I wish to cause any difficulty while I travel in this realm."

Embarrassed by the apology he should have made first, the older son of Halion regarded her with as much dignity as he could manage under the circumstances. "We both chose our words ill," he said after a moment. "Let us forget this unpleasantness and start anew, my lady."

Melia's gaze touched his and she nodded in acquiescence. "I would like that, my Lord."

Aeron relaxed visibly and offered his older brother a smile of gratitude. "Thank you, brother."

"You and your companions," Hadros shook his head with a resigned sigh. "Come on then. Let us go together to Eden Iolan. Lord Gavril will be pleased to see you."

Chapter Seven

A Night in Eden Iolan

As Hadros, Melia and Aeron passed through the Veil and into Eden Iolan, Melia found herself gaping in awe at the resplendent beauty of the elven city. Even Hadros's insult was distant as she stared in wonder at the settlement that seemed to have sprung forth from the land like the great trees of Iolan. She knew that, unless the elves permitted it, a traveller moving within this space would see nothing of the colony, only the trees within it. The enchantment of the Veil ensured the elves could live here safely without anyone being aware of them.

Despite his brother's apology, which Aeron knew was for the benefit of his men and any report to Arianne, he reminded himself to clarify the nature of his relationship with Melia. The last thing he wanted was for Hadros to report to the court of Eden Halas that Melia was his lover, particularly when she was not. She had behaved like a lady throughout their entire journey and he would not have her virtue slandered, as Hadros was likely to do after she insulted him so properly.

Ascending a spiral set of stairs that coiled around the trunk of a behemoth tree, they stepped onto the floor built above the thick branches strong enough to support it. The rest of the house was built with logs fallen naturally, ornately carved with intricate patterns, resembling marble instead of wood. Seated on his throne was Lord Gavril, an elf dressed in robes that did not differ from his guards save for some gold embroidery along the cuff. At the sight of them, he left his seat and met them half way across the floor.

"Young prince," Gavril greeted with genuine pleasure, clutching Aeron's shoulder as he spoke, "it has been too long."

"Likewise, Lord Gavril." Aeron bowed to Gavril, whom he respected, even if the former captain answered to Halion. Melia bowed without speaking, wishing to fade into the background while Aeron and Gavril made their greetings. Flanked by both Aeron and Hadros, she felt very much out of place and was convinced all eyes were fixed on her, trying to decide what she was to their young prince.

"We stumbled upon my brother and his," Hadros paused as he threw a glance at Melia before continuing, "his companion approaching from the river. I almost thought he had lost his way home."

"Very funny brother." Aeron gave him brother a look. "Melia is a watch guard and she needs a guide through these woods. We were both in Sandrine at the same time and I offered to help her."

"Watch guard?" Gavril turned to Melia, who immediately wished she was anywhere else because she expected a reaction akin to the one she had been given by Hadros. "The same one who aided Queen Arianne on her quest to fight Syphia?"

"The same," Aeron confirmed, pleased because Gavril's knowledge of Melia's part in that affair would help smooth the way for her in Eden Iolan.

"We are in your debt then," Gavril said, taking Melia's hand in his and gazing down at her with warmth. "It is no small matter to face a Primordial. Trust me, I know."

She supposed he would, since he had fought at Halion's side during those wars. "Thank you." She gave him a smile of gratitude at his acceptance. "Arianne is my queen and my friend; I was honoured to be of service to her."

"It appears she considers you a friend as well," Gavril replied. "Arianne has made some inquiries on your behalf. Is that why you have come here? To see Tor Iolan?"

Aeron turned to Melia, his eyes showing his hurt that Gavril knew more about her mission to Tor Iolan than he. After all, he was her travelling companion and guide. Melia saw his reaction and immediately felt a pang of guilt at revealing her purpose at Tor Iolan. She wished Gavril had not disclosed what Arianne had done for her, since it only complicated matters between them.

"Yes," she swallowed thickly, aware of the prince's eyes upon her as she spoke. She knew she would have some explaining to do once this audience with Gavril was done.

"There is nothing there," Hadros stated before Gavril could. "It has been completely emptied. The fortress stands, but nothing more. We swept it clean after thc Aeth War."

"I must go there nonetheless," she replied, directing her answer at Gavril instead of at Hadros – or at Aeron, for that matter. "I have to see it for myself."

"Your mother will not be found there," the Lord of Eden Iolan declared.

"Your mother?" Aeron blurted out, unable to hold in his shock. "This has been a search for your mother?"

"I told you," Melia met his gaze. "It was a personal matter."

"Melia, no human survived Tor Iolan," Aeron insisted. It saddened him to dash her hopes, but she needed to hear the truth. "The Disciples were very thorough."

Melia wished she did not have quite so much of an audience when answering him but she felt badly Gavril should know more than he, especially since he had guided her this far. He had earned the right to know. "My mother was not human, Aeron."

"Not human?" His eyes widened in shock. "What was she? Elvish?"

"Not elvish," Gavril answered for her, seeing Melia's difficulty in explaining. "Melia's mother was a river daughter."

A river daughter. He knew the legends. They were vassals of the Water Wife, the Celestial Dalcine. "The ones who serve the Celestials? Does that make you an immortal as well?" He asked her.

It was ridiculous the hope he felt at the possibility.

"No," Gavril unknowingly quashed hope promptly. "Melia's father is mortal and so is she."

Aeron hid the disappointment he felt hearing that. If Melia were a true river daughter, then she would possess a life span ensuring he would never lose her to Father Death the way he would eventually lose Dare and all his mortal friends.

"Why could you not tell me?" he asked, his voice reflecting his hurt.

"I did not want anyone to know," Melia answered softly, deciding he deserved an honest answer. "For so long I was not even certain that river daughters were real. I did not want to appear foolish for believing in a fantasy, and perhaps I feared what I would learn about myself in discovering what they are."

Aeron could see her point. Even to the elves, the river daughters were something of a mystery. It was said that they were vassals of the Water Wife, but few had ever been seen. If Melia had made her parentage known, she would have brought undue attention to herself, or worse yet, been the object of ridicule and disbelief. She was too proud for that. Nonetheless, knowing the truth explained much as to why she was so determined to see Tor Iolan for herself.

"As you can see," Aeron turned away from her and faced Gavril, still absorbing what he had just learnt. "We have some ways to travel before we arrive at our journey. We ask for passage through your realm and shelter for the night."

"You shall have it," Gavril replied without hesitation, aware that Aeron need not ask. He was touched by the respect, nonetheless. "Tonight, you will rest here and enjoy our hospitality. I am eager to hear what progresses beyond in Carleon."

It was an offer Aeron was happy to accept. It had been a long day, and the comforts of a bed were welcomed after travelling rough and with many days still ahead before they arrived at Tor Iolan. He had no idea what would happen once they reached that desolate place because he knew there was nothing there to find. Aeron had been part of the force clearing Tor Iolan after Balfure's fall, and saw for himself its dungeons were emptied during that sweep.

Finally, he understood why Arianne was so insistent he accompany Melia on this quest. She should not be alone when she arrived at Tor Iolan and found nothing.

* * *

It became apparent, after their arrival, that Gavril did not have much opportunity to entertain guests, for much pomp and ceremony went into the feast he ordered to celebrate their presence at his court.

For the second time in as many weeks, Melia found herself needing more formal wear than the breeches she was accustomed to wearing. Unfortunately, this situation was even more nerve-wracking than the gathering at Sandrine Keep because there, at least, she was among friends. In Eden Iolan, the only person she knew was Aeron, and everyone else probably saw her as a barbarian Easterling.

Once again, Melia was forced to wear the same gown and felt self-conscious Aeron would recognise it when he saw her in it. She supposed she could have accepted the offer of a gown from one of the elven maids, but Melia preferred to wear something of her own, even if it was the only dress she had.

She studied herself in the mirror and was pleased by her decision to wear her hair loose. It was in keeping with elvish fashion, and she wanted to stand out as little as possible. There were some pretty white flowers in her room and she used one in her hair, deciding it was all the embellishment her dark locks needed.

Still, if it were possible, she would have remained in her room all night, because she did not relish having to emerge from its safety into the company of people she did not know. It was too long since Melia was required to be in the presence of so many and she knew much of her social skills were eroded away by years of living rough in the wilderness. Out there, there was no need for airs and graces, of being polite and diplomatic. There was only herself, and she was not easily offended.

Unfortunately, the knocking at her door meant there would be no escape from this ordeal. Melia drew in a breath to brace herself for the evening before going to answer the door.

She expected to find Aeron standing outside, but instead it was Hadros waiting in the hall beyond her doorway. Melia grew immediately wary at his presence, recalling his insult at their first meeting and knew that, despite conciliatory gestures on both their parts, appearances could be deceiving. She wondered why he was here and was suspicious at what he might say now they were alone.

Hadros seemed to stare at her for a moment, taken by surprise by how she looked in a dress, and Melia steeled herself for another biting remark at her expense.

"I thought I would escort you to the hall," Hadros said stiffly, although he was making no effort to hide how his eyes were raking over her form from head to toe. "I behaved harshly to you at our earlier meeting and I thought I should make suitable amends for my conduct."

Melia was convinced he had an alternate agenda.

"Fine," Melia declared, sweeping past him, deciding the only way to end this ordeal was to begin it as quickly as possible. "Let us be off then."

"I must confess," Hadros remarked as he fell into stride with her, "you do not look so much like a barbarian when you are properly attired. I commend my brother's taste."

Melia stopped short and turned around to face him with clear annoyance. "Your brother and I are travelling companions," she stated firmly. "Nothing more."

Hadros returned her fierce gaze just as intently, "That is a pity. You are in your way beautiful, for an Easterling that is." His hand reached for a strand of her hair, causing Melia to flinch slightly but not pull away. Did he think to unsettle her with his advances?

"Come now," he lowered his hand, noticing her ambivalence at his touch. "We are not children. Surely you would have enjoyed the comforts of a warm body on some cold night out in the wilderness? You are a watch guard. There cannot be much opportunity to make attachments in your chosen vocation?"

His voice was no longer arrogant but husky and, try as Melia might, she was affected by his closeness. She had paid little attention to Hadros physically during their first meeting because she found him rude and arrogant. Now that she was in the mind to take note, she decided he was handsome, though the beauty of him was different to that of Aeron's.

"There are not," Melia admitted without shame, aware of what he was alluding to and suspecting he was attempting to seduce her. She wondered if he would dare make such assumptions about her sexual intimacies if she were noble born instead of a mere Easterling. "I have shared my bed when I met someone I liked enough."

"That is all I seek to offer you, a night of comfort satisfying your needs and my curiosity. I have never had a woman of the Rayan," his eyes filled with suggestion.

"I am not Rayan," she corrected. "I am Nadiran."

She should have been offended by his offer, but she was not. If she were, she would have never consented to travel with Aeron alone. She was not a maiden untouched. She did not consider herself wanton even though she knew physical intimacy, seeing no need to bind herself in marriage because of it. Nevertheless, she chose her dalliances carefully and never out of simple lust.

"I thank you for your offer but I have to decline," Melia said politely, feeling less intimidated by him now that she knew what he was about. She had no wish to satisfy his curiosity about Easterling women, if that was his purpose. For all she knew, this could be an ill-conceived way for him to determine her loyalty to his brother, or was it a game of brinksmanship between brothers? Whatever it was, Melia had no wish to be caught in the middle of it or, for that matter, betray the prince.

"Because of Aeron?" Hadros asked pointedly.

While he would have liked to bed her, he was not terribly disappointed she refused him, especially now he knew there was his younger brother to consider. Despite both Melia and Aeron's protestations that their relationship was platonic, Hadros could tell Melia's refusal almost certainly had to do with Aeron. Besides, there were many others would oblige him if Melia was unwilling.

"No," Melia stated more hastily than she should have.

She saw his eyes narrow in calculation and knew immediately he did not believe her. Melia cursed inwardly at her inadvertent revelation and said nothing for a few seconds as she gathered her thoughts, trying to find an answer to convince him she and Aeron were just friends.

"I have no desire to bed an elf. It is dangerous," she said finally.

"Only if you love him."

Melia had no answer to that.

Instead, they maintained their silence as they continued walking towards the hall, two former antagonists finding an odd sort of neutrality. They achieved an understanding that, in their mutual dislike, they had more in common than either expected.

"Has anyone ever told you that you are a very vexing elf?" she declared, resigning in this game of verbal chess.

"As often as you have been told that you are evasive," Hadros replied like a gracious winner. "I believe that places us on equal footing."

"Equal?" She craned her neck to look at him and noted that he was smiling at her wryly. "I thought elves were better than us mortals in every way."

"We are, but it's impolite to repeat it in your company."

Despite herself, Melia laughed. "I see now where your brother gets his ego."

"Oh, it is a family trait," Hadros grinned. "You should meet our father."

* * *

When Melia entered the hall in Hadros' company, Aeron could not help feeling a little disturbed by the sight of them together, particularly when they appeared to be getting along. It was a far cry from the antagonism displayed when they met earlier that day in the woods. What was worse, Aeron recognised the familiar gleam in his brother's eyes as he regarded Melia, and tensed. He had seen Hadros wear such a look when he was attempting to woo some maid at court into his bed.

The idea that Hadros might have similar designs on Melia tugged jealously at Aeron.

The celebration was modest in comparison to some of the feasts Aeron had attended during his lifetime, but the atmosphere was warm and entertaining. Gavril was always an amiable host and it was clear he enjoyed entertaining. Despite being Lord of Eden Iolan, he conducted his gatherings as if he were still the captain of the Forest Guard; they were light-hearted affairs, devoid of ostentatious formality. Aeron had often wondered if

Gavril would be happier if he were still a soldier instead of the leader of his own realm.

Even before Hadros delivered Melia to his arm, Aeron could hear the speculation running through Gavril's court at who she was to him. Was she simply a friend or more? No doubt, there would be much gossip and rumour-mongering about what the youngest son of Halion was doing in the company of a mortal female, particularly an unattached female.

He knew that for many years, especially at Halas, there had been those who questioned why he had not presented any maid as his favourite. Unlike Hadros, who seemed to have a different flavour every month, and Syannon, who was happily married. Aeron's reasons for remaining unattached were due entirely to his parents.

He did not think the match of Halion and Syanne was well made. Although the span of his parents' marriage stretched across millennia, they never seemed suited to each other. The affection between them was certainly lacking, and Aeron wondered if they simply tolerated each other. If there was love between them, Aeron never saw it.

He did not even think they were bonded, but never dared to ask his mother. Once an elf found his or her soul mate, the bond between the two would last for all time, even after one of them was dead. Some elves were known to die after the loss of a mate, while others moved through life a shadow of their former selves. While his parents produced children and ruled Eden Halas together, Aeron was certain neither were happy with each other. It made him more selective about whom he would choose for his own mate, because eternity was a long time to be trapped in a loveless marriage.

If Melia noticed the stir being seated next to him had caused, she did not show it. Instead, she remained silent during the first hours of the feast, adding to the conversation only when addressed directly. Aeron suspected she was somewhat overwhelmed by the company of so many of his people, when it was entirely possible Arianne was the first elf Melia ever met. Most mortals went their whole lives without even encountering the elves, let alone being allowed into one of their cities behind the Veil.

Despite Melia's desire to remain a quiet observer in the proceedings, she was undoubtedly the centre of attention. As strange as the elves might seem to Melia, she was similarly a source of great interest and fascination because of her Easterling heritage. The first contact between the Western Sphere and the Easterling nations took place during the battle of Astaroth. Before that, none had ever come this far. Melia was most likely the only Easterling female any of them had seen.

Unfortunately, Melia's heritage was nowhere as fascinating to the court of Eden Iolan as the nature of her personal relationship with Aeron. After all, there had to be something between them for her to be travelling with him alone. Aeron supposed it did not aid matters that he paid her such close attention while she sat next to him during the feast. He made the request because he knew she would be nervous in such unfamiliar company. She was by nature a solitary creature, slowly becoming accustomed to having people in her life again.

Still, he would be lying if he denied he enjoyed having her next to him.

* * *

"Tell us of Nadira, Melia," Miriel, a young maiden, asked once the meal was done and they were waiting for evening's entertainment to begin. The question drew a general rumble of interest from those present and Miriel's inquiry originated from a place of genuine curiosity.

Melia swallowed thickly, wishing she was not singled out in such a manner. She was still trying to accustom herself to their ways, and she did not wish to be the focus of everyone in the room. Still, there was little she could do to avoid it, since Miriel was waiting for a response.

Meeting Aeron's gaze, she saw his encouraging smile and supposed that if she was capable of fighting Berserkers and a Primordial from Sanhael, she could face answering a simple question about her homeland. The elf maid appeared young, even for an immortal, and waited with rapt interested for Melia to speak.

"Well," she spoke after thinking up a suitable answer. "My father's tribe were originally of Rayan, but we broke with them five hundred years ago and journeyed north towards the Castellan Sea. We had peace with them for many centuries, until Balfure decided he wanted us to join his armies. When we refused, Balfure set Rayan and our neighbours against us. To many of the Easterlings, Balfure was an ally. He showed us how to reclaim water from the air and how to survive in the desert when our tribes were young."

"It is hard to imagine him as being benevolent," Gavril remarked. "Not after what he wrought in the west."

"I agree," Melia answered. "It was a means to an end. We understood his aid came at a price, and once he had the devotion of the others, he indoctrinated them with hatred of all things in the Western Sphere. He had them believing if they did not defeat the kingdoms of the west, the West would come for them. My people were not swayed by Balfure's lies, but we paid the price for them. Our refusal to submit resulted in Rayan becoming determined to conquer Nadira, and we have been at war ever since

"That is a terrible fate," Gavril declared with genuine distress, because he knew what it was like to be embroiled in a conflict that never seemed to end. He could not imagine it for his people, or any other for that matter, simply because they wished to be free. "It is a wonder your people were able to survive."

"Our survival came at a price," Melia said sadly and continued her explanations. "When the Rayan were allied to Balfure, their raiding parties included Berserkers, and many of our women were taken and despoiled. After a time, it was decided that, to protect us, we should remain hidden always."

"How primitive!" Miriel gasped, unable to imagine such a life where she would have to remain cloistered away from the eyes of all. "Was it this way for you?"

"Yes," Melia nodded slowly, remembering those days when she had only be allowed out of her home in the company of her father; and he was more tolerant than most regarding the treatment of women in Nadira.

"My father spent some time in the west, so he saw it was possible to raise daughters differently, which is why he taught me how to defend myself. In our lands, women may not fight or use weapons, because Berserker raiding parties would kill anyone with a weapon. It was believed that if we did not bear arms, we would be safe from that fate at least."

"That is a shame, for I have seen enough women in combat to know they can carry themselves in battle as well as any man. Celene of Angarad is equal if not better than most men in combat," Aeron remarked, remembering the Lady of Gislaine in a battle.

"As I said, it was for our protection to begin with," Melia explained, having never really considered the traditions of her homeland so deeply until now. "But as time went by it became an excuse for men to have their way and have absolute command over their women."

"If we were to attempt such practices here, I do not think we would survive the night," Gavril said, laughing and receiving resounding agreement from those at court by the chorus of nods and soft replies. "I think it would grieve me if I did not have the counsel of my lady during the times of ages past."

Gavril tried to hide the sadness in his eyes, and it was opportune when the elven musicians began to play their instruments for the entertainment of those present. When the sweet melody of their song filled the air, it distracted everyone from the Lord of Eden Iolan's sorrow over the loss of his wife. She was taken in childbirth, and Lord Gavril mourned her still. It was a common misconception among the younger races that elves were completely immortal, when in fact they could succumb to serious illness, injury and unnatural death.

Gavril did not allow his melancholy to hinder the mood of the evening, and prompted his people to enjoy the music. Very soon some maids were invited to the floor by their suitors to dance. Once this celebration of life bloomed around him, Gavril's cheer returned to the table. Aeron was glad for this. In his youth, the Lord of Eden Iolan had been far more approachable than his father, and many a time Aeron had come to him for counsel.

Aeron turned to Melia to invite her to dance; he realised, much to his chagrin, someone had beaten him to it. His eyes searched the floor in front of him and found, much to his annoyance, that she was dancing. With his brother.

Hadros had his arm about her waist, his fingers entwined in hers and they were moving in concert across the floor amongst the other couples. What was even worse was that Melia appeared to be enjoying his company. Wasn't it this morning that he had called her a barbarian and, worse yet, Aeron's whore?

Seething with jealousy that she could forget a slight so easily, Aeron watched the couple with growing irritation. He could not help but feel incensed at the radiant smile she was giving his brother as they moved across the dance floor with perfect rhythm. Even his brother's typical arrogance appeared diminished, and there was real warmth in his eyes when he looked upon her. Hadros seemed enchanted, and Aeron bristled at the continued contact his brother had with Melia's waist.

He bore it for as long as he could but, when the music paused, Aeron was on his feet and striding across the floor towards them. Tapping Hadros' shoulder before he and Melia could resume dancing, Aeron did his best to ensure he showed his older brother no sign of jealousy. His efforts were in vain, and Hadros flashed him a smug smile when he stepped aside for Aeron.

"Why are you dancing with him?" Aeron demanded as soon as Hadros was out of earshot and the music resumed playing. This was no easy thing to do, considering the sharpness of elven hearing. In a proprietary gesture, Aeron slid his arm possessively around her waist when he saw Hadros watching them together.

Melia raised a brow at the question and the tone behind it.

"Because you reminded me earlier today your brother is the crown Prince of Eden Halas and I should be courteous," she replied, staring at him with puzzlement as she tried to grasp what was running through his mind. "I am after all a guest here, and was repaying our host's hospitality with some measure of courtesy."

"Hadros is not your host," Aeron pointed out with some irritation, not meeting her gaze because he was busy searching the floor for Hadros to see if his brother was lurking about like a spider in wait for its next meal.

"He is your brother," Melia declared, bewildered by his tone. "He asked me to dance and I saw no harm in it."

"He insulted your honour. Did you forget that when you chose to dance with him?"

"I did not," Melia said, becoming annoyed at his tone until it dawned on her what was behind his behaviour. In understanding his motivations, her anger was diffused and Melia's irritation shifted to amusement.

There were moments when she really did not know what to do with this elf.

"We have reached an understanding of sorts," she responded calmly. "Hadros is quite tolerable once one learns how to deal with him."

This did not please Aeron in the slightest. He did not like the idea of Melia tolerating Hadros on *any* level. "Hadros is a philanderer. He uses women for pleasure as if they were trophies he is collecting. He would use you in the same fashion."

"I guessed as much when he asked to bed me," Melia agreed casually. Aeron stopped dancing in mid step and gawked at her.

"What? He would ask that of you while you were with..." he stopped speaking before the word he wished to say slipped out and would be too difficult to explain away.

"I said no," Melia declared, uncertain whether or not she should be flattered by this display or furious he would think her so incapable of handling herself. Around them, the other elves at the celebration were staring at them questioningly, wondering why the guests of honour had stopped dancing so abruptly. Only Hadros had any idea, and he was too satisfied with himself to explain.

"You said no," he cleared his throat, embarrassed.

"I *said* no," she shook her head at him before she broke into a little smile. "You are very sweet when you are jealous."

Without another word, she led him away from the eyes of everyone watching them. Melia had no desire to continue this conversation before the entire court of Eden Iolan. Already too much was being made of their arrival together, and Melia did not wish to provoke any further rumours about their non-existent relationship. They stepped out through large doors leading to a balcony that gave them a glorious view of Eden Iolan.

"I was not jealous," Aeron defended himself feebly once they were alone. The sight beneath them was breathtaking, with fireflies dancing through tall trees that resembled ladders leading into heaven. "I have known Hadros for longer than you have been alive. He has always been a favourite of the ladies."

"I do not doubt that." Melia knew he was jealous, no matter what he would have her believe. "His only interest in me was to satisfy his curiosity about Easterling women. When I declined his offer he was hardly crushed by the rejection."

Now that the moment had passed, Melia found his jealousy more touching than amusing. She noticed he still could not meet her eyes, but his hand remained entwined in hers, as if he feared letting go might allow someone else to stake their claim upon her. "Are you going to sulk all evening?"

"I am not sulking," he said petulantly, appearing like a little boy who was doing just that.

"I do not see why you are jealous," Melia replied as she stared into his eyes and saw how easy it would be to lose herself in them. They said that the elves came to the world as stardust. When she stared into his eyes, she could well believe it. "I have enough difficulty trying to tolerate you. Why should I wish to vex myself with the company of another? One, I might add, who is even more arrogant than you?"

"True," Aeron agreed, his earlier irritation diffusing. With the music in his ears and her hand in his, he found he did not much mind her teasing. He would be her fool tonight if she wished it. "Not to mention I have claimed you as mine," he added matter-of-factly.

"Of course," she humoured him, glad that he had overcome his little snit. "I forgot that. I should have told Hadros."

"That would have made him more insistent, if I know my brother," Aeron snorted before his tone returned to its usual eloquent manner. "I am sorry for doubting you. You deserve better than my suspicion."

"Do not trouble yourself. It was flattering, and Hadros means nothing to me, just as I mean nothing to him. Even though you drive me to distraction, you and I are friends."

"Friends." The word stabbed at him unpleasantly.

"Yes," Melia nodded.

"I do not wish to be friends," he met her gaze, finally daring to speak what had been in his heart since he met her.

The shift in the conversation put Melia in retreat and she started to pull away, wishing to retrieve her hand. He gave her no chance to escape. Pulling her to him by the waist before she had chance to protest, he leaned forward and pressed his lips to hers in a soft but insistent kiss. She stiffened against him, her uncertainty lasting only as long as the demand in his lips crumbled her resistance. Before sense prevailed, she was parting her lips and giving him leave to continue.

His kisses had power, Melia thought dizzily as his tongue slid past her teeth and began exploring her mouth with passionate chase. He was not unskilled in the art, she soon discovered. His lips continued to plunder hers, tasting her like she was something to be savoured. Melia tried to respond in kind but he was in complete control and for once she did not mind relinquishing hers to let him take from her everything he wanted.

Aeron could tell she was afraid, even when she had allowed him the kiss. She was filled with the same inhibitions as he, but he doubted even she knew the effect she was having upon him. His mouth devoured hers. He tasted her and felt his whole world shrink into sensation when she began to kiss him back.

There had been other women in the past, of course, but there was always a barrier holding him back from forging something lasting. While the encounters were always enjoyable, Aeron yearned for the emotional substance to transcend the experience into something special. Like now.

Since their first meeting they had flirted with each other, skirting the edge of possibility out of fear that admitting their true feelings would open the floodgates to emotions they could never deny.

"We cannot do this!" She pulled away from him, leaving him shocked she had actually retreated.

For a few seconds, Aeron was left reeling by the loss of their contact.

"I'm sorry!" She cried, mortified at letting things get this far. Melia's heart broke at the confusion in his eyes. "I want you so much I cannot bear it, but we are both doomed; you know that! This thing between us can only end badly."

"It does not have to," Aeron tried to convince her, but his effort was half-hearted because she was right. "I am in love with you. You must know that by now."

"I do know," Melia answered, wiping the tears from her eyes. "I have fought hard how I feel for you. I cannot deny feeling the same, but we have no future together. You must know that too."

"Dare and Arianne had a future," Aeron pointed out, grasping desperately at any semblance of hope, not merely for her but for himself. He knew of what she spoke, of the obstacles lying before them, but he loved her and he did not know if he could stand to be without her. Whatever the consequences.

"You and I are not Dare and Arianne! I am just a woman. I will grow old Prince! I will grow old, and one day I will die, perhaps far sooner than either of us know. You will go on, and if you bind yourself to me, you will mourn me for eternity or die because of it. I cannot let you suffer that."

"That is my choice to make," he argued, anguish in his heart because he knew she was far more sensible than he.

"If you believe I love you," she met his eyes firmly, "then believe I will not sit by and let you make such a choice."

And with that, she turned and walked away.

Chapter Eight

Mother Trees

To the casual observer, nothing appeared amiss between the young prince of Eden Halas and the watch guard Melia when the duo departed Eden Iolan the next morning.

When dawn broke over Eden Halas, the two travellers thanked their host, Lord Gavril, for his kindness and hospitality and set out from the elven settlement as if nothing unusual had taken place between them. Hadros noted some tension between them and inquired if all was well out of brotherly concern, but Aeron told him nothing. Gavril made them the gift of two horses, which pleased Melia to no end, since it meant they would arrive at Tor Iolan sooner rather than later.

Considering what lay between them, it was probably for the best.

Aeron rode on silently, keeping his gaze fixed ahead because it was far safer than facing her. If he did, he would only be revisited by the images of the previous night, when his need for her had been so fierce he would have done and said anything to take her on that balcony. After she had left him and retired for the night, he found himself talking solace by walking through the wood, trying to understand why she was so afraid of anything between them.

Of course, he knew what obstacles lay before them if they chose to pursue any relationship.

His father would probably disown him for the sin, though that was the least of Aeron's concerns. He wondered if Melia knew he was just as afraid of the consequences as she. With all due consideration to her worries about him, it was nothing compared to the actual pain he would experience when she was gone. If she allowed him, he would remain with her all her life, even if it meant having to someday watch her die and then go on without her.

Did she not think he knew the risks?

For a long time, he thought how sad it was Arianne was forced to surrender her immortality to be with Dare. She would never know what the future held, because she chosen to bind herself to a mortal man. He knew many were angered Arianne, the only daughter of the High Queen, should squander her existence away on a mortal, to die with him when his time had come. Until now, Aeron had not understood how easy it was for her to make that decision once her heart was given to Dare, or how fortunate she was to be able to make such a choice.

He would have given anything to have the same privilege.

Melia sought to save him by pushing him away, not understanding it was already too late. He loved her as he had loved no one in a millennia. He knew if he had Arianne's choice he would do the same in a heartbeat, but it was not to be. It was a hard thing knowing he had lost Melia before she was ever his, but he understood she had good reason for her actions the night before.

One thousand years old and he had no idea what to do.

Aeron might have taken comfort in knowing Melia felt just as miserable as he was about their situation.

The watch guard was furious for allowing herself to fall in love with an elf of all people. She knew the heart seldom permitted anyone to choose on whom it decided to bestow its affection.

Still, she had hoped for a less insane choice than an immortal, let alone a prince of Halas! She could not have made a more complicated choice if she had tried.

Yet, against her will, she had become drawn to this handsome elf beside her, who by his nature and his good humour claimed her heart as if it was always his to own. Melia knew it was entirely possible that she would love him for the rest of her days, but for her the time did not seem terribly long as it would to him.

As they rode through the wood in silence, Melia wished more than anything that what had transpired between them had not happened. She found herself studying his profile as he rode by her side, secretly examining the contours of his face and imagining how soft his lips were to the touch.

This would not do, she told herself. Out here in the wilderness, her mind needed to be sharp, not lost in daydreams like she was a virginal maid. She was far too experienced and seasoned in life to be distracted this way, and this silence between them was not aiding matters. Despite how much Melia loathed the notion, she and Aeron needed to clear the air if they were going to continue this journey together.

"Prince," Melia let out a heavy sigh. "We need to talk."

She saw his posture slacken a little in the saddle, as if he had been waiting to say those very same words to her.

"Yes," he agreed sombrely. "We do."

"I am sorry for last night," Melia apologised, feeling like the wanton for leading him on and then pulling away so abruptly. It was not fair to him. "I was swept away in the moment and allowed myself to forget how things are with us."

"How things are with us?" He turned his eyes towards her. "How things are with us, is that I love you."

There. He had said it and the world had not ended.

"If it were that simple," she countered wearily.

"It would be simple if you were not so afraid," he replied. "Do you not trust me to know my own heart and decide how I should choose to bestow my love?"

"I am afraid of nothing," she said hotly. "I just know that tragedy can only be the outcome of anything between us. I do not wish to watch you stay young and beautiful while the years turn me into an old woman who is nothing like the Melia you care for. I cannot bear to watch your love for me diminish as the years pass. I would spare myself that pain and you the sorrow when you realize you lost me long before I died."

"It would not be that way," he tried to argue desperately, wanting her above all else to know that could never happen.

"Can you say so for certain?" Melia returned tautly. "I cannot, and I will turn from this path before it becomes irrevocable to both of us."

"You do not walk the path alone," Aeron replied just as sharply. "I am there with you and I do not wish to abandon what I feel for you in the fear of what may happen tomorrow."

Aeron had wrestled all night with her words after she left him. Yes, it was true, they were not Dare or Arianne, and she was probably just as right their love would only succeed in breaking both their hearts one day. Yet it was better to know a few years of bliss rather than a lifetime of feeling nothing at all.

For so long, Aeron had been chained by duty, bound to his responsibilities as a prince of Eden Halas. But this one thing he would have, no matter what the consequences to himself. He loved her, and though they had not lain with each other to complete their binding, he knew he was lost and it was already too late for him.

"You hardly know me, or anything of me. All you know is how you feel," Melia shook her head, wishing that she did not feel this way lightly. "We have not known each other long enough to be able to say that we will stand the test of time. All you are to me is an elven prince whose life I know nothing of, save to say that you have lived through far greater times than I."

"Do you love me?" he asked her pointedly.

Melia hesitated in her answer. She knew that she did, but she did not see why it was necessary to say it. He awaited an answer, hoping what she spoke of the night before was no figment of his imagination borne of passion. It was also the first time the question was put to her so bluntly.

"Yes," Melia admitted after a long pause, "I do love you."

She saw Aeron's chest swell with happiness for a brief instant before his expression hardened again. "If you love me then that is all you need to know. You are right, I know nothing of who you are other than what you have deigned to tell me, but I know without doubt I love you. I will until the day all things are done between us. If we know this about each other, cannot we take a gamble upon a future together, however short that time is?"

"No," she replied and faced front again.

"Why not?" he insisted, unable to believe she could be so stubborn about this.

"Because I will not have you end up like my father," she said, finally, and dug her heels into her horse, leaving him behind to contemplate her words.

* * *

They did not speak for the rest of the day except to exchange short words regarding their journey. While Aeron burned with curiosity about what she meant by claiming he might end up like her father, he held back the question. Too much had been said already, and both of them were mired in conflicting emotions that made clear thinking difficult. Aeron was by no means ready to give up on her just yet but, for the moment, their argument was in abeyance until they could both catch their breaths.

They rode for as much as they could, but the woods of Iolan were vast and it was almost nightfall, and Tor Iolan was still half a day's ride away. Aeron knew they would have to spend the night out in the open and, while he had been careful to ensure their route through the woods took them nowhere near danger, he could not be certain it would not find them if they camped for the night. As the sun began to set, there was little choice in the matter and they found a suitable campsite near a stream and a large boulder providing a good lookout for whomever was on watch.

"I will take watch," he said shortly as she started a fire, noting her anxiety as her eyes scoured the trees surrounding their small clearing.

"Eat something first," she offered, as she reached into her saddle bag for supplies.

"I am not hungry," he replied more abruptly than he intended.

Melia opened her mouth to speak but thought better of it. "Fine," she said just as tersely. "It will be here if you are hungry."

"I would not cook if I were you my lady," he spoke, and his formal tone infuriated Melia to no end. "The scent will give us away. The fire at least will give the creatures here some reason for hesitation. The aroma of food will not."

Melia stiffened, snapped closed her saddle bag, and glared at him. "Is that all?"

Her acerbic manner stung but he ignored it. He was angry too, and he would have her know it. "Get some sleep; I do not require it, so I shall be able to keep watch until morning."

"I can do my part," Melia retorted. "Wake me in four hours."

"As you wish," Aeron muttered, and stalked off into the darkness beyond the glow of their fire.

* * *

Still lost in thought, Aeron remained on his perch atop of the boulder, watching everything in sight. Like most elves, his ability to see through the dark was far superior to that of men, and nothing moved without his notice. So far the hours had passed without incident, and none of the menaces he warned Melia about appeared to plague them. Aeron was not so foolish as to assume their presence in the woods would go unnoticed. The woods of Iolan might be vast, but he had every reason to believe the monsters in the dark would pick up their scent.

Shortly before the hour Melia expected to be awakened for her turn at the watch, the forest fell deathly quiet.

Leaning forward on his perch, he saw no further movement of any life in the darkness, save the slight rustle of leaves by the wind. Listening closely, the only sound he could hear were the cackling of the fire in their campsite, the quiet babble of the nearby stream and their horses, snorting and neighing in short bursts as they stamped their hooves nervously. They seemed almost afraid to call attention to themselves, wanting to join the exodus of other animals in the wood to escape the path of unnatural beings moving through the trees.

Climbing off his rock, Aeron reached the ground and quickly strode into the circle of light radiating from the dying campfire. Dropping to his knee as he reached Melia, who was still asleep and unaware of any danger, Aeron shook her gently awake.

"Melia," he lowered his lips to her ear and whispered urgently, "wake up."

Melia's eyes flew open almost immediately. She was accustomed to being awakened quickly when sleeping in the woods. The urgency in his voice drew her abruptly out of her slumber, and by the time she looked up at him, Aeron was already taking a step back from her. Judging by the serious expression on his face, she knew even without having to hear him say it that the monsters he had warned her of only days ago had found them.

Reaching immediately for the crossbow near her sleeping place, Melia surveyed their campsite and saw nothing amiss. The fire was beginning to diminish, telling Melia just how long she was asleep. She felt a fleeting moment of annoyance at Aeron not waking her to take over the watch for the night. Then again, considering their current predicament, perhaps it was for the best he had not.

Aeron stepped away from her, his keen hearing trying to determine from where the attack was coming. He armed his bow and took up his usual archer's stance as he prepared to shoot. Throughout the night Aeron had sensed danger, but it was difficult to determine if the peril was approaching them specifically or emanating from the woods all around them. At this moment, there was little doubt something was coming for them.

Melia joined him after she had retrieved the pouch containing the bolts for her crossbow and hooked her sword in its scabbard to her belt. He did the same, and seemed to take no notice of her beside him. His eyes were too steadily fixed on the darkness ahead to be distracted by her arrival.

"Do you know what it is?" she whispered softly, confident his superior hearing would make out her words.

"I think they are the spawn of mother trees," he replied back in a low voice, not looking at her.

Mother Trees. She shuddered, recalling his tale of man-eating trees able to send out parts of themselves to scour the woods for victims. She wondered if there was one nearby or had its spawn spent the night searching the forest until it found them. It mattered little, she supposed as she armed her crossbow: they were still coming.

"Listen," he told her.

Melia obeyed and spoke no more, concentrating hard with her human senses to hear what he did. She heard the fire, spitting and crackling as the logs burning upon it broke apart into ash; the slow, ambling trickle of the stream in the nearby distance;

the horses fidgeting uncomfortably on their hooves, wishing eagerly to get away from here. Beyond that, she heard nothing, though that in itself was telling.

No sounds of crickets, owls or any other creature save themselves. It felt as if all the life in the forest had abandoned this place, running for cover from whatever was approaching.

"I hear nothing," she whispered.

"Because the forest animals leave when something unnatural moves about," he replied, his gaze still sweeping across the woods surrounding their campsite before he noted the fire almost burning itself out. "Melia, keep the fire going. We will need the light."

Or rather, she would need it.

Nodding, she darted to it quickly, picking up one of the logs they had piled safely past the ring of stones around the campfire and adding it into the flames. A cloud of burning embers rode the night wind, displaced by the log. Melia returned promptly to his side and adjusted her stance to shoot when the creatures finally arrived. Her heart was pounding as his vivid descriptions menaced her thoughts, while they waited for the danger she knew he sensed but she could not see.

They had not long to wait. The attack came so suddenly it caught both of them by surprise.

Arrow and crossbow swung in concert as the creature leapt past the long shadows crisscrossing their campsite and landed a safe distance away from the fire. It was shaped like a man but that was where the similarity ended. Its skin was brown like bark, and its eyes shone like the fat bodies of fireflies. Its face was featureless, save the slash of mouth that bore teeth of sharp splinters, jagged and capable of tearing flesh. It landed on one knee and raised its head to glare at them.

Neither Aeron nor Melia waited to shoot. Both arrow and bolt flew at almost the same time, with Aeron's projectile striking first. His arrow struck the spawn in the chest, while Melia's bolt dug into its shoulder. The creature opened its mouth and uttered an unearthly howl, like the low moan of a dying animal, making Melia's blood run cold. She saw its luminescent eyes narrow in hatred before it flung its arms forward like whips.

Unfortunately, the distance did not appear to be an obstacle, as it lengthened and tapered like branches with sharp, claw-like hands at the ends. They lashed out at Aeron and Melia with such speed neither had time to escape its reach. The tendril-like fingers clamped around Melia's ankle yanked back with such force that she was swept off her feet. Landing hard on her arm, she once again felt the familiar pop of her shoulder and was barely able to keep from screaming in pain when it started to drag her across the ground.

Aeron, on the other hand, had dropped to his haunches in an effort to avoid being impaled through the chest by the claws. Only then did he see Melia being dragged across the dirt away from him.

"Melia!" He made a wild lunge to grab her wrist, but she was too quickly out of his reach. The wooden appendage attempting to impale him did not give up, and came at him again. Aeron rolled over as it drove its sharp point into the ground where he would have been. He flipped onto his feet and unsheathed his sword. Swinging the blade, he cut the deadly spike away from the rest of the appendage. Another agonised howl followed as it retracted its limb and gave Aeron time to reach Melia.

Dragged across the dirt like a sack of flour, Melia tried to maintain her calm when she saw an arrow flying over her head to strike the spawn in one of its eyes. Glowing yellow fluid exploded viscously from a ruined eye as the creature uttered a scream of pain and fury, releasing its grip of her ankle. She scrambled to her feet, finally able to draw her own sword, and running to protect Aeron as he rearmed his bow.

She stopped short when she saw another spawn appearing through the woods behind her prince. It appeared the creature in the middle of their campsite was not alone, and that the other had lain in wait to attack at an opportune moment. Aeron had yet to see it, too preoccupied with coming to her rescue. The new arrival closed in, extending its spiked limbs. There was barely enough time to warn him before she bolted forward, ignoring the pain in her shoulder as she ran to intercept the thing.

"Prince!" she cried, and shoved Aeron aside just as the branch reached them. There was a moment of blinding pain when she felt the point of it press against her jerkin and then penetrate the leather to reach her skin. What ability she had to hold back her scream vanished as the jagged point tore through her shoulder and then out again.

Melia screamed without even realising she had done it.

The agony of it was all-consuming, and she could think of nothing as her knees buckled beneath her. She became aware of the sensation of warm blood spreading across the fabric of her shirt, and the stench of iron-rich blood almost made her gag.

For a split second, Aeron could only stare.

Nothing registered. Not the fact that her wound was not mortal, or that it was her shoulder impaled, not her chest. She had stepped into the path of danger for him and his mind could not process the realisation she could have died for him. When the creature retracted its limb, bark glistening with blood, *her blood*, something inside Aeron snapped and rage he did not believe could exist inside him surfaced like bile in his throat with mind-numbing fury.

"I am alright!" Melia managed to cry out, because the danger was not over and, if they were to survive this, he had to shed that look of horror on his face and act quickly. There were two of the things now, and this injury meant she would be next to useless. He had to save them both.

Hearing her say it did not abate his fury. It was a fireball inside him, needing expulsion. One of the creatures came at him again and his blade was there to meet it, severing its limb with one hard strike. The other was going after Melia and, though she was managing to fend it off, he could tell she would not be able to do it for long. One strike, perhaps two, but no more. Her arm was hanging limply at her side and it required strength to cut through bark. He needed to make a quick end of these creatures.

It came to him in a flash. Aeron sprinted across their campsite, stopping at the fire and tossing his arrows into the flame, quiver first. The spawn, guessing his plan, attempted to stop him, but Aeron hacked through the branches lunging at him with elven speed. Glancing at the arrows in the fire, he saw they were ready. Plucking one out of the fire, he aimed it at the spawn Melia was fighting and released. The flaming arrow struck the creature in the middle of its body and, for the first time, Aeron saw fear in its eyes as it came face to face with its most primeval fear.

He spared no further thought as he swept up a second arrow and fired it into the other creature, the arrow embedding itself in its body like the first. Both monsters were too panicked to try and put out the fire, instead running towards the stream to extinguish the flames. Aeron gave them no such quarter, and fired arrow upon arrow into both of them with each step they took. Each new arrow drove them into a further state of panic, until they lost their sense of direction entirely and the dry bark of their skin ignited like tinder.

Once they were consumed in flames, Aeron retrieved his small axe from his saddle bag and began hacking at them with merciless determination. The burning children of the mother tree flailed their limbs about desperately as they attempted to fend off the blows, but dismemberment and fire soon ended their struggles, and they sank to the ground as small pyres of flame.

Melia let out a sigh of relief and stumbled away from the con-flagration, sinking to her knees a short distance away, finally surrendering to the agony in her shoulder. Gritting her teeth, she had forced herself to stand because he needed her help; but now that the danger had passed, she yielded to her pain. As soon as she had dropped, Aeron glanced over his shoulder to see where she had gone. Upon realising she was down, his rage subsided, replaced by a new emotion—fear.

"Melia?" He skidded to her side, the sight of the blood slick against her jerkin provoking a fear so thick he could choke on it.

"I am alright," she assured him, seeing the naked fear in his eyes. "It hurts like anything but I think it just pierced my shoulder, not anything, more serious." Of course, she was no healer and she could not say for certain if she was really injured or not. It just seemed important at this moment he hear it.

"Let me see," he told her, finding their places reversed from days ago when it was he who had been injured and needed help with his broken ribs. Of course he was an elf and healed rapidly, while she did not. Never more than at this moment did Aeron feel the fragility of her mortal existence. How easily he could lose her to the perils of this world.

She did not offer protest when he opened the buttons of her jerkin and then her shirt to see the wound. There were splinters in it, he was sure, but it was impossible be certain in this dim light. In fact, if they were closer to Eden Iolan, Aeron would have taken her straight there, but at the moment Tor Iolan was closer. Even though it reeked of evil, the fortress itself was empty and it would provide them with some shelter from another attack. If they rode now, they could reach it before dawn.

"I will dress this quickly for travel," he said to her, kissing her gently on the forehead and noting the sweat against his lips. He needed to bind this wound quickly to prevent any further loss of blood. "We are leaving as soon as I am done."

"You will have no argument from me," she said weakly, closing her eyes as the pain throbbed against her shoulder in wide, burning pulses. She did not realise she was shivering until he examined her wound. Her throat felt dry, and it felt like there wasn't enough air in her lungs.

"That will be a change," he added with a small smirk as he covered her up once more and set to work. They had a long ride ahead, and he did not want her condition to worsen before they arrived at Tor Iolan where he could properly attend her injuries.

For once, going to Tor Iolan would save a life instead of ending it.

Chapter Nine

Tor Iolan

For thirty years the fortress of Tor Iolan was the singularity to which all evil in the north was drawn.

Constructed almost immediately after the fall of House Icara, Balfure built the fortress for his Disciples to oversee the occupation of the Northern Province. From Tor Iolan, Balfure directed his attacks against Angarad and Eden Halas while maintaining control of Cereine by ensuring dissenting voices were soon screaming within its walls. The Disciple Kalabis, a sorcerer himself, was known to have conducted many a dark ritual using the prisoners brought here over the course of three decades.

When Aeron approached the ancient fortress, he could see the silhouette of the building against the sky, though there were no lights in its windows to indicate any habitation. This did not surprise him. Tor Iolan had been abandoned since the end of the Aeth War. Some Berserkers took refuge within its walls for a time, but the elves eventually drove them out. Forced into the woods, they soon discovered there were far more dangerous things in the old forest than themselves.

The tower itself was rectangular, with turrets at each corner. The top of the keep was partly demolished by the assault of a trebuchet during the final battle between the elves and the Berserkers. The land on which it was built was devoid of vegetation. The dark spells conducted by Kalabis sapped life-force out of the earth when the victims sacrificed for the purpose were not enough. The ruined land remained spoiled, defiantly refusing to allow the forest to reclaim it.

Aeron led Melia's horse behind him while Melia herself was pressed against his chest as she sat astride his horse, his arms around her as she slept. As promised, he attended her wound enough to keep her from losing more blood, making her fit to travel even though a more permanent treatment was needed. Unfortunately, with the scent of her blood wafting through the forest, Aeron knew to remain where they were was to invite every creature hungry for flesh back to their campsite. Leaving was the only option they had.

For once, she had not protested when he'd swept her off her feet and put her on his saddle, a testament to the seriousness of her condition. Instead, she had allowed him to ferry her all the way here without complaint and, at some point, succumbed to exhaustion. One hand on the reins while the other held her firmly to him, he spent the journey breathing in the scent of her hair and feeling the rise and fall of her chest against his. Somewhere in the middle of the night, he offered a silent prayer to the Celestial Gods for her continued survival until they reached the fortress.

Upon arriving, his first order of business was to make a quick scout of the building to ensure they were indeed alone here. While the Berserkers were known to be driven away, there was nothing to stop anyone else from taking up residence. Aeron would leave nothing to chance before bringing Melia into the keep.

When he was finally satisfied that it was safe to do so, he brought the horses into what was the great hall and allowed the animals to be stabled there while he took Melia upstairs to the solar and the private chambers of Kalabis. It was in all likelihood the one place in the entire fortress that did not reek of misery, death and torture.

Even an evil Disciple needed to sleep, Aeron supposed.

Returning to the hall, he unpacked the horses and then, using his elven ability to speak to them, directed them to the river where they could drink and graze in open country. They would return when they were needed and, truth be told, with Melia's injury, they might well be in this place for some days. Still, despite their unsavoury surroundings, Tor Iolan would afford them some measure of protection during the night, since the cursed land surrounding it kept most creatures away.

The solar had been ransacked of anything valuable before the Berserkers quit the place. What furniture was left, a chair or an upturned table, was of little use to them. Aeron cleared a corner of the room of debris and dust before he laid out Melia's bedroll. Once her sleeping place was prepared, he finally set her down.

Melia was now in a deep sleep that had much to do with the *rhoeas* tea he had made her drink during their journey. He had found the dried leaves in what appeared to be a healing pouch in her saddle bag and was aware the plant possessed certain properties that dulled pain and apparently induced sleep. The limited quantities of it in her possession indicated he did not have to use very much, and he was right. It had let her lapse into a peaceful sleep, sparing her the pain of her injuries while he rode hard toward relative safety.

While the room was almost empty, save for the chair and table, there were also pieces of wood left over from furniture that was broken up to light a fire. It was quite ideal for their needs, for the window gave him a good view of anyone approaching from the trees.

No traces of its former occupants remained, for which Aeron was grateful. Despite being abandoned, Tor Iolan radiated a sinister atmosphere that did not die with the Disciples. Even when the sun was out and glaring across the barren land, one could still feel the anguish and horror this place had wrought during its day.

Once they were settled, he went to the well, which had as its source the nearby river, and was grateful to find the water was still fresh. Then he set to work tending to Melia. Fortunately, twenty years at Dare's side had given the elf some experience in tending to wounds acquired by humans. The Circle had often joked Dare needed a royal physician more than an army, due to the frequency of his injuries. Of course, why Dare became injured so often had to do with the fact he was always the one charging ahead into any peril to spare his friends.

As expected, the spawn's limb had speared her shoulder right through to the other side but had damaged only muscle, not bone this could be healed in time. He removed the splinters, cleaned the wound and stitched the raw flesh. Applying a poultice to the wound to reduce any chance of a fever, he bandaged her up again and let her sleep some more. Only then did he allow himself to relax as he sat next to her, sipping tea and wondering whether or not she would be alright.

Whether he really understood what it was like to love a human.

When he'd thought the spawn had killed her, his heart had stopped beating in his chest. The despair threatening to overwhelm him had been so complete he did not think he would survive it. How would it be if he lost her after a life time together? Would he die? Was he willing to die? He knew of elves who lost their mates and succumbed to death because the grief was too much, too overwhelming. Was he willing to place himself in the same position?

Yet, as he watched her sleep, he knew it was too late. He loved her. It had probably happened when he met her at the Frozen Mountains. Kyou, that damned dwarf, had seen it, but Aeron refused to admit it, because back then he still had sense enough to fear the price for loving a human.

Now, he did not care. The heart seldom required permission or appropriate timing when it chose to love, and Aeron was too far gone in his feelings to protest.

Whatever the pain it would ultimately bring.

* * *

The woman was weeping.

She was crouched in the corner of her cell, weeping terrible tears.

The creature standing before her was not a man. He was the progeny of Syphia. From a litter of what she considered to be her lesser children, he was the oldest and protected his younger siblings from Syphia's more powerful creations, who would have devoured them if given the chance. It was he who listened to the Master's warning they needed to leave Sanhael soon because the Celestial Gods were coming. He made the choice, spared the litter the fate that befell many of Syphia's children in Sanhael that day.

The woman was not the only one in such torment this day. Echoes of other voices, men and women, weeping elsewhere created a windstorm of pain swirling around the creature causing it. He was not alone though. There was someone else with him. A dark man, with skin so flawless in its colouring it was like looking into the richness of dark soil. He wore rich amber robes and his brown eyes lacked the indifference to the woman's tears that so unmoved his unholy companion. His eyes were haunted, bearing the look of someone who was damned for all time and knew it.

"This will not work," he implored the creature before him, the one who wore black like an endless chasm of darkness. "I cannot do this."

"You have begun," the creature answered, and his voice had the will to drain the life from anyone who heard it. It was all the things hidden in the night and lurked in dark places waiting to bite.

"I cannot finish," he replied. "They will die before I am done, and what good will they be to your Master, unformed?"

The woman continued to weep, heeding nothing.

"He is your Master," the creature reminded. "You chose to serve him in this place. We have been good to you. You have had your fill of subjects to work your magic. Now it is time to pay the price for that."

"I never intended this!" The man cried out. "I only wished to make something greater than elves or men combined. Your master had no right to twist my work into this abomination!"

"My master has right to do anything he pleases!" the creature shouted, and its menace sent fear through the man.

The man started to touch the woman, to ask forgiveness before his courage left him, but she did not look at him and there was no forgiveness when he had not even done his worst. "I am sorry," he whispered. "I never meant for this to happen, Ninuie."

At the sound of her name, she turned her head and looked at him with tear-filled eyes. "Not as sorry as we are Mage, not as sorry as we."

* * *

It was in the middle of the night. Melia repeated the restless tossing and turning in her sleep Aeron was now accustomed to seeing. But the intensity of this particular nightmare differed. She was thrashing and calling out names, repeating the word Ninuie over and over again. Then the seizures started, and as he tried to calm her down as she thrashed on her bedding senseless, he saw blood running a red stream from her nostrils, and her eyes widened, seeing nothing.

She seized violently until he was forced to shake her, harder and harder, trying to snap her out of whatever fit she was experiencing. His heart was beating so loudly in his chest he was surprised the sound alone did not wake her. Tears were streaming down her unseeing eyes, wetting her cheeks as she stared straight past him into some terror to which he was not privy.

Cursing himself for not taking her back to Eden Iolan, he had never felt so helpless in his entire life.

"Melia! Wake up I beg you!" Aeron implored, once again gripped by that terrible despair she might die in his arms if he could not help her.

Suddenly, she gasped out loud, her body arching in his grip, trying to draw as much air into her lungs as possible. When the need for air subsided, she crumpled in his arms again and started to cough as if she could not breathe. The sound broke the panic in the room, and Melia's coughing soon descended into weeping as she cried in loud sobs and clung to him as if he were all that stood between her and complete madness.

"Melia, are you alright? Are you hurt?" he demanded, needing to help her but uncertain of how.

For a moment, she was uncertain how to understand the chaos of the last few minutes. The images were all flooding to her. It was like a tidal wave of pictures, and she was drowning. When he continued to beg her for an answer, Melia used his voice as an anchor, used it to drag herself back to some form of lucidity. When the confusion cleared, it was quickly replaced by another emotion almost as devastating: despair.

"Oh, Prince," she burst into tears and buried her face in his shoulder, sobbing. "I saw… saw… it!" she stuttered, "I saw what happened there! I saw what happened to my mother!"

Bewildered, Aeron had no idea what to say to that. They had gone from one situation to another so quickly that he needed to catch up. The only thing he could do was hold her, to provide her the comfort she needed as she wept, and try to understand what she had seen in her sleep. Had being here prompted some kind of memory?

"Tell me from the beginning," he said, when she was composed enough answer coherently. "What did you see?"

"If I am to explain what I saw," she said, still shaking in his arms, "then I must tell you everything."

"I am listening," he urged, rubbing her arm with one hand to stop the trembling. "Tell me, Mia."

She blinked at what he called her and reached for his chin, her fingers brushing against the line of his jaw, and she nodded before she began speaking. "For as long as I can remember, I have dreamt of my mother. The dreams were always vague, unclear, and I could not say for certain what they meant. But one thing was clear in all of them: she was screaming."

"Screaming?" he exclaimed, understanding now why her dreams had been so terrible throughout their journey here.

"Yes," she swallowed, drying her eyes, only to be rewarded with the sight of blood. Reaching for a cloth near her bedding, she dabbed at the blood and resumed speaking. "In them, she was always screaming, as if something terrible was happening to her. I never told my father any of it. He spent all my life devastated by the thought she chose to leave him instead of returning with us to Nadira. I do not think he could have endured knowing she may not have had a choice in the matter that something might have happened to her."

Aeron was unconvinced her silence was a kindness, but he said nothing, since it was a deed done. Melia's father was no longer alive for amends to be made.

"You said you know what happened to her. Did you see it in your dreams?" he asked, wondering if being here had somehow unlocked something in her mind that allowed her to learn her mother's fate.

"She was here, Prince." Melia met his eyes with sorrow. "She was here with others, I think. They were all weeping. There was so much fear and suffering! I think what I saw was always inside me, but it required being here at Tor Iolan to open the door. I do not think she is dead; I do not feel it."

"But you saw her in torment," Aeron reminded. "If she was here, the Disciples would have killed her, killed all of them. We found no one here, Mia. They were all killed."

"Something was being done to her," Melia explained, trying to mine her memory for every detail of that tortured vision. "She was weeping and there was man. She called him 'Mage'."

Aeron's eyes widened. "Did you say 'Mage'?"

"Yes," Melia nodded.

Aeron stood up and walked away, disturbed beyond all reasoning. Melia realised that he knew something, and stood up shakily, her shoulder pulling at her as she stood. "Aeron, you know something. Tell me!"

"It is impossible." He turned to her after a moment, not knowing what to say. "Tamsyn is the only mage left in Avalyne. All the others were killed, presumed dead during the Primordial Wars. I do not believe one has been sighted since then. Are you sure?"

"She said 'mage,' " Melia insisted. "He was about the same age as Tamysn, except his skin was dark."

"Like an Easterling?"

"No," she shook her head. "Not any Easterling I have ever seen. His skin was far darker than any of the people in the Eastern Sphere. It was beautiful! So flawless, almost like the richest mahogany, and he wore amber robes."

"We encountered no mage when we destroyed Tor Iolan," he answered. "Only Disciples."

"He was here!" Melia insisted. "If you say you love me, if you believe that I am all that you will ever want in this life, I swear to you I know what I saw. It was real! He was here, doing something terrible to my mother and all her people! I have searched for years to find some trace of a river daughter and I have found nothing. What if they were all somehow brought here to Tor Iolan? What if it was his will to destroy them all? Would that not explain why no one has seen or heard of a river daughter?"

"Mia," he took her shoulders in his hand and made her look into his eyes. "I believe what you saw, but if what you say is true then she would surely be dead along with the others."

"She's alive!" Melia exclaimed. "I know it! If we find the mage, then we can find her. I have to find him!"

"Mia," Aeron stared at her in exasperation. He wanted to help, but what she wanted to do was next to impossible. "If you saw a mage, he could be anywhere in Avalyne. He has remained hidden for centuries without any of us, not even Tamsyn who is of his own Order, having any idea of his existence. How do you expect to find him?"

Melia stared at him, the words sinking in at last.

He was right. It had taken years to learn this much. How could she possibly imagine she could find a wizard who had remained concealed for so long? The pain in her body made her pull away from him as she returned to her bedding. Shoulders slumped, she felt deflated of her earlier spirit. When she lowered herself to the sleeping place he had prepared for her, he saw her eyes filled with tears.

Seeing them broke his heart, and Aeron cursed himself for being so harsh with her. Now, he too had questions that burned beyond finding her mother. If Melia was correct and she had seen a mage in her vision, how had Tamsyn not known of it? He was certain the members of the order were known to each other. All of them should have been connected by the power of the Celestial Enphilim. Worse than that, the mages always fought against evil. Yet Melia believed this mage had helped Balfure slaughter the river daughters.

"Mia," he knelt before her. "I am sorry," he apologised. "I do not mean to dash your hopes, but these are the realities we face if we are to continue this search. I will go with you to the ends of Avalyne if we know where to look, but we do not."

Melia believed him. She only had to look into his eyes to know that he would do exactly that. Whatever obstacles lay before their future together, at least she could not doubt his devotion. But even that was not enough in the face of the despair she now felt. "This cannot be all there is, Prince," she said softly. "I cannot have come so far only to learn I cannot go any further. I feel in every part of my being that she lives, that somehow there is something left in her capable of reaching out to me for help."

Aeron took her hands in his, caressing them gently. "If you are right, and she lives, then we need to know where to search. Finding a mage is going to be exceedingly difficult. I have not heard of another in my lifetime, and certainly Tamsyn never spoke a great deal about them. He woke from his hibernation to learn that they were all gone."

"We never saw any of them in the East," Melia replied, taking comfort from Aeron's touch. It was soothing in the face of her melancholy. "The only man of magic we ever saw was Balfure."

Aeron wanted to help her, but nothing in his memory explained the disappearance of the mages. It was assumed they were all killed by Balfure; but even before that, tales of the order had been scarce. Perhaps what was needed was to hear from those who might remember when the order was at its full power, but he worried about giving her false hope.

Some hope was better than none at all.

"Mia," he looked at her and hoped she took his suggestion without argument. "Come home with me to Eden Halas. My father lived through the Primordial Wars. If there is anyone in Avalyne who might know the fate of the Order, save Queen Lylea, it would be Halion. Perhaps he might have some idea as to where they might have gone."

For the first time since she had awakened from her nightmare, it was not her mother or the Mage she was thinking of as she listened to his proposal. When she had entered the court of Eden Iolan, much speculation had been made as to her relationship with the prince. What would be the result if she entered the court of King Halion of Eden Halas, Aeron's father? How willing would he be to help her if he for one moment thought his son might have feelings for a human? And not just any human but, as Hadros had pointed out, a barbarian?

"Is that wise?" she asked tentatively.

For a moment, Aeron was taken back by her question. He'd thought that suggesting Halion might have the answers she needed would put her in better spirits, but now he saw a different kind of trepidation in her eyes. "Why would it not be?" he found himself asking, puzzled.

"Prince," she loved him for the simple fact that he could not see the trouble. "Your father may not be eager to see me at his court."

"What do you mean...?" He almost did not grasp what she was saying until he thought about it a second more.

She was worried about his father. Halion would not be pleased if he thought his youngest son was bonded to a human. It did not matter; he was not the first person in his family to defy his father. His mother had set the precedent, and he was willing to follow in her footsteps.

"Let me worry about my father." He assured her, "I am certain that if he is going to be angry with anyone during this visit, it will most likely be me."

At least he hoped that was the case.

Chapter Ten

Eden Halas

They remained at Tor Iolan for another two days before setting out for Eden Halas.

During that time, she continued to dream of her mother's disappearance without any new insight into the whereabouts of the mage who might well be responsible for the disappearance of all the river daughters. Melia felt at the tipping point of either being swallowed up by the visions or being denied learning anything new. In the end, Aeron's suggestion to go Eden Halas, to learn if his father or mother knew of the mage she described, seemed the best course of action.

Of course going to Eden Halas presented a whole different set of anxieties for both Melia and Aeron.

The two day trip to cross the East Yantra, and their arrival within the pristine woods of Halas, did nothing to raise Aeron's spirit. While it was good to travel the forests of his childhood playground, it also saddened him to know he would soon be leaving this for good. Through all his travels, Eden Halas was the one constant in his world. And now, through his own devices, he was about to cast off the last anchor keeping him tethered to this place.

The decision would anger his father, no doubt, but it was his mother whom Aeron worried for most of all. His brothers would not be much surprised at his decision. They had always known he bore the explorer's spirit, much like the elves of old who charted the world before the Primordial Wars. It was the queen who would be most affected by his decision. He and Dare were her favourites, and leaving her alone bothered him.

Yet Dare was right. He would never be happy living under his father's rule. Even in his youth, he differed from other elves, because he burned to leave when most of his people preferred to remain cloistered away behind the Veil.

If that was not in itself troubling, Aeron began to consider how Melia would be received when they reached Eden Halas. Despite his confident words to her – that his father would be too preoccupied by his announcement to concern himself with the relationship between his son and a mortal – Aeron knew better. While nothing was decided between the two of them, there was no hiding how he felt for her. His mother would certainly know it, and if Hadros could suspect it at Iolan, then Halion would be just as astute.

And how would he react to it?

His father tolerated Dare but made it clear the orphan babe brought into his court was not a part of his family, despite his mother's claims otherwise. Aeron knew Dare had felt the distance all his life, and it had formed part of the reason he chose to depart Eden Halas at first opportunity. Aeron was of Halion's blood but, as his youngest son, understood alienation. He was too much like Syanne for Halion's liking, and so very different from Syannon and Hadros. Halion never knew what to do with him, and never seemed to object when he spent his time in Eden Iolan or Eden Taryn with Queen Lylea.

As difficult as it was for Halion to show it, Aeron knew his father loved him. Whether he loved him enough to tolerate his youngest son binding himself to a human for all time was another matter entirely.

Melia spoke nothing of her insecurities to Aeron, even though she had them. During the quest to the Frozen Mountains, Celene and Keira (before they knew she was actually Syphia) told Melia of their reception at the Court of Halion. While the King was polite enough, it was clear he cared little for Arianne's companions. She feared how well he would tolerate an Easterling in his city, even without the knowledge of his son's affections. Melia decided that, for all their sakes, it was best that she and Aeron revealed nothing about their feelings for each other.

It would only complicate the situation.

"How far are we from your home?" Melia asked as their horses traversed a well-travelled path through the forest.

Once they crossed the river, the dangers that plagued Iolan seemed to vanish. Aeron revealed that Halion and his Forest Guard had seen to it that the ancient menace was never able to taint these woods. Even when Balfure released the spiders of Syphii into Halas, the menace was driven out with ruthless efficiency. Halion's love of this forest had no equal, and he would tolerate no desecration of it.

"Less than an hour's ride," Aeron remarked as he cast a knowing smile at the trees flanking them as they travelled.

"An hour from Halion's court and not one guard?" she asked, voicing her growing puzzlement at having seen none of Halion's famed Forest Guard. "That is hardly a safe situation. Surely there must be sentries of some kind."

"You think so?" He tossed her smug smile.

"What do you know that I do not?" she demanded, staring at him suspiciously. He had that look of playful mischief, implying she had missed something.

Aeron broke into a grin and called out to the forest, "Shall we tell her, Syn? Or do you and your men plan on hiding in the trees all the way home?"

Almost immediately a ripple of laughter moved through the trees like a breath of wind before Melia saw the leaves rustling around them to reveal the elves that were perfectly concealed there. One by one, she saw them emerging from the canopy of the trees, descending to the ground like falling leaves to surround the two of them on their horses. Aeron flashed Melia a look of guilty admission, as he'd been aware of their escort for some time now.

Melia, in turn, felt completely ineffectual. She'd not had the slightest suspicion they were being watched. As a watch guard, she prided herself in being aware of any enemy before an ambush, and not seeing even one of the Forest Guard made her feel clumsy and useless. Still, she reminded herself, even the best mortal tracker in all of Avalyne was no match for the skill of the elves.

The leader of the group, approached Aeron's horse, and Melia immediately knew that he and Aeron were kin. In build he was slightly stockier than Aeron, but his features bore similar characteristics even if his eyes were different. All three sons of Halion had the same dark hair, she noticed.

"I was starting to think your time among men had made you forget all your skills," he greeted.

"I do not need any skill to find you," Aeron retorted as he dismounted his horse. "I could hear you scratching yourself like you had fleas," he teased, causing another burst of laughter from the elves around them. "It is good to see you, Syn," Aeron said as his brother reached him.

"And you, little Princeling," Syannon returned, ruffling Aeron's hair before both brothers embraced each other warmly. "It's good to have you home. Mother will be pleased. She misses you."

"I miss her too," Aeron admitted readily enough, and then saw Syannon's gaze shifting over his shoulder in Melia's direction and realised introductions needed to be made. His brother seemed to be sizing her up but, unlike Hadros, there was no contempt or suspicion, merely curiosity. That was not Syannon's way. His middle brother was much like his father in many ways, but he had a more personable manner.

"Syn, I would like you to meet Melia, she is a watch guard of the Baffin and my travelling companion."

While some of his men had been staring at her hard because they had fought at Astaroth and were familiar with Easterlings, Syannon did not regard her with the same scrutiny. If anything, he appeared fascinated by what she was to his younger brother.

"Welcome to Eden Halas, Melia of the Watch Guard," he greeted her with a genuine smile of greeting and Melia saw that, behind him, Aeron visibly relaxed. She supposed he had been worried his older brother might give her a greeting similar to that of Hadros in Eden Iolan, and was glad to be proven wrong.

"Thank you, Prince Syannon." She bowed her head slightly as she answered him politely and added further, "I must commend your men on their skill. I am rather ashamed I had no idea that any of you were there. As a watch guard, it is somewhat embarrassing."

"Please call me Syn, and please do not feel that you are any less for not seeing us. We have had a very long time to perfect our ability to move unseen," he said kindly.

"That does make me feel a little better." She smiled at his attempt to console her and decided Syannon was very different indeed from Hadros.

Even though Aeron had told Melia he felt as if he had little in common with his older brothers, he shared more than he knew with Syannon, she decided. They both had the same easy-going manner. His easy acceptance put her a little more at ease with what sort of reception she would receive in Eden Halas when she met the king and queen.

* * *

Melia did not have long to wait to find out.

No sooner had crossed the Veil than the king and queen were waiting for them at the foot of the spiral stairs that coiled around the Great Tree of Eden Halas. The Great Tree was one of the oldest and tallest trees in Avalyne and, on its mighty shoulders, it carried the city of Eden Halas. It was said that Halion had journeyed south after the Primordial Wars with some survivors of Sanhael almost two thousand years ago and began constructing the city in the very place they were standing. Since the destruction of Eden Ardhen, Eden Halas was now the oldest elven city in Avalyne and its people took pride in that.

Melia, who had never been in an elven city before, gaped in awe and wonder at the grandeur of the place. She had never seen trees so magnificent or strong that they were able to hold an entire city on their enormous branches. However, not all of Eden Halas was constructed on the Great Tree.

Some parts of the city were built on the ground and the path through these terrestrial dwellings were framed with beautiful shrubs and plants, filling the forest floor with colour and the scent of flowers. With the sunlight streaming through the canopy of leaves above, Melia thought neither Arianne's or Aeron's descriptions did it justice.

As Syannon directed his men to see to their belongings and their horses, the three of them went to greet the king and queen. As she approached the regal couple, Melia once again wished she could disappear into the forest as effortlessly as Syannon's men. They appeared as unreal as their city, elegant and ageless. Next to them, she felt as if she were this crude, clumsy thing that had stumbled into their presence, a place she had no business being. Steeling herself for whatever came next, she reminded herself she would bear any slight for Aeron's sake.

When she laid eyes on the king of Eden Halas, it was staggering to imagine that he was more than four thousand years old.

To begin with, he bore the appearance of a man barely past his fortieth year, who looked far too young to be father to three grown sons. Hadros and Syannon inherited his features and intense dark eyes but, while they wore their emotions on their faces, King Halion was a cipher. She could not tell what he was thinking when he regarded her. He was most likely maintaining a facade of polite interest while taking her apart with his steely gaze.

It was easy to see why Aeron considered his parents such an ill match when one compared the king to his queen. Where he was dark and serious, reminding Melia of the coolness of the moon, his wife was like sunlight captured in the palm. A porcelain beauty from whom Aeron inherited his handsome features, her hair was the most recognisable thing about her. Its fiery lustre matched her warm personality and, under the sun, it shimmered like polished copper. She stared at Melia with her son's blue eyes before taking Melia's hands in her own, welcoming her to Eden Halas.

With that one gesture, Melia knew they had concealed nothing from the queen, despite their attempts to feign a platonic relationship. Melia suspected Aeron's mother had questions and, in due course, would wish them answered. But, at present, Syanne treated her with kindness that did much to put her at ease. The queen placed a friendly arm around Melia's shoulders and led her to the steps circling the Great Tree, revealing why she was so loved by her son.

As they ascended into Eden Halas proper, the king immediately called for a feast to celebrate the return of his youngest child. The idea of appearing before the entire court of Eden Halas did little to settle Melia's nerves, but she knew it would mean much to Aeron for her to be there with him and it would be the height of rudeness to refuse attendance. Besides, after all he had done for her since leaving Sandrine, she could not deny him one night at his arm.

* * *

The royal family occupied a solar attached to the Hall that contained several chambers and private rooms for them and their guests. It was one of these Melia was assigned for her stay in Eden Halas and, once again, she found herself in awe at the elegance and beauty of elven architecture. The room was constructed with tall fan-shaped windows facing the forest to provide its occupant a panoramic view of Halas, while the wooden walls were treated with some kind of wax to bring out the lustre of the grain. She guessed elves designed their homes to ensure they never felt wholly separated from their woodland surroundings.

She was perusing the one dress she owned with a frown when she heard a knock at her door. Crossing the floor, she answered it, expecting to find the prince coming to see how she fared being a guest in his parents' keep. He knew she was anxious about coming here after the gossip that followed their arrival at Eden Iolan. But when she swung open the door, it was not the prince waiting. It was the queen.

"Your highness," Melia exclaimed and then quickly swallowed away her surprise to offer the lady a customary bow of respect. "How may I help you?" she asked, trying not to sound more nervous.

"Hello, Melia," Syanne greeted, realising her sudden visit had placed the girl in state of anxiety. "May I come in?"

It had taken only the briefest of interaction between Melia and Aeron for Syanne to guess the nature of their relationship. While Syanne's first reaction was that of concern, she also knew she should not have been surprised. When it came to her youngest son, he had never done anything expected of him. From the very first, Aeron had stood out among his brothers by being his own creature, even when he obeyed his father's bidding and performed his duties as a prince. Why should she now be surprised that, even in love, Aeron would defy convention to make his own choices?

How could she berate him when it was she who taught him how to be this way?

"Of course," Melia said without hesitation, stepping aside to allow the queen entry into the room. She waited for Syanne to step inside before closing the door behind them and turning to face the lady, hoping that this meeting would not be as terrible as she feared.

Syanne stepped into the room and noted the pale blue dress draped over the bed. "That is a lovely dress," she complimented.

"Thank you," Melia said graciously, wondering if her lady was here to warn her away from her son. "I am afraid it is the only one I have for this evening's feast. I do not have many occasions to require more than one dress."

"Oh?" Syanne declared as she went to sit down at the end of the wooden seat facing the window and patted the empty space beside her so Melia would join her. "If you permit me, I would be happy to arrange something for you. After all, it is a woman's right to spoil herself when the occasion allows it."

Melia had no wish to trouble the queen with such a thing, but Syanne was attempting to be kind and Melia had no desire to insult the lady's hospitality. "If it is not too much trouble," Melia agreed and sat next to her, "I would appreciate that, my lady. You are most generous."

"Nonsense," Syanne said dismissively with a smile. "I know what it is you did for my Dare's wife. Even in Halas, we have heard the tale of Arianne's quest and your part in it. Dare is my son too, and I consider Arianne my daughter. You have helped her and my grandchild. For that I am grateful."

Melia did not know what to say. The Queen's gratitude was unexpected, but it did relax her a little. "Arianne is my queen and during the quest both she and Celene became my friends. I could not sit by and let either of them do this thing alone if it was in my power to help them."

"You are very brave, my dear," Syanne patted her hand gently. "I see why now my son cares for you so much."

That revelation made Melia exhale loudly and she stood up abruptly, as if Syanne's words were an unpleasant truth they had to face before going any further in their talk. She stood up and walked to the window, unable to look the woman in the eyes when she answered, "I wish he did not."

Syanne stared after her. "Do you not care for him?"

"Oh, my lady," Melia spun around and faced her again, "I do care for your son a great deal! I love him, but you cannot think his love for me is a good thing. I am mortal and your son is not. Anything between us will only end in pain."

At least she understood, Syanne thought, even if Aeron did not. "Melia, please sit down," Syanne bade her.

Melia obeyed. She had not intending to reveal to Syanne the true depths of her feelings for Aeron, but since it was out there now, it was also quite liberating. Far more so than if they were sneaking around each other for the entirety of her stay in Eden Halas.

Syanne covered Melia's hand with her own and squeezed it gently to show there was no animosity in her heart over the situation.

"My son loves you. I saw it every time he looked at you. He is my child and I love him. I would do anything to protect him and, were it were possible to change his mind about the folly of loving a mortal, I would do so, because you are right. If he binds himself to you, he will know pain when you are gone from this world. But Melia," Syanne's brushed a strand of hair from Melia's face, "that is *his* choice to make. He will still love you whether you are with him or not. I cannot speak for either of you but, sometimes, a brief moment of happiness is worth an eternity of emptiness."

Melia had no words to counter her, but she suspected that Syanne spoke from experience and wondered if that was what her marriage to Halion was like, full of emptiness.

* * *

The dress presented to Melia for the feast was possibly the most beautiful gown she had ever seen. It was brought to her room by one of the queen's ladies in waiting and Melia could not suppress the gasp that came from her lips at the sight of it.

The fabric was the colour of sunset and the silk so delicately woven that it seemed to glide over her skin and was luxurious to the touch. The cut of it was also flattering, clinging to her waist with a scooped neckline that was tantalising but not scandalous. Melia was certain there were aristocratic ladies in Sandrine who would have paid their eyeteeth to wear such a dress. When she slipped it over her shoulders, she wondered if it was perhaps too ostentatious for the likes of her.

The dress was presented with a small velvet pouch Melia opened only after she donned the gown and released her hair from the braid she customarily wore during travel. When she pulled the drawstring and emptied its content into her palm, Melia found herself staring at a single strand of a gold holding an exquisitely crafted butterfly pendant.

The craftsmanship was so fine and intricate that Melia was almost afraid to touch it. She wondered if this was a mistake until she saw the note from Aeron asking her to wear it for him. At first, she debated obliging him, because this was only encouraging him, but it looked so lovely that Melia could not resist. Furthermore, it would hurt his feelings if she did refuse.

This time, when someone knocked at her door, it was Aeron. She supposed she ought to have been surprised to find him there. He knew she was anxious about being in Eden Halas with his family and seeing him brought a grateful smile to her lips.

"Prince, should you not be at the feast instead of lingering outside my door like some loiterer?" she teased.

Aeron turned around, preparing to make some clever jibe, and was momentarily struck silent by her appearance. He had thought her lovely when he had seen her attend Arianne's dinner in Carleon but, now that she was attired properly in elven clothes, the effect was breathtaking. He wondered if she knew how beautiful she was when she was not hiding beneath the jerkin and breeches.

"I came here to escort the watch guard Melia to the feast, but I have no idea who you are my lady," he teased in return, trying pathetically to cover how taken he was by her appearance. "However, I am certain she can find her way there herself. May I escort you instead?"

Melia laughed and shook her head, chuffed at his approval though she would never admit it out loud. She was so rarely able to show this side of herself. It was nice to be reminded there was a time when such things were important to her.

"You are very funny," she remarked, stepping out of the room into the hall. "I suppose if you are the very best Halas has to offer as an escort, I will have to manage," she feigned resignation.

Aeron grinned and offered her his arm. "Why thank you, my lady. Shall we?"

"Oh do not start that again," she grumbled as she took his arm and they started down the corridor towards the hall.

"You look beautiful, Mia," he spoke quietly, his voice devoid of humour or teasing. "You will take everyone's breath away this night."

Melia blushed despite herself. "Well, you have your mother to thank for this dress. She was kind enough to lend it to me."

"It is very becoming," he complimented again. "My mother likes you. She thinks you are far more sensible than I."

"Well that goes without saying," Melia teased, unaware her fingers were intertwined with his as they walked. "I like her as well. She is very kind."

"She is," Aeron agreed, and then shifted his gaze towards Melia's neck. "I am glad you wore it."

Melia's hand instinctively went to the chain hanging around her neck, her finger tracing the smooth finish of gold. "It is beautiful, but perhaps a little too much for the likes of me."

"I think it is exactly for the likes of you," he said brushing aside her self-deprecation. "It has been in my possession for a long time. Finally, I have met someone I truly wish to have it. It belonged to my mother and came from Sanhael with her. It was one of the few possessions she managed to save before Mael took the city."

Aeron did not add that the butterfly was the perfect symbol for Melia. Like her, the small, delicate insect was very beautiful and very brief.

"Your mother's?" Melia exclaimed, suddenly very self-conscious about wearing it. Already, they were seeing other elves heading towards the entrance, dressed in finery, while the sound of chatter and music emanated from the room. "Prince, is this appropriate?" She had to ask, knowing what kind of reaction the pendant was going to produce from the court of Eden Halas when they saw it about her neck.

"I do not care whether or not it is appropriate. It is mine to give, Melia, and I wish that you wear it," he said firmly, giving her a look of determination indicating that she would not convince him otherwise.

Melia decided against pursuing the matter because they were almost at the hall. "You are exceedingly stubborn. You know that?" she grumbled, conceding defeat.

Sensing victory, Aeron threw a sidelong glance at her and said smugly, "I am not the only one."

* * *

The celebration was less nerve-racking and far more enjoyable than Melia expected it to be. The elves of Halion's court were eager to hear of everything taking place in the world outside and particularly Aeron's adventures with Dare and the Circle. It appeared the prince had acquired some fame at home because of his adventures and much of the night was spent with Aeron recalling some of those stories, down to the most recent adventure in the Frozen Mountains.

Despite Halion's famously cool relationship with Dare, the rest of his court were eager to hear news of how things fared with Dare. They still thought of the High King of Carleon as the delightful babe Syanne rescued from death and raised as her own. The long life of elves meant children were few and the spirited child Dare had endeared himself to all of them. Melia also noticed that, while Halion could never consider Dare family the way Syanne did, there was genuine pride in his face as he listened to Dare's achievements.

She guessed that, while he might never admit it, he did have some affection for Carleon's king.

Melia was also surprised when she was questioned not just by the court but by Halion himself about the Eastern Sphere. For many of them, she was their first contact with an Easterling and there was genuine interest in learning about her people. Melia explained what she could—about Balfure's influence on the eastern lands, appearing as a benevolent teacher who helped them survive the harsh desert terrain while he secretly moulded them into his private fiefdoms. To the Easterlings, Balfure appeared as a god and his indoctrination of them was so complete that it was a blow to many to learn he could die.

"Father," Aeron asked after Melia explained her reasons for coming to the west. "Have you met any mage of the Enphilim that may have been in these parts?"

Halion seemed surprised by the question and set down his goblet on the long table.

"Not for a very long time. During the war, we encountered them, of course. The mages aided us against the Primordials by weakening the creatures long enough for us to kill them. Alas, Mael was cunning, and soon directed Syphia and Balfure to hunt them down and kill them. Why do you ask?"

Aeron glanced at Melia, seated next to him, and nudged her to tell her story. "When I was in Tor Iolan, I had a dream about my mother being imprisoned by the Disciples, but also present was someone they called a mage. He was helping them keep the river daughters imprisoned. "

"A mage helping the Disciples!" Syanne exclaimed with shock. "It cannot be."

"Are you certain, my dear?" Halion asked, not about to discount the girl's dreams. Elves put much stock in dreams and a vision was nothing to take lightly.

"The Disciple called him 'Mage' but he was unlike any race I have seen in my lands. His skin was dark but much more than that of my people."

Halion blinked in recognition, "I do know of a mage whose skin was as you described, but I have not seen him since the end of the war, when I spoke of my desire to come south. His name was Edwyn and he spoke about exploring Avalyne, but that was almost three thousand years ago. I have heard nothing of him since then. Knowing what Balfure did to the mages he knew of in Avalyne, I assumed that Edwyn was killed too."

She had gained a name, but that was all. Melia could not hide her disappointment. Still, it was more than she'd had a moment ago. "Thank you, my Lord," she said gratefully.

"We will find him, Mia," Aeron assured her, reaching for her hand and squeezing it.

The gesture was not lost on King Halion.

* * *

When King Halion asked her to dance after the meal was eaten and the musicians had taken over the hall, filling it with music and happy couples, Melia could not refuse.

Even as he led her out onto the floor, she suspected an ulterior purpose and guessed he was taking the opportunity to have a private word with her, away from the rest of his family. As they took the centre of the floor, she glanced at Aeron and saw that the prince was watching them closely, trying to appear indifferent even if Melia knew better. She could read him well enough now to know he was nervous.

Until now, the king showed no reaction to his son's obvious attraction to her, but Melia noted Halion's observations during the evening. As they began to move, lost amidst the other dancers, Melia braced herself for what was coming.

Halion did not mince words.

"He loves you."

Since he was so frank with her, Melia decided the best course was to return his honesty in kind.

"Yes, he does. I am sorry for that."

A part of her railed against having to apologise for Aeron, since there was no controlling the heart when it decided what it wanted. Neither she nor Aeron had committed any sin by falling for each other. It was only their origins that made their love so tragic.

"Do you love him?" Halion asked, surprised by her apology.

"Yes, I do," she confirmed, refusing to insinuate that this was a one-sided affair when she knew better. She loved her Prince and might well love him until death, even if everything about their romance was doomed.

"Then I am sorry too," he replied and it was Melia's turn to be surprised. She saw genuine sadness in his eyes. The aloof mask he wore for the benefit of his people lowered momentarily and Melia glimpsed the man behind the king.

"I have nothing against you, daughter of Hezare," Halion explained. "I know something of the loss he will carry if he does not abandon you and I will not see my son endure such grief if it can be avoided. If you remain with him, rest assured he will love you for all of your days. When you are gone, he will be alone for the rest of his, if the grief does not kill him first."

Melia blinked. The pain of such a fate befalling Aeron so acutely in her chest it felt like a knife through the heart. She glanced at him, her Prince who loved her for some reason she could not fathom, who was willing to throw caution to the winds just for a few short decades with her, and knew she could not let him suffer that way. Even now, he watched her with his father, his eyes showing his worry when the rest of him was maintaining its cheerful facade for the benefit of the court.

"You tell me nothing I do not already know, King Halion," she admitted, her voice lowering to a hoarse whisper. "I have tried to tell him that there can be nothing between us, but I cannot dissuade him."

"Then break his heart," the king stated coldly.

"Break his heart?" She stared at Halion and saw the return of the cold, rigid king that Aeron described to her. As his dark eyes bore into Melia's own, she could well believe this was the King that was driving away his son and had once prepared a mortal infant to die alone in the woods.

"I do not understand," she declared and she really did not perceive what he was alluding to.

"My son feels things deeply, as you well know, and his trust when given is absolute. If you break it, it will not be easily repaired. You are a woman. I am certain you know of how you can do that." His gaze felt like the point of a knife, drawing blood.

Melia almost snatched her arm away from him when the king's meaning fully dawned upon her. Remembering that they were being observed, she quickly averted her gaze from father to son and saw that Aeron was standing up from the table. The prince had seen her reaction and needed little prompting to cross the floor to come to her defence.

As it stood, Melia had intended leaving Eden Halas as soon as possible. When Aeron had revealed where the necklace she wore around her neck had originated, she knew she had no choice, but Halion's way would do considerable harm if she chose to follow it.

"I cannot," she retorted, "I *will not* do that to Aeron."

"If you truly care about him, then you need to be strong enough to make the right choice for you both. Sometimes, Melia, to be kind you must be cruel."

"May I cut in?" Aeron suddenly appeared through the crowd.

For a few seconds, father and son stared at each other as if they were locked in combat.

"Of course," Halion said, relinquishing his hold of Melia and stepping aside for his son. "Enjoy your evening, my dear." His eyes brushed Melia's slyly as he drew away.

Melia did not speak as she felt Aeron take his father's place, unaware that even though he was retreating, Halion had already won.

* * *

"Well, that was not so terrible, was it?" Aeron asked as he walked her to her room when she was ready to retire for the night. Even though it was on the tip of his tongue, he refrained from asking her what was said between her and his father. Whatever it was, Aeron could tell Melia was unsettled.

As Aeron guessed so accurately, Melia was shaken by her discussion with the king, but composed herself enough to feign enjoyment for the rest of the evening. Despite her abhorrence at his suggestion, his words lingered in her mind throughout the night. Worse yet, Aeron's attentiveness to her throughout the feast and Melia's responsiveness to him seemed to prove his point that, unless something drastic was done, they would both reach the point of no return and be doomed to the tragedy that followed.

As the celebration stretched into the night, the hour grew late enough for Melia to excuse herself without offending her hosts. According to Aeron, the feast could continue into the small hours of the night and not all the guests were expected to have to remain for the duration. Thus, Melia could excuse herself without fanfare. After saying her goodnight to the royal family, no one was particularly surprised when Aeron escorted her back to the room.

"What was?" Melia asked, glancing at him when they reached the door to her room.

"Being with me," he answered, trying to keep the mood light even though the shadow that had fallen over her face following her dance with Halion remained there all night. He hoped to distract her with less demanding conversation until he was ready to ask her what upset her so. While Aeron could guess his father's words, his own arguments with Melia during their journey here indicated there was nothing Halion could say that should have surprised her.

"Being with you is easy," Melia said, smiling at him as she opened the door and stepped inside, expecting him to follow. "I enjoyed myself. It reminded me of the celebrations my family used to have when my father came home from battle. I had forgotten what it was like to get dressed up and dance all night."

It was not simply the memories of the past that made her smile. Even though she knew it was folly, it was so easy to fall into his eyes and forget everyone else. When they were not burdened with heavier matters, she felt so carefree and complete in his company that it was hard to imagine a time when he was not a part of her world. Together, they were able to laugh and joke, take playful delight in each other's eccentricities, and feel a connection apparent to everyone at the table. It was frightening how attuned to him she felt. It was frightening and exhilarating at the same time.

"You should do it more often," Aeron said, following her in, taking up the unspoken invitation. "We elves love our ceremony, especially when we have guests," he replied, glad to hear she enjoyed some of the evening.

As she turned to face him, he caught her hand and slid an arm around her waist. "We could dance in here," he said, pulling her gently towards him. "I can still hear the music."

Melia smiled, not resisting the touch because she too could hear it, carried on the wind through her open window. "I did not know that, apart from being an expert archer, you were such able dancer," she teased, allowing him to twirl her around in his arms.

"I would say the same thing about you," he pointed. "Who knew that, under all that watch guard, there is not only a beautiful woman, but a lady of court?"

"I was not always a watch guard," she reminded him. "My father was a nobleman among the Nadira; I was raised a proper young lady."

"Mia," Aeron said, holding her to him, their bodies swaying as if they were still dancing. "When you are done with your quest to find your mother, come with me on my journey."

"Your journey?" Melia raised a brow in question. While completing her quest seemed very far away, she was intrigued by the mention of his mission. She knew that he had plans beyond remaining in Eden Halas but, until now, Aeron had not told her what they were.

"Yes," he said seriously. "I spoke to Dare before we left and I am going to the woods of Ardhen when this all done. I intend to take all the elves that will go with me to those woods and rebuild Eden Ardhen. If Tor Ardhen is to ever lose its power, then the woods must be reclaimed. I intend to do that and I know there are many of my people who tire of this hermit's existence behind the Veil. They want to live in the world too, not hide from it."

Melia paused and brushed his cheek, her eyes dancing with pride at his decision. "I think that is a wonderful idea, Prince. I think the world would benefit from it as much your people."

Her approval filled him with pleasure and he pushed further, "Then come with me, Mia. We can build something together there. Be my wife and I promise you, you will not have cause to regret it."

What he proposed went right to the heart of the difficulties between them. For a moment, Melia actually considered a life with him. Taming the woods of Ardhen together, chasing out the Berserkers and putting an end to Tor Ardhen once and for all. Building a new home with him in the woods, something that was exclusive, theirs alone. She envisioned the danger and the excitement and all of it was terribly inviting. It was what came afterward that disintegrated the dream.

He would enjoy their kingdom alone because she would be dead. Eden Ardhen would be a monument to the suffering he would feel at her demise. Letting go of that dream, even briefly, tore out her heart.

Melia stopped dancing and stared at him. "Prince, you know I cannot."

His expression was one of disappointment, which she had expected, but he was not about to give up, not when he had finally voiced what he wished for them in its purest form. "Why? Because of my father? What did he say to you?" Aeron demanded. "I know he said something. I saw your face."

Melia turned away from him and went to the doors leading to the balcony outside. She stepped out into the night and saw the beauty of Eden Halas before her, the lights of the arboreal city competing with the stars above. Surrounded by all this, it was easy to be lost in the moment, but that was their trouble. Moments were all they had.

"Nothing that I did not already know," she said, standing at the wooden rail, and shrugged.

Aeron's cursed under his breath, a lifetime of unresolved anger at his father surfacing more acutely than had ever before. He was furious with his father, but he also wished Melia had more faith. Stepping into the open air with her, he curled his arm around her waist and whispered in her ear.

"Mia, my father's opinion matters little to me. I love you and I want to be with you. Can you not trust in that?"

Melia sucked in her breath, wishing he would not do this. "I trust you, Aeron," she turned around and faced him, wishing he understood why she was so adamant. He did not see she could not bear the thought of leaving him alone. "But I will not live with the guilt of knowing that, when I am gone, I will be the cause of so much pain."

"Yes," he nodded, not denying it. "There will be pain, Mia, but I am not a fool. I still want a life with you. When you are gone, I will be able to take comfort in the years we had together."

"You say that now," she returned, "but it will be different when it is a reality. I do not want you to spend eternity in misery. I do not want that for you."

"So you take the choice away from me?" he demanded, pulling her hand away from his jaw.

The action wounded her and, whether or not it was hurt or Halion's words that prompted it, she reached for the chain around her neck and ran her fingers along it. "You should take this back. This is not mine to have, Prince."

With that, she broke away and retreated into the room again. However, Aeron's ire was up and he was not about to let the argument end there.

"I wish you to have it," he declared in exasperation as he chased her in. "Can you not let me have my way in this one thing?"

"Someday you may want to give this to someone you care for…" she started to say before he cut her off savagely.

"I already care for you, Mia! Whether you are at my side or away from it will change nothing of my feelings. There will never be anyone after you. Do you not know that by now?"

Once again, Halion's words came back to haunt her and she knew that there was no other course left to her. The Celestial Gods forgive her, the king was right. To free Aeron, she had to be cruel.

"Yes, I do," she swallowed down the anguish and took up the action she had sworn only hours ago she would not do. Turning to face him once more, she suddenly closed the distance between them, saying nothing as she approached. When she reached him, Melia coiled her arms around his neck and drew him to her so that she could plant a soft, tentative kiss upon his lips.

"I love you," she whispered after that initial contact was made, "I will always love you."

Aeron regarded her with puzzlement for a moment, uncertain what she was about until she kissed him again with greater urgency. He felt her tongue probing past his lips as she tugged at him more insistently, until he could feel her nails in his back, drawing him into a sweet trap of pleasure and pain. Her breasts pushed against his chest, until he was aware of every part of her body pressed against him, waiting for reciprocation. She was seducing him with her mouth, plying his skin with small insistent kisses that ran along his jaw and up his cheek before culminating in a playful nip of his ear.

Considering the arousal that surged through him at that action, he was rather surprised he was able to pull away from her lips at all. He needed to understand what was going on here, what had suddenly changed between them to warrant this passionate display. Yet, another part of him was throwing caution to the winds. The part of him that was very male wanted to revel in the pleasure of her, wanted to bask in it more than his next breath.

"What is this, Mia?" he managed to ask, despite the shortness of breath coming in his increased excitement.

"This is just us, Prince," she said, holding his gaze, trying to convince him her intentions were pure. "Let us not think about tomorrow. We keep looking so far ahead that we are forgetting right now is all that really matters. Let's just be Aeron and Melia for tonight, nothing more. We can worry about what follows tomorrow."

Aeron wanted to point out it was she who was more concerned with it than he, but if this was what she wanted, he could accept these terms. Perhaps if she saw how good they were together, how much pleasure they could take from each other's bodies, she might realise it did not matter what would happen in the future. The moments they had to share with each other was all that was important. There would be plenty of time for him to face the days ahead when she was gone.

What mattered, now, was the time he had with her.

Aeron surrendered at last by reclaiming her waist and pulling her hard against him, until he could feel her hips pressed against his own. Once he relented and gave, her mouth bloomed beneath his and he uttered a soft growl of appreciation when he was allowed to explore her more fully. Finally, the pent up frustration harboured since that night in Iolan was allowed expression and he revelled in it. His fingers ran through her hair, slid down the graceful curve of her back before clasping the firm flesh of her rear.

His mouth upon Melia's was dizzying and, though there were a thousand reasons why they should not be embarking on this intimate undertaking, Melia could not think of even one at that moment. Once she banished the last of her dark thoughts from her mind, she was swept away by the incredible touch of him against her body. She also knew she had been truthful in her words to him—she would love him until the day she died.

Aeron continued to taste her, caring no more he would have her for only a splinter of time. At this moment, she belonged only to him. His lips were brutal with need, plundering the territory as he steered her towards the bed, guiding her into it so that they could continue this exploration more completely.

When she saw where they were headed, Melia smiled, showing him she felt no doubt or harboured any hesitation at what would come next. This was one journey with him she would not protest. As he drove them towards the bed, she slid her hands down his shoulders, savouring the curve of bicep, before tugging at the buttons of his shirt and freeing them enough for the fabric to flap open. His chest was smooth and Melia relished running her palms along the hard muscle, admiring the beauty of him.

Their lips did not leave each other as they continued to undress each other. Just as she had freed him of his shirt, Aeron slid the dress he so admired from her shoulders, watching it glide over her skin and fall, pooling around her feet as if she were standing in flame. Divested of the silk, his breath caught as he laid his eyes upon her bare flesh in appreciation. Her colouring made a blush difficult to discern, but there was enough of a tinge for Aeron to realise she was self-conscious at being seen unclothed.

Wishing to allay her fears, he leaned forward to kiss her shoulder delicately, his eyes closed as hips brushed the skin. Though they had both had lovers before this, those felt like a need simply satisfied, lacking the emotional connection this promised to yield. She reminded him of a fawn, beautiful and lean, but still easily frightened. Trailing kisses along her collar bone, he lowered her against the soft sheets of her bed and spent the next few minutes after their descent, charting her flesh like an explorer in a new land.

Melia was gasping. Her entire body was caught in a wave of fire as she felt his insistent mouth doing things to her while his hand kneaded her flesh with aching caresses. She tore at his remaining clothes in a mad frenzy, desperate to feel every part of him as fiercely as he was indulging in her. Lowering her head when his ear was within reach, she traced the ridge of his tipped ear with her tongue and was rewarded by an unexpected groan of pleasure that made him pause. When he resumed his oral assault once more, it was with feverish intensity.

Seeing that neither could take this foreplay much longer, Aeron reclaimed her mouth and gave her no quarter when he took her leg and hooked it over his hip. By now, the evidence of his arousal was plain for her to feel and, looking into her eyes, he saw they were dark with urgency. Poised on the edge of a coupling that had the power to drive all reason from their minds, he needed to know this was what she wanted before he went any further. After all her protests, he needed to be certain.

There would be no turning back for either of them after this.

Gods how she loved him, Melia thought as she stared at him and saw the naked vulnerability there. So many people mistook this physical exchange for lust when most never really saw it for what it was. The one time when two people could see each other as they really were, peeled down to their most exposed selves. What she saw now was that, between the two of them, it was the thousand-year-old elf that was more afraid. He was an immortal who could have anyone he wanted and all he wanted was her. Even now, she saw the wonder in his eyes, the pride he felt at being chosen to be with her in this way.

"Are you sure you want this?" she asked. Of the two of them, he was the one with most to lose.

Aeron's answer was a single, hard thrust into her body.

Melia's back arched at the penetration, her fingers clawing at his shoulder blade as he pushed deep inside of her. How he felt made her past lovers pale in comparison and Melia knew that, from this day forward, she would go to her death never wanting anyone but him. She loved the smell of him, how he tasted on her lips and the fullness of him inside her. The soft groan of pleasure that escaped his throat when he could go no further and his breath against her neck. The glazed expression in his eyes and the strain along his jaw as the pleasure rippled through him.

To her, he was never more beautiful than at that moment.

Gods, he never thought, never imagined, she could feel like this!

While he was almost undone by the slick journey inside her, she was the calm in the middle of storm. As he held her gaze, he was anchored by the certainty he saw there, the love for him as she waited for him to adjust to the warm, clenching heat of her that was all around him. Steadying himself, he pulled her even closer, until his fingers were digging into her thigh. A soft whimper escaped her and the sound nearly broke his concentration apart once more. The sheer intensity of the experience was further heightened by her nails raking across his back. Pleasure and pain creating sweet agony.

"I love you, Prince," she said softly in his ear.

Aeron was not so lost that he could not appreciate the sincerity of her words. Despite the overwhelming urges from the rest of his body, he kissed her chastely on the lips, a paradoxical gesture of tenderness when the rest of him was burning. His blue eyes sparkled like the sun bouncing off the ocean and he smiled at her before the urgency of their coupling overcame him and he began to move.

"As do I, Mia. Until the end of the time, I promise you," he managed to say, punctuating each word with the forward thrust of his hips.

They moved in perfect harmony, dancers moving to the rhythm of an ancient song. Since meeting her, he had wanted this, and now it was here, far sweeter than anything he could have imagined. They fit together so perfectly he could have been forgiven for thinking that the Gods fashioned her for him alone. Fingers intertwined as Aeron pressed them into the bed, they were a sweaty tangle of limbs as they became one creature moving towards completion.

Melia was soaring higher and higher with each hard thrust of him into her, until she could hardly breathe for the pleasure of it. It had been so long since anyone had been able to make her feel so much. Like all secret romantics, she longed for that one person with whom she could share her desires and her soul, who would look into her heart and capture it the way she wanted. She never imagined the one to do so would be an elven prince. Even if she had to let him go, she could live on this for the rest of her life.

Aeron could not think at all. His jaw was clenched as beads of sweat ran down his forehead and a fine sheen of moisture formed against his skin. He continued to move, his breath shallowing, and he sensed by the tension that was crushing him with agonising pleasure she was nearing the place he wished her to be. Suddenly, Melia's muscles clenched around him as her fingers dug into his hands and he knew she was there and would take him with her.

Tumbling over the precipice together, they fell into an abyss of lust, love and something undefined binding them together forever, despite what sense might have them believe later.

"I love you," he whispered when it was done, knowing in his heart that, while nothing was resolved between them, everything else had changed.

Chapter Eleven

The House of Halion

The moment he woke up and found himself alone in her bed, he knew she was gone.

They had spent the night before making love into the small hours of the morning, matching each other for stamina and pleasure. With Melia, Aeron experienced a sense of connection unlike anything he had shared with anyone else in a thousand years. Their intimacy was assured and comfortable, like they had been lovers for years, not merely a single night. By the time, they collapsed into each other's arms shortly before dawn, being together felt like the most natural thing in the world.

Or at least *he* felt that way.

When he opened his eyes the next morning and discovered the warmth of her body was not against him, his mind snapped quickly to full alertness. It was a credit to her ability as a watch guard she was able to slip out of his embrace without waking him. Then again, Aeron thought bitterly as he sat between the empty sheets, attempting to overcome his utter disappointment at her betrayal, when it came to fleeing from him, Melia was an expert.

Next to him on the pillows, was his mother's necklace abandoned without even a message to say goodbye. Not that one was needed; he understood her intention clearly enough.

Aeron did not know how long he spent simply staring at it, his jaw clenched as the shock of her actions threatened to sweep him away in a tidal wave of despair. Inside his chest, his heart turned into this icy cold thing keeping him rooted to the spot, unable to move, unable to think or dismiss the anger he felt at not seeing what she had obviously intended to do all along.

How much of this had she planned before giving herself to him last night? Was that why she allowed him to make love to her, because she was leaving him in the morning? He was not foolish enough to believe anything was solved by their intimacy the night before, but he had hoped her willingness to trust him with her body might smooth the way to trusting him with her heart.

Now, it appeared, that had always been his dream, not hers.

His fury at her departure kept the pain at bay for the time being, but using its momentum Aeron dressed quickly and stormed out of the room, with every intention of going after her. He was not going to allow her to arbitrarily decide that this was the way things were going to be end between them. He was done trying to appease her, trying to prove he loved her. What she had done had provoked in him a state of indignant fury he was not repressing for once.

It was time she listened to what he had to say instead of deciding for both of them that she knew best.

Aeron stormed down the hallway towards his own room and he heard his father beckoning him from the king's study. Aeron froze in his steps, having not intended to confront his father, who he held just as responsible for Melia's flight as the lady herself. Still, it would be useful to know what exactly Halion had said to distress Melia into believing making love to Aeron was the way to make their parting more palatable.

Entering the study, Aeron slipped the necklace still clenched in his fist into the pocket of his breeches and marched up to Halion, who was seated behind his desk.

"What did you say to her?" he demanded, not mincing words.

Halion eased back into his chair and let out a heavy sigh. "I take it she is gone?"

"What did you say to her?" Aeron repeated himself, leaning forward on his father's desk, palms pressed against the wood as he stared down at Halion.

"Nothing that surprised her," Halion answered.

Aeron straightened up and glared at his father. "You two are much alike." Aeron's voice was low, a stark contrast to the anger threatening to spill over his restraint like a bursting dam. "You both deny me the choice to make my own decision."

"I am protecting you," Halion returned smoothly, not at all repentant over what had transpired. If anything, he was pleased that Melia had followed his guidance so well. Perhaps now, Aeron could see an end to this business. "You are my son and I ensured you will not have to suffer an eternity of regret. How do you not see what she did is for the best? This thing you feel for her, it will pass even faster now that you've shared her bed."

Aeron stared at his father in complete disbelief. "Are you implying that by bedding Melia I have now satisfied my need for her like some itch I had to scratch?" He glared at his father, appalled.

"Son," Halion stepped out from behind his desk and went to his son, perhaps wanting to show the boy that he did not mean for the remark to sound so crass, even though it was mired in some truth. "I spoke hastily. What I meant to say is that this infatuation you have will pass. Once the love-making is forgotten, you will find someone you care for and she will be a memory."

Aeron stared at his father in disbelief. "I will love her until the day I die, father, and I will not substitute anyone else for her. Do you think I wish to go through my life mimicking the joyless facade that has been your marriage to my mother?"

It was Halion's turn to stare in shock. "What did you say to me?"

"You heard me," Aeron continued, too far over the edge of disaster to pull back now. "You cannot tell me you and my mother are bonded. Do you think I am blind? I know you do not care for her. I have seen how you regard her all my life. That is *not* love."

Stunned at the accusation, Halion returned somewhat feebly, "I care for your mother and she understands the term of our marriage."

"The terms of your marriage?" Aeron asked, realising he might have stumbled upon some uncomfortable family secret. "You choose to lecture me about being ill-bonded with someone when you describe *your* marriage like it is an agreement for services rendered?"

Halion's expression darkened. "Remember to whom you are speaking, *Prince*," he warned. "Believe what you will, but you do not know everything."

"I know enough to say that *you* of all people have little right to tell me anything when it comes to matters of the heart. You have no idea what I feel."

Halion flinched but did not answer. "Perhaps not, but you know anything between you two would ultimately end in tragedy."

"My relationship with Melia is my personal affair! Not yours. You had no right to say anything to her! Do you know how difficult it was for her to even admit she felt anything for me? She had enough fears in her heart without you making things worse!"

"Do you have any idea what you are embarking upon by choosing a mortal, my son?" Halion defended himself with just as much determination. "Can you truly endure the pain of watching her grow older with each day, knowing that she will die and there is nothing you can do to prevent it? Do you know what it is like to lose someone you have been bound to? At least if you loved one of us you could be reunited, but we do not know if we will see men in the afterlife. You may never be with your Melia again."

"Do you think I do not know that?" Aeron barked in turn. "It breaks my heart to know one day I will be without her, but I can accept that if it means having her even for the small span of her life. I know I may not see her when the world is done but, for as long as she is alive, I will treasure the moments. No one can say for certain what will happen when we pass from this world, but I am not going to dwell on what cannot be when all I have is what is."

"It is not that simple," Halion protested, wondering how Aeron could be so naïve, even if he was just a thousand years old. He was truly his mother's son. Halion frowned. "You may delude yourself," the king insisted, "but you know it to be true."

Aeron did not have time to argue. Each moment he spent debating the point with his father was precious time during which Melia was widening the distance between them. Perhaps his pursuit of her would be for nothing; that, upon facing each other, they would find themselves caught in the same stalemate. However, Aeron had to try.

"I am going after her, father," he said finally, drawing away from the King's presence. "I ask your leave to depart, but know that if you refuse me, I shall go anyway."

"This is foolishness, boy," Halion retorted. "Let her go. Let it be finished."

Aeron turned on his heels and started to walk, pausing enough to add. "Goodbye, father, this will be the last time that we speak."

Halion's expression was troubled when he realised his son was deadly serious. "What do you mean?" he called out, but Aeron did not stop walking or answer. "AERON!"

* * *

The queen entered the hallway just in time to see Aeron storming out of his father's study ignoring Halion's calls for him to return. The furious expression on his face almost prompted her to call out to him herself, but Aeron was so quick around the corner he was gone before she could finish the thought. Fearing what might have transpired between father and son, Syanne decided it was prudent to deal with Halion before she attempted to resolve the quarrel with Aeron.

Upon entering Halion's study, she found her husband, the king, leaning against his desk with an expression she rarely saw, but recognised. He was shaken. That took some doing, she thought to herself as she approached him. They had been husband and wife for almost two thousand years, but she could count the number of times that she had seen him unsettled by a situation. He was always in charge of every situation, even when it did not require his interference. He raised his eyes towards her when he saw her enter the room and the mask of uncertainty vanished immediately, replaced by the disciplined King she always knew.

"What has happened?" Syanne demanded. "Where is Aeron going?"

"He is going after that girl," Halion answered with no small measure of contempt in his voice. "She left this morning after bedding him."

It took a moment for Syanne to process that information before she could respond, "She left? Just like that?"

Syanne could not believe Melia would do something so unkind after being intimate with her son. She had seen the girl's eyes. Melia loved Aeron. Her feelings were no lie. "I cannot believe it," she exclaimed, "she loved him. I saw it!"

"She loves him," Halion confirmed, "but we agreed it was the best decision for her to make. After all, what good can come of it? She is a mortal and he is one of us. Love will be of no good to him after she is gone."

Syanne's eyes narrowed and she stared at her husband hard. "What do you mean you *agreed* it was the best decision to make?"

She, too, had noticed Halion taking Melia to dance and knew something was said the night before that distressed the girl enough for Aeron to go to her rescue. After speaking to Melia, Syanne had reached the conclusion Melia was a strong woman—she could handle herself and needed no one to fight her battles for her. Hearing Halion's words now made her chide herself for not speaking up sooner.

"I told her that, for his sake, she needed to leave him and to be cruel about it so Aeron would not follow her," Halion replied, describing the exchange with brutal honesty. "So she bedded him and left."

The queen said nothing at first, and then she raised her hand and slapped her king.

"How could you do that to your own son?" Syanne demanded, stifling any protest made by Halion at her actions. "How could you tell her to do that?"

"It was necessary!" Halion bit back, more shocked than hurt she had actually struck him. "Do you want him to suffer needlessly for the rest of his life, pining over a love he can never have again?"

"Better that he pine for love than live his days in emptiness!" Syanne retorted.

"Is this you're doing, then?" Halion retorted. "Have you been the one encouraging him in this foolishness?"

"Foolishness?" Syanne roared. "I have done nothing to encourage him in any of this! I did not need to! We have hardly set good examples for him, have we?" she challenged.

"We are not the subject of discussion here," Halion returned automatically, but he recalled what Aeron accused him of. "You know what will happen if he chooses her."

"Husband, are you so blind?" Syanne stared at him with a mixture of pity and disbelief. "He has *already* chosen her and now you've driven him away. If my son does not return to Eden Halas, know I will never forgive you."

"Syanne," Halion exclaimed. "I did not do this to drive him away."

"I don't care! He has been the only comfort to me during this facade of a marriage. I do not blame you, of course. I was the one who chose to be with a man who did not love me…no, *cannot* love me." She bit back, hoping perhaps he had the words to change her mind, but it was the truth. Years ago, Syanne had made peace with her decision, but knowing how it had affected Aeron, especially now, made her revisit the subject for the first time in centuries.

Halion turned away because that accusation he could not refute. Not even a little. "You know why."

"Yes," she nodded, "I know that you loved someone else before me and I am sorry I am not her. I married you because I wanted to leave the ruin of Sanhael and because I *did* love you. I have always loved you, but I understood you were bonded before me. I hoped for some semblance of affection, at least, but you seem only capable of giving that to our sons. Aeron and Dare are the only things that have given me comfort these last few years but, if they are gone too, then there is nothing else."

"Syanne," Halion found his voice. "State your terms and I will gladly do whatever you wish to make you happy."

The queen shook her head in sadness. "There are no terms you can give me that will make me happy, husband. This is as much my fault as it is yours. I should not have married you, because all we have done is shown our son that a lifetime of emptiness is worth the love he has for Melia. The damage is already done."

* * *

It was not difficult for Aeron to discern where Melia was going, once he set out upon her trail. She was easy to locate because he knew the terrain she was crossing so intimately. He also knew which tracks were hers, because the elves travelling across Halas did not leave markers of their presence. They were more adept at moving through their realm than any other creature and Aeron was schooled in this art well. Although Melia had taken care to ensure her departure from Halion's court was as discreet as possible, not even a watch guard with her skill could remain hidden from the Prince who was determined to find her.

While her tracks were easy enough to read in the woods she travelled, the reasons for her course were not easy to ascertain. All signs pointed to Melia returning to Tor Iolan, though Aeron for the life of him could not understand why.

There was no reason for her to return to the place, since it was apparent nothing remained there of her mother, nor was there any clue leading to the whereabouts of this mysterious mage who was at the centre of everything. Melia was no fool. She had understood this when they were at Tor Iolan together. Why would she return there when there was clearly nothing to find?

Once again, Aeron was greatly troubled by the possibility of a mage being involved in this foul business. In her vision, Melia had revealed the presence of a mage at Tor Iolan in clear alliance with the Disciples. While it was possible a mage might have cast his lot with Balfure, it made Aeron wonder why a wizard who was in service to the dark lord did not make his emergence during the Aeth War. Why had he remained silent when his master required him most? And why was he hidden still?

His old friend would have been able to solve this mystery swiftly, but Tamsyn was travelling through Avalyne in search of acolytes and had not been seen for some months now. Unfortunately, Aeron sighed as he continued his pursuit of Melia, he would have to solve this riddle himself. Without Tamsyn, it became apparent to Aeron that Melia was the key to everything, though he was uncertain how she could be used to unlock the mystery.

Aeron considered Melia's dreams. She believed without doubt her mother lived. What if the dreams were Ninuie's way of communicating with her daughter, drawing her across Avalyne to the Yantra? Melia's dreams in Tor Iolan were violent. He remembered the blood seeping from her nose during the experience. Something more than dreams had touched her mind. Perhaps Melia's human self was only able to cope with such communication through the nightmares she experienced. Furthermore, it was only at Tor Iolan the dreams had become clear enough for her to see the mage and discover the abduction of the river daughters by the Disciples.

By Cera!

Why she was returning Tor Iolan came upon him like a blow to the head.

With that one realisation, the imperative to reach Tor Iolan became desperately urgent, with Aeron driving his horse hard to reach Melia quickly. He had no idea if what she was attempting to do could kill her, but he remembered the seizures she'd endured during her first vision. There was no telling in what condition he would find her if he was not there to wake her this time. Melia would ignore the consequences to herself in her quest to learn her mother's fate. Especially now she had no other alternative.

Aeron cursed his foolishness as he forced his mount through the woods, trying to maintain a devastating pace he knew could not continue for long. Melia was hours ahead of him and she was an experienced traveller. She knew how to pace herself and possibly suspected he might be in the mind to follow her. The prince of Eden Halas wondered how a woman he loved with such untold abandon could be the cause of so much exasperation.

Not even the Celestial had wisdom enough to answer that question.

Chapter Twelve

Dungeon

This thing she intended to do was pure insanity. She knew that.

And yet here she was, standing before Tor Iolan, with a descending blanket of darkness behind it, preparing to face evil the likes of which she had only ever seen when confronting Syphia in Sanhael. Alone. More than anything, Melia wished Aeron was here with her. Despite her shameful behaviour towards him, she craved Aeron's ability to give her strength when she needed it most. Arriving at her destination, she needed his support more than ever, even if she deserved none of it.

When he had brought her here after being injured by the spawn of the Mother Tree, Melia was kept inside the ruined keep and saw little of it during her brief convalescence. When they left at dawn, the sunrise blunted the foreboding look of the place. Now, with only the moon for company as she approached the fortress in near pitch black darkness, Tor Iolan felt utterly sinister. Melia shuddered as she nudged her horse ahead, imagining all the tortures and cruelty that took place here during the occupation.

When she finally dismounted, Melia took no chances. She crossed the piles of stones that made up the fortress walls with her crossbow in hand. She wished she still carried Aeron's dagger with her, but it was left behind in Eden Halas, along with the broken remains of his heart. It felt necessary to have one at this moment and even if she was not terribly good with a blade, she was capable of defending herself if pressed. Melia made a promise to herself: if she survived this, she would have to see about acquiring one herself.

During her last visit to Tor Iolan with Aeron, she'd had little opportunity to explore the fortress because she was still recovering from her injuries. Nevertheless, she did not require the experience of any earlier reconnaissance to navigate its grounds. She knew where she was going and the rule of castle-building always ensured dungeons were located in the lowest part of the keep. Tor Iolan was no different, she noted, glimpsing the stone steps leading into the bowels of the fortress.

Descending into the underground dungeons, Melia was overcome with mind-numbing terror as she ran her palm against the stone walls. The sensation was intense but also odd because it did not feel as if it were coming from her at all. For an instant, she considered fleeing to Eden Halas and into the comfort of her prince's arms, but knew she had to remain strong. She needed answers and this was the only way to get them.

Barely able to see in the darkness, she used the walls to guide her path until her hand grasped a torch mounted against the rock. Fumbling through her satchel until she found her tinder box, she removed the torch from the wall and was grateful to see there was some wick left to burn. It did not take her long to give life to a small, steady flame, flickering to life and illuminating the tunnel with an amber glow.

Continuing onward, she returned her thoughts to Aeron and what had passed between them in Eden Halas. It helped her to focus her thoughts and diffuse her fear as she continued down the dimly lit staircase. Thinking of him sent a fresh surge of anguish and regret at her actions.

It began the instant she slipped away from his embrace and started riding towards Tor Iolan.

Melia had hoped the yearning for Aeron would diminish when she put some distance between them, but she still felt raw inside. Two days after leaving Eden Halas, the need for him remained undiminished. Melia bore the pain stoically, reminding herself this was for the best. King Halion was right; she needed to be cruel to be kind.

Nevertheless, until she left him, Melia never thought a heart could be cut without a knife.

* * *

By the time she reached the dungeon floor, not even thoughts of Aeron could assuage the cold, naked fear, coiling tendrils around her spine. The sinister gloom emanating from its walls felt like a living, breathing thing, choking the air with the atrocities committed by its former masters.

The cruelty of the Disciples bled into the walls, stained the brick with malice and anguish. She shuddered, remembering Balfure himself once walked this very floor and his evil seeped into the earth like poison rotting healthy skin. No amount of time would ever cleanse this place fully. It would always be a scar upon the world, reminding its inheritors of the evil that once walked amongst them.

Yet as she forged ahead, Melia began to realise it was not stubbornness that compelled her forward—something was calling her. It was daring her to solve the riddle in the darkness. Invisible threads tugged at her limbs, forcing her feet forward despite her courage threatening to fail her at every turn. Something wanted her down here. Without understanding how she came to this conclusion, Melia believed it nonetheless. She continued on, drawn like a moth to a flame, until she stopped at a cell at the far end of the hall.

This was her mother's, she realised, and once again there was nothing but this feeling to convince her.

Whatever I am to find here, she told herself, *I must surrender to it.*

Whatever the consequences, she was ready to accept them. If death was the result, there would be no regrets. She had lived a life of freedom most women would never know. Her destiny had been hers to choose and there was love too, a great love during her one night with her prince. She only hoped that if the worst came to pass, he would understand why she needed to do this. Steeling herself for what came next, Melia closed her eyes and wrapped both her palms on the bars of the cell and let what had to be, happen.

Its effect upon her was far more potent than even her most violent nightmares. The searing pain that filled her mind upon contact forced a scream from her lips without Melia even realising it. It tore through the night and, if anything stirred in the wood around Tor Iolan, it certainly did not care. Melia had been right about one thing when she embarked upon this course, and that was that she was alone.

Utterly and truly alone.

* * *

There was no weeping. Just screaming.

Loud, anguished wails of pain and torture, tearing the night apart like the shriek of a soul being ripped apart, one piece at a time. To those who ruled Tor Iolan, its sound was music. For everyone else forced to listen, they could only shudder in fear and feel pity as its assaulted their ears.

The Disciple Kalabis watched the Mage use his magic for a purpose it was never intended to be employed. There was some satisfaction in knowing that he, a child of Syphia, commanded so much power over the servants of the Celestials gods. The serafs, who were called Mages in Avalyne, and the river daughters. One was supplicant to him while the other – the other was a prisoner.

The river daughter was chained to the wall, far from the source of her strength, the Yantra-hai. Her power found its source in the Celestial she served – in this case, Dalcine, who held mastery over all the waters of Avalyne. Once she was taken from its presence, she was weak as any mortal. She and her sisters were systematically hunted and enslaved before being brought here in secret. The capture of the river daughter was a task almost as laborious as the continuing search for the Exiled Prince, but it was what Balfure commanded.

The mage clearly did not have the stomach for what needed to be done, which was why the Disciple was required to supervise his work constantly, ensuring the transmogrification spell continued. He needed to ensure that the execution of the intricate spell currently making the river daughters scream with such agony did not falter due to the mage's misplaced compassion.

Kalabis smiled beneath its hood in what was almost pleasure at the mage's attempt to hide his anguish. Kalabis had selected this river daughter as the first subject to endure the spell because she was the mage's favourite. The mage protested bitterly but, upon realizing he had no choice in the matter, grimly obeyed without further protest.

The spell was sending waves upon waves of power through the room and even Balfure's servant was impressed by how powerful the mage could be when properly motivated. If the wizard wanted, it was possible for him to leave Tor Iolan, and no Disciple would be able to stop him. Yet his fear of Balfure was too strong, even when the Aeth Lord was far from these walls.

Even as she screamed fiercely, the river daughter's strength showed signs of waning. Her flesh was boiling under her skin. It bubbled like the dark sludge of a marsh bog and lifted muscle and sinew from her bones as the spell's purpose began to reshape her form. Only the chains shackling her kept her upright. She wasn't strong enough to stand, let alone break through them.

There was no turning back once the spell began

Carleon was in open revolt.

The exiled prince was no longer hiding from them. At long last, he had come forth and the whole of Carleon was rallying behind the last son of House Icara. Kalabis was immediately recalled to the Iron Citadel for orders on how to regain their power over the kingdom. In the meantime, the work that had continued steadily for so many years was disrupted and the mage was left to his own devices in Tor Iolan for the first time.

The spell he devised to create something beautiful had become a twisted abomination. What should have been his crowning achievement was now the bane of his existence. He was trapped as helplessly as the unfortunate souls he corrupted to make his spell possible. The mage began to fear the possibility Balfure might be unable to regain control of Carleon. Such a defeat could prompt the Aeth Lord to return to Tor Iolan and retrieve his creations, to use them against his enemies to turn the tide.

It had never been the mage's desire to create a soldier. He wanted to fashion a form of life possessing the singular beauty of the elves and the fiery passion of men. In his determination, he never considered once how such work could be twisted terribly enough to threaten all the peoples of Avalyne. Now that the Disciples overseeing his work were absent, he began to contemplate what came next.

The mage stood within the cell occupied by his favourite. She was his favourite because she had fought the hardest against her incarceration. Later on, after the transformation had broken her will, he learned her name and realised her desperation stemmed from her determination to return to her husband and child. In the end, the only thing remaining of them in her mind was their names, uttered as she wept her ruined state. It made what he did even more reprehensible.

What was left of her remained trapped in a cocoon of flesh, with only the faint outline of her body to show that what was once beautiful had now become a horrific parody of life.

There was only one chance to end this before this nightmare became any worse and he took it. There was only so much time before she and the others would emerge from the pods in which they were transforming. The Berserkers who remained here in place of the Disciples were of little threat to him. He could take his creations and disappear.

Avalyne was on the brink of war. It was entirely possible Balfure would be too busy defending his territory to bother with one mage and the twisted fruit of his misguided dreams. The mage would take them far away from Tor Iolan and hide in the belly of the earth, perhaps in the distant Gahara Plateau, and be forgotten. Perhaps, with enough time, he could undo what he had done to them. He could save them.

He did not know if this hope was any more misguided than the one that led him to this place, but he knew he had to try. He had to do it before they emerged from their cocoons.

Before they woke up.

* * *

Scrape.

Scrape.

Scrape.

The sound filled the world almost as completely as the overwhelming darkness. The darkness was the world, its sides pressed against her, wet sliminess against her skin. She pushed against it, but it would not yield. It was like being a fly trapped in ointment. She could move inside its hollow innards, but she could not escape it. Her nails scratched at the membrane, but it would not tear, it simply stretched, taunting her with the possibility of rupture. It became her world and she could not escape it. She took a breath and *it followed the path into her lungs, making her cough. She opened her mouth and it flowed down her throat, blocking her scream.*

The need to escape was overwhelming, but she could not even see where she was because the darkness was everywhere. There was a faint memory that it had not always been like this. There was a time when there were light and sounds that were not this slow, turgid flow of liquid filling her eardrums. There were memories buried in a place so deep it was difficult to see them, if not impossible. She felt them in her heart, felt the life that existed in a faraway place.

Sometimes, she almost felt someone else.

The contact was brief, but she was certain of its presence. Someone beyond her prison was trying to reach out to her, but she could not answer, not directly. The other was able to reach through the wall and touch her mind, creating a brief but weak connection. The other was just as confused as she, so neither could help each other. Yet someday, she knew, she would escape and she would find the other.

All she had to do was keep scratching at the walls, searching for the tear that would help her escape.

Scrape.

Scrape.

Scrape.

* * *

Melia woke up gasping.

Her first impulse was to scream, but somehow she maintained enough composure in the dreamscape to avoid it. There was so much, and it almost swallowed her whole. Melia was shaking as she struggled for breath and tried to cope with the images swirling about her head. There was so much of it, and she felt like she was being drowned at the bottom of the river.

For the first time, what she saw in her dreams did not diminish with wakefulness. The vivid images of things she could not possibly know, yet knew with utter certainty to be the truth, remained in her mind. Somehow the lingering magic in the walls of the cell allowed her to see what she needed. It had been her intent to open her mind to the visions, but she never expected the sheer intensity of the connection. At best, she had hoped for a clue as to where her search should take her next, but now she had more than that.

She had a destination.

It was only after she quietened her mind and regained her composure that she realised where she was.

She was no longer in the dungeon. She was in the forest. The sun was shining above her head through the canopy of leaves and she was surrounded by trees in the middle of a clearing. She was sitting on her bedroll with a blanket draped about her body. The tasty aroma of something cooking made her glance at the fire in the centre of the campsite.

Her horse and another were waiting patiently under the shade of a nearby tree, nickering at each other in their secret language. She recognized the animal beside her own and supposed she should not be surprised by the gelding's presence. Sweeping her gaze across the immediate area, Melia saw no sign of its rider.

After taking a moment to contemplate what she would soon be facing, Melia attempted to stand and found her legs rather shaky. She wondered how long she had been unconscious. The drowsiness in her eyes lingered and it was a few seconds before she was able to brave standing up. When she did, her legs ached from the sudden demand of activity. As she walked gingerly towards the horses, they raised their heads in interest at her approach.

Melia stroked the brow of her horse gently before running her palm over the gelding's flank.

"Where is your master?" she asked gently.

The horse had no answer other than to snap its head back in reaction to something behind her. Melia turned and saw Aeron staring at her from across the fire. He was carrying his bow, indicating his return from a quick scout of the area to ensure they were safe. His first reaction upon seeing her was one of relief, but then his blue eyes bore into her mercilessly as they hardened. Under the scrutiny of that gaze, Melia had no defence.

"You came after me?"

"You left," Aeron returned shortly. "I had little choice but to follow."

"You found me?" She ventured a guess and then imagined the fear he must have felt finding her in the condition she'd been. She felt an immediate surge of guilt at making him worry so.

"Yes. You were unconscious for almost a day. I thought your mind might have been lost forever."

"I am sorry to have made you endure that," Melia apologized and somehow guessed it would not nearly be enough to soothe his anger. Despite his deep concern for her, Melia could also see his rage. Rage he was keeping under tight restraint for the present. "It was the only way I could find him."

"Did you?"

"I did." She was overcome with the fear of the child about to receive punishment for particularly bad behaviour and was unable to meet his gaze. "I think the mage went to the Gahara Plateau to hide. I am not certain of everything I saw, but he did something to his prisoners, something he did not intend. He hopes to help them there."

"I see. Then we will go." His voice was curt.

Melia raised her eyes to his. "We?"

"We," he repeated, his jaw ticking in controlled rage. The tension between them was so thick it could have been run through with a sword. "We will go there together and deal with what menace he has wrought upon your mother's people."

"I cannot ask you to do that…" she started to say and realised her mistake, but it was too late. The words seemed to be the last straw and the dam of his rage finally burst.

"It seems that there is very little that you can ask me. You have been making decisions affecting us both since we met. I suppose I should hardly be surprised you chose to simply ride off without the decency of a farewell or, for that matter, an explanation. The irony of it should not be lost upon me. After all, how many times have I left some lady's bedchamber in similar fashion? Still, you could have at least left the customary benefice. What is the going rate for a prince these days?"

"I thought I did what was best!" she returned. The remark was harsh, even from him. Of course he had a right to be furious. She *had* behaved badly. The more determined she was to her keep away from him, the more she seemed to hurt him.

"What was best? Do you know how sick to death I am of hearing what is best for us?" he shouted, making her jump. It was quite something to hear the controlled elf suddenly lose his temper. Aeron crossed the distance between them and was standing over her in seconds.

"I woke up that morning filled with hope. I thought perhaps we might find happiness together. You speak as if I have a choice in my decision to love you. I have no more ability to harden my heart than you do! You wish to spare me, but what you do not understand is it is already too late! I love you! I will love you until the end of time, whether or not you stay with me or run to the ends of Avalyne. I have done all I can to convince you. If it were possible for me to become mortal like Arianne, I would do so without a second thought, but that way is denied me. So I seek desperately to reconcile our lives so we can share what time we have together."

Melia did not know what to say. All she knew was that, since leaving Halion's court, her heart had been a heavy stone inside her breast. When her mind drifted, it would inevitably drift to him, her prince of Eden Halas. He was a part of her now, no matter how much she sought to deny it. Yet despite how much she loved him, her doubts remained the chief source of her refusal. Nevertheless, the time had come for them to be honest with each other. She owed him that at least.

"I am scared," she replied simply and it was the truth.

His gaze softened. "Of what are you frightened, that I will hurt you?"

"That you become like my father."

"Your father? I do not understand." He stared at her puzzled.

Melia exhaled deeply. It was so hard to speak of something she'd lived with all her life and confided in no one.

"My father met my mother on the banks of the Yantra River where I was born. When I was an infant, he chose to return home and wished her to go with him to Nadira. The morning we were to leave, she vanished. He waited for weeks for her to return, but she never did. Finally, he had no choice but to leave without her. It broke his heart, Prince. He never recovered from it. I do not wish you to suffer the same way because of me. I will leave you, Prince, that is a certainty. What I do not want is for you to spend the rest of eternity mourning the loss, trapped and unable to move on."

Aeron placed one hand on her shoulder while the other touched her cheek before he spoke. "When you pass from this life, it will hurt me. I will not lie to you. But I would also have a lifetime of happiness to take comfort in. Furthermore, if we have children, they may see me through the days ahead. I would not trade that for anything."

Why did he always say the right thing? How could he be so sure? Was it the age of an immortal, or did he simply love her so completely he could not see anything else? The magnitude of it staggered her and left her awestruck as well as ashamed, because she did not feel worthy of it.

"I do not know what to do! I love you so much, but I don't want to be selfish!" She blinked away fresh tears.

The tears he saw running down her cheeks were enough to break the back of his anger, until all he wished to do was bundle her in his arms and hold her to his heart forever. He wished she would believe he would never regret being with her. It was this belief more than anything that kept them apart.

"I only know that I fear someday this woman you love will disappear and perhaps you might be angry at yourself at binding yourself to me," she whispered against his chest.

Aeron took her face in his hands and kissed her tenderly. "I promise you on all I hold dear, I will never regret loving you, Mia. If this is all we have, I will gratefully accept it as long as we spend it together."

Melia could not see so far ahead but, for now, she chose to believe him. Perhaps the love they held for one another would be enough to sustain them through the years, and perhaps it would not. Melia needed time to consider his words. This decision was too large, too momentous, to make in the spur of the moment, despite how earnestly he spoke.

"Give me time, Prince. I cannot think of my future until this quest is done. For now, please know I love you and I will not run from you again. I swear to you when this is all done, you will know my mind. You said we would do this together. Do you still mean it?"

"Of course I do." He understood her need for time. The revelation about her father and her fears of condemning him to the same fate went a long way toward explaining her actions, even if it did not absolve her. What he asked was a tremendous step and Melia's willingness to give the matter thought was encouraging. If she needed time, he could oblige her.

It was the one thing an elf had in abundance.

Chapter Thirteen

The Wilds

At dawn's break, they set out again, this time bound for the Gahara Plateau. The mage had fled there with his charges and Melia was convinced her mother was still among them.

Aeron was simply grateful she was accepting the idea of being a part of his life. His faith in their life together was unshakeable, despite her fears of it being folly. With the agreement to belay any discussion of their future for now, Melia relaxed and became accustomed to having him by her side. Their nights were spent under the stars, adjusting to this new part of their relationship, exploring each other without friends and family watching closely. It was very liberating. Alone, they were simply Aeron and Melia, not the elf and mortal bound for tragedy.

Aeron wished it was like this always.

The journey to the Gahara Plateau lay would take weeks. It required reaching the Wilds, the sparse, friendless region that acted as a buffer between Carleon and Abraxes. Much of the Wilds was eroded escarpment and the plateau itself was nestled in the Nazkaad Gorge. The Gorge was a maze of narrow canyons and rocky hills covered in deciduous trees that came to life only during the spring season. The vegetation across the escarpment was seasonal and confined to waist-high shrubs, watered by thawing ice from the top of the plateau.

It took only a few days into their journey before they saw the gradual transformation of the lush green hills of Carleon into the sparse, harsh landscape of the Wilds.

Aeron had travelled this far east only once in his lifetime and it was to track a goblin party that dared enter the border of Eden Halas. Halion was so affronted by the incursion, he demanded his Forest Guard make an example of the trespassers. Aside from the canyons preceding the plateau, it was also home to the Syphii Chasm, home of the spiders responsible for the decimation of Caras Anara.

The goblins originated from the caverns beneath the Gahara Plateau, but they were not the only predators to occupy the mesa. It was also home to a nest of animals known as the *krisadors*. They were four footed beasts, large as horses, with tusklike teeth, and possessed the surefooted agility of a mountain goat. On first sighting, one would think they were lizards, but they were warm-blooded creatures who nursed their young with milk and stalked the hills for their favourite prey. Goblins.

As they journeyed eastward, it was still the goblins that concerned Aeron the most. Since the conclusion of the Aeth War, goblins were driven from the lands along the eastern borders by elves, humans and dwarves. Instead of returning to the caverns of Gahara, they took refuge in the Nazkaad Gorge. The reasons for this were unclear, though it was assumed the goblins were trying to avoid falling prey to the krisadors, whose number had grown large during their absence.

Upon reaching the Gorge, Aeron found himself in a heightened state of wariness. He saw no way to avoid the goblins en route to their destination. Even though he did not see them, his elven senses felt the danger the instant they entered the gorge, reeking the many cracks and fissures in its canyon walls. There was something else, something he did not voice to Melia. There was danger, but it was not all coming from the goblins or the krisadors. There was something else lurking at the edge of his consciousness.

Something was awaiting them at the Gahara.

* * *

"What is it?" Melia asked as they travelled through the gorge, noticing the growing uneasiness in the prince the further they went into the Gorge. By now, she had good instincts about his moods and the serious expression constantly on his face was very telling.

"Nothing," he answered promptly, having no wish to alarm her unnecessarily while he surveyed the area, trying to determine where they could camp safely for the night. The sun was already making its way towards the evening and the darkness would follow soon after.

"You do not have a face that says nothing. You have a face that tells me that something is worrying you, but you do not wish to tell me because you are trying to spare me undue concern."

"I have a face that says all *that*?" He stared at her.

"Oh yes," she smirked and added, "You cannot hide anything from me."

"I will remember when we are married." Aeron was uncertain whether he liked being read so well.

"You had better." She winked playfully, but her tone soon became sober once again. "So, what is it you do not wish to tell me?"

"There is an ever-growing threat in my mind. I can feel it pressing against us. It is coming from the Gahara."

Melia stiffened immediately, her gaze following his own to rest on the plateau in the distance. "I know of what you speak. I feel it too."

"You do?"

"Not in the way you do," she clarified quickly. "Since Tor Iolan I have felt the pull of something whenever I am close to the places my mother might have been. It is the same as when I went into the dungeons and was drawn to her cell. She is trying to speak to me. I can feel it."

"It is not merely this place that concerns me, Mia. Until Tor Iolan, I never gave much thought to some of the stories I have heard coming from these lands since the end of the war. Since we learned of your mage and the possibility he came here, I am revisiting those reports and some of the implications are disturbing."

"Of what do you speak?"

"Since the war, the goblins have taken refuge in the canyons that surround us. What puzzles me is why have they not returned to their former home? The Gahara Plateau is the perfect ground for them and yet they do not go there. If anything, they appear to be avoiding it. It was thought perhaps the krisadors numbers were too large for them to settle safely, but goblins are a canny race. Could the numbers of krisadors be that much of an obstacle to them?"

Aeron had a point and she, too, wondered what was the real threat keeping them away?

Could it be because of the mage who used his magic on her mother and the other river daughters? What exactly had he done to them that he needed to spirit them away like thieves in the night? Melia was almost afraid to voice her thoughts, but in the end decided she needed to tell Aeron of them. He was risking his life to help her and he knew a great deal more about mages than she did. Perhaps together, they might shed some light on what happened at Tor Iolan.

"Aeron, what do you know of Balfure?"

Aeron looked at her sharply. So much had already been said about the Aeth Lord, but if the truth were told, accounts of the great enemy were more myths than fact, so he understood the question, if not the timing of it.

Balfure was such a big part of their lives, Aeron forgot not everyone knew the truth about him. No doubt in years to come, Balfure's legend would see many distortions, but Aeron was long-lived enough to remember the truth. Melia's people had only seen the facade Balfure had presented to them to gain their loyalty. Indeed, he had deceived the Eastern Sphere into thinking he was a god, and a kindly one at that.

"Before his corruption, he was a *seraf*, a trusted vassal of the Celestial Gods. The mages are serafs too. Balfure was seraf to Maelog when Maelog was still one of the Celestials. When Mael broke with them, Balfure joined him and was the first of Mael's Dark Three during the Primordial Wars. Following him were Syphia and then Attean."

"The Dark Elf," Melia nodded in recognition, having heard the tale of Arianne's uncle who was disowned by his family when he became swayed by Mael's promises to rule. "What changed Balfure? Was it simply loyalty to Mael that caused him to fall into darkness?"

"Surprisingly no," Aeron continued. "Tamsyn does not like to speak of it, but he does tell us Balfure did not set out to rule. He wanted Avalyne to remain untouched. He believed the world Cera made was perfect enough without the ruin that elf, man and dwarf would bring. Initially, he joined Mael to vanquish the elves from Avalyne so it could be returned it to its former glory. Of course, as the power corrupted him, what noble purpose he intended to achieve was lost to his ambitions. Before the Celestials banished Mael, Balfure disappeared into the Burning Plains, along with anyone who wished to join him. Some of these were the Disciples."

"Such noble intentions twisted so terribly," Melia shook her head, thinking that Balfure was not the only seraf who was susceptible to this particular conceit.

"I do not think Tamsyn could even comprehend it," Aeron said sadly. "Balfure was one of his own and I think it was an affront to all the serafs that one of their own could fall so irrevocably. I think there is a moment when one must know what line not to cross and, sadly for Balfure, he did not see it until it was far behind him."

"They say that he created the Berserkers by breeding men and goblins. Is that true?"

"I am afraid so," Aeron nodded, grimacing at the horror of it. "It was said he took prisoners of both races and use dark craft to create a new beast. I suppose that it was the only way left to him after Syphia was supposedly killed."

Melia winced and could see now how the mage they were seeking in Tor Iolan fell into the same trap. While Balfure wanted to create a new type of soldier for his armies, this mage had sought to create perfection. The hubris of believing himself to be the equal of Cera in such craft appeared to have brought him to the same ruin as Balfure.

"Prince, I have always known my mother was not dead. I knew this with utter certainty, because in my dreams I feel her mind touching mine. I am convinced she is being held against her will and, now I know what transpired in Tor Iolan, I realise what befell her."

Aeron saw Melia's eyes fill with emotion and felt his heart ache, seeing that the realisation was still hard for her to accept, finding her mother in pain. If she dreamed of a happy reunion with her mother, that hope was now completely dashed. What she would find, instead, was a terrible tragedy demanding resolution. From astride his horse next to hers, Aeron reached for her hand and gave it a squeeze.

"Tell me," he coaxed gently.

"The mage wanted to create something better than elves and men. He likened himself to Cera. I think Balfure learned what this mage intended to do and tricked him into fashioning something that has not walked the world before. I think that, whatever he sought to create, he did so using my mother and the other river daughters."

The enormity of what Melia was suggesting horrified Aeron, for it was more than just evil. It was abomination. A cold chill spread down his spine at the idea. River daughters and serafs, like the Celestials, were children of Cera, intensely powerful, with their power linked to the many aspects of the world: the sea, the earth, the wind and air. Each played a part in the Cosmic Thread Cera had used to weave the Universe.

What did it mean when one strand of that tapestry was corrupted?

"You think that the mage has turned your mother into a creature of darkness?"

"Creature, yes," Melia nodded. "Darkness, I do not know. I only saw it was against their will that they were turned into whatever the mage intended. After it was done, he became deathly afraid of their power. At first opportunity, he took them from Tor Iolan, to prevent Balfure from unleashing them upon his enemies."

"If that is so," Aeron questioned, "where have they been all this time?"

Melia shook her head and was about to answer when suddenly Aeron lurched towards her from his saddle. He toppled them over to land on the rocky ground with a heavy thud. Melia was about to demand what he was about when her horse reared up on its hind quarters, braying in pain at the arrow that was now lodged in its neck. She had just enough time to register the blood when another arrow struck again, causing the animal to buck with pain once more. Aeron's horse, sniffing the blood, began to stamp its hooves in panic, wanting to bolt.

"Goblins!" Aeron declared, recognizing the crude workmanship of the arrow shafts.

"Now?" Melia exclaimed in confusion. It was still daylight! Then she realised nightfall was not far away and, if the goblins crippled or killed their horses, they would be forced to escape the Gorge on foot. They could not hope to get far enough away before the goblins tracked them down, most likely in large numbers.

Melia's horse, a grey mare, had taken the worst of the enemy's marksmanship. The animal was on its haunches and was breaths away from succumbing completely to her injuries. Wasting no time, Aeron grabbed Melia's hand and pulled her towards his horse, aware their survival rested in putting as much distance between themselves and the goblins as possible, then carrying out their assault from the safety of the fissures and cracks in the canyon walls.

Aaron mounted his horse just as another arrow flew past him and embedded its point into a nearby tree. Melia lingered long enough to retrieve her crossbow but she agonized at leaving a wounded beast to the ministrations of the goblins. However, there were enough arrows in the poor animal to ensure that it would not be alive when the goblins came. Hurrying away from her mount to his, she caught Aeron's outstretched hand and he pulled her onto the saddle with him.

The horse bolted as soon as she was seated, with arrows flying after them. One tore through the fabric of her breeches, cutting close enough for her skin to bleed. Melia winced in pain but knew the injury was minor. Her arms slid around Aeron's waist as he rode hard through the Gorge, intending to reach the river if possible. Another volley of arrows flew at them from a different direction, forcing him to steer away from the easier path to the embankment.

Melia glanced over her shoulder and glimpsed the goblins moving in between the shadows of the rocky hills, peering through them from cracks and shaded rock shelves. Her heart froze at just how many of them there were, waiting for the sun to go down before they swarmed the area in search of food. In search of *them*, she thought. The goblins were taking full advantage of the hilly terrain surrounding them as they escaped the Gorge.

Leaving the narrow passage did not aid their case when the rocky hills hid many places from which the goblins could continue their attack. As arrows flew at them, Aeron steered the horse away, hoping to reach higher ground. He could hear water rushing and knew that, if they had to, they could use the river to escape. Goblins did not like water and most did not know how to swim.

More arrows came at them and Aeron shifted their path again, even though he suspected there was some method to the goblins' actions. He and Melia were being herded. The arrows were forcing them to a place where they would be surrounded and trapped. As they went higher, he dug in his heels and forced their mount to burst through trees, determined to find an alternate route to the river and penetrate the goblin blockade.

"Keep your head low!" He barked at Melia. She took refuge in his shoulder as he himself lowered his head to avoid the branches snapping at them as they rode past the trees.

The horse thundered forward through the uphill track, past trees and rocks, a slave to its master's demands. Too late did Aeron see what it was that made the animal try to stop so suddenly, but could do nothing to prevent what was coming. In the split second before they went over the edge of the cliff, he came to the unhappy conclusion that perhaps goblins would not be the death of them after all.

The fall would.

"What's going on…?" Melia demanded. She felt herself being propelled forward by the combination of their great speed and the sudden stop that followed it. Her words turned into a scream as all three toppled over the edge of the cliff into the dark waters of the churning river below.

* * *

Aeron's horse reached the water first, breaking the tension with a great splash before the braying beast disappeared beneath the frothing river. Aeron and Melia followed, plunging feet first into the water below. A blanket of cold water immediately swirled overhead and drove them to the bottom. It was hard to keep stock of each other after such a tumultuous landing and all Aeron could do to get his bearings was to follow the direction of the bubbles rising from his mouth through the water.

When he broke the surface, he immediately sought out Melia and saw their horse struggling to reach the embankment. There was no trace of Melia and her absence filled him panic. The strong current of the river did not help matters, sweeping them further down its winding length with each passing moment.

"Melia!" He tried to call after her over the churning white water.

There was no answer and he was ready to call out again when he heard her voice crying out frantically behind him.

"PRINCE!"

Aeron whirled around in the water and followed the direction of her desperate call to find she was not far behind him. Melia had managed to surface long enough to utter that terrified cry but was soon sinking under the water again. It took a moment for him to register why she was so frightened. She was neither swimming nor threading water. Instead, she was thrashing about wildly, unable to maintain any buoyancy. She disappeared under the water again, only her arms visible as the rapids crashed over her.

She can't swim! Aeron realised with a burst of clarity. Melia can't swim!

Surging ahead, he broke into powerful strokes as he fought the current to reach her. The white frothing waters fought him every inch of the way and he finally decided if he continued this way, she would drown long before he ever reached her. Taking a deep breath, Aeron dove beneath the waves, descending deep enough to avoid the chop so that he could swim to her.

Aeron reached Melia just as she went under again, her body bobbing up and down as it lost its battle to stay afloat. Melia's effort to call him only resulted in more water rushing down her throat as he heard her coughing hoarsely. With far more speed than he thought himself capable, Aeron wrapped his arms around her waist just as she became completely submerged in the icy water. Upon noticing his presence, Melia immediately wrapped her arms around his neck and held on for dear life as he used their collective buoyancy to push them both to the surface.

When they broke the surface, Melia gasped greedily for air. If he had not arrived when he did, she had no doubt she would be drowning at the bottom of the river. She clung to him tightly as he swam towards the embankment, but her added weight and the strength of the river would not allow them to break free of its powerful currents. Their horse had gained the far bank further down river, still shaking off the river from its body.

"Hold on," he ordered over the sound of the rushing water and she complied with a frightened nod. Aeron let himself relax, no longer fighting the flow of the water and positioned himself to float, with Melia doing the same. The river swept them further downstream, until they were moving so fast it was difficult to keep track of the enemy and almost as difficult to keep the river from claiming them permanently.

Neither Aeron nor Melia could say how far down the river the current took, them but they soon reached a point where they were unable to endure the freezing water any longer. They had to reach shore before both were stricken with frostbite. They were on the edge of the world, perhaps even beyond it. There would be no help here if either of them fell ill. Aeron knew if his elvish endurance was at breaking point, Melia would be in even worse condition.

It was still light, but the day was fading and soon their pursuers would be out in force. He could sense danger all around them, though not from any specific place, so it was difficult to decide whether it was safe to make an attempt to reach the embankment. When he caught sight of their horse at the embankment, Aeron decided to risk it and headed towards it. The steed appeared exhausted. Its hooves dug into the shale beach, as it tried to find its master.

He started swimming towards the edge, deciding that the nearest shore was as good as any to make their emergence. Fortunately, his bow and arrows remained fastened to his body, as Melia's crossbow did to hers. If they were to encounter the enemy, at least they wouldn't be defenceless. After what seemed like an eternity, they reached the shore, almost completely exhausted due to the added weight of water in their clothes and weapons.

Crawling onto the embankment, they collapsed heavily against the sand, succumbing briefly to their ordeal in the river. Melia was already starting to shiver, thanks the icy cold water soaking her skin, but she was doing her best to tolerate it.

"How is it," Aeron asked through his exhausted breath when he finally turned to her, "that you can fight as well as any man, shoot a bow better than most *and*, I might add, curse like a Lenkworth sailor, but somehow forget to learn how to swim?"

Melia scowled at him, "I come from a dry country, Prince. We used our water for bathing and drinking, not anything as frivolous as swimming!"

"But you have been in Avalyne for some time. Did you never think to learn?"

"No!" She declared defensively, feeling unbelievably stupid for not learning the skill.

"If you don't mind, if we survive this, I think I had better teach you."

His offer earned him a shove.

"We need to get out of here," she grumbled, wringing the water out of her hair and quickly scanning the surrounding trees.

Aeron was already on his feet and striding towards their approaching horse. The animal had found them, drawn to their familiar scent, waterlogged as it might be. For someone who was soaked to the skin, he moved with surprising speed and made Melia swear under her breath when she stumbled about like an infant on unsteady legs in her saturated clothes. She needed to get warm, but a campfire was out of the question until they were well away from here.

The sun was setting and the goblins would not be far behind.

"The saddle is gone," Aeron stated as he ran his hand across the bare back of the animal. Only reins still remained. Everything else was swept away by the river. Elves were accustomed to riding bare backed, but he was uncertain if Melia was capable.

"You first," he stated as he took hold of the reins and steadied the animal.

Melia nodded, loosening the fasteners holding her crossbow in place across her back. Her stores of bolts had dwindled substantially after being washed away in the river. Only a handful remained in her pouch and she was not pleased by this fact. They were hard to replace at the best of times and, out here in the middle of nowhere, this was all she had. Aeron helped her mount the horse, since she was used to doing it with stirrup, before he climbed up in front of her.

"We must move now," Aeron suddenly exclaimed, digging his heels into the horse's flank and sending the animal surging towards the cover of trees.

She did not need to ask why. The sun had disappeared behind the mountains and, though there was some light left, it was not nearly enough to keep them safe. No sooner than he had spoken, a band of goblins burst out of the bushes near the embankment. The closest one ran across the ground with surprising speed, brandishing a cruel-looking mace meant to disable their horse.

Melia raised her crossbow without thought and let fly a bolt of steel. It embedded itself in the goblin's forehead before the creature had time to shriek. It dropped dead where it stood.

They were already moving, but the horse was struggling to pass the goblins who were quick to bar its way. Breaking into a gallop nonetheless, the steed's pace struggled for haste as its hooves sought firmer ground than the soft shale of the embankment. Nostrils flaring, the steed neighed in dislike at the goblins in its way, stamping its feet as it charged through them. The orkish creations sought to push Aeron and Melia off the animal.

From the corner of her eye, beyond the chaos caused by the goblins in front of them, Melia caught sight of two of the foul creatures closing in from the rear. One brandished a dagger to impale either the horse or its rider. Melia wasted no time putting a bolt into him. Meanwhile, Aeron kicked away another and returned his attention to escaping their trapped position. He reached for one of his own daggers, tucked neatly with his bow, and slashed wildly at the horde attempting to converge upon them.

"Back, you foul things!" Aeron cursed and slammed a boot into the jaw belonging to one of them, shattering bone with his heel. Another swung at him, but the elf turned in time to catch the blade, returning it with a far better aim. Melia was shooting her steel bolts at the enemy, but he could tell by that taut expression in her eyes that she was running out of them. They needed to get away from here now.

A sharp glint of moonlight caught Melia's eye. It was heading towards her prince. Melia saw it an instant before it struck. She pulled Aeron out of its path without thinking and they both fell off the horse just as the creature broke into a run, dragging goblins with it in its desperate attempt at escape. The arrow that would have killed him was now embedded in the steed's neck, blood staining the white of its hide. The remaining goblins were now closing in for the kill.

Anticipating their retreat to the river, the goblins ensured the path was closed to them and, before they were completely surrounded, Aeron grabbed Melia's hand and started towards the trees. In the wood, there was a chance he could lose them amongst the trees. A goblin attempted to intercept them, but Aeron made quick work of it, swinging his blade at the creature and tearing open its insides. Melia was also accosted and she reacted just as swiftly, slamming her crossbow, now exhausted of its supply of bolts, across the face of her attacker.

The action gave them the precious seconds of a cleared path and they took advantage of it, running faster than either had ever run in their lives. They could hear the goblins falling into pursuit behind them as they tore through the woods. While Aeron left no tracks, Melia certainly did, and those tracks were easily followed by the enemy. Had they the time, Melia would have been able to disguise her path, but their main goal at this moment was to put as much distance between them and the enemy as possible. Dusk was finally upon them and there would be no safety until sunrise.

Trampling through the forest, the terrain towards the mountain was hard and it was with dismay Aeron saw the canopy of trees would soon come to an end. The goblins would move with greater speed over the cleared ground and they would have no place to hide. He could feel the creatures behind them, relentless in their pursuit.

They are ravenous with hunger, he realised, *almost on the verge of turning on each other.*

The revelation of their desperation meant they would not give up until they captured their prey. There would be no hiding from them.

They were close behind and, as he came to a stop, he saw Melia knew it too. Her fear was great, but she was too proud to show it. This journey on foot would not do, Aeron realized, and he searched the trees. They were as strong as they were old.

Some of the branches were spread out like giant palms upturned towards the sky, their leaves a blanket of green. The branches were thick enough to hold the weight of two and if there was to be any escape tonight it would have to be in trees. In the bosom of the meagre forest, they might be able to double back the way they had come and reach the safety of the river.

"Follow me," he instructed as he reached the tree that would suit their purpose. "Put your foot where mine has been and nowhere else. Fail in this and we will both die tonight."

Melia did not argue and obeyed without question. Aeron started up the tree, scaling its branches with such speed he almost looked like he was flying. He was well off the ground when his hands reached for her and he pulled her up into the cover of the leaves. Poised on the thick branch, they moved as silently as was possible. Even the slight rustle of leaves felt too loud. Below them, the goblins continued the search. When sounds of them drew too near, they froze in silence, praying it was enough to maintain their concealment.

Aeron seemed made for the trees as he remained crouched within its branches, blending in as if he were one with its life. She watched him, still as the night air, eyes burning in the dark as he studied everything. He was an image of beautiful concentration. He would always be this way, she realised. It gnawed at her as she rubbed her callused palms and glimpsed the scratches on her skin. Aches would become more acute, joined with wrinkles and crow's feet. All were markers to remind her time was catching up to her.

He said she was beautiful, but she knew it wouldn't last.

One day, she would be old.

"I think it is safe," Aeron whispered finally, breaking the silence after what seemed like hours. "We should remain here until sunrise."

Melia could not hear the goblins, but that meant nothing. Goblins knew the art of stealth as well as they did. She looked up into the sky and saw that the indigo night was well underway.

"Then what?" she asked softly. "Do we continue?"

"We must," Aeron nodded. "We must put some distance between ourselves and the goblins, for they will be roaming these woods as soon as the night falls again. Without the horses, it would take too much time to retreat. We are safer continuing ahead."

"I have never known them to be so relentless," Melia declared, somewhat mystified.

"They are hungry," Aeron explained. "Did you not notice how there is no large game here? All the life we normally expect to find in a wood this size is absent. I have seen nothing larger than a rabbit. Such a diet cannot be enough for goblins who are used to larger fare for their bellies."

"It was the same in the Frozen Mountains, but those were caused by the spawn of the dragon," Melia remarked, remembering how barren the foothills had been before she, Arianne, Celene, and Keira reached the mountain range. They had learned, eventually, it was caused by the worms living there, sired by a dragon of ancient times.

"There are no worms in the Gahara, but there are the krisadors."

"Krisadors?" she exclaimed and then cursed herself for not keeping her voice down. "What are those?" This time, she kept her voice to a whisper.

"Creatures living in the plateau," he answered. "They are dangerous, but I prefer to take my chances with them than the goblins."

Melia smiled despite herself. "I admire your ability to make so measured a choice."

Aeron returned it before his expression sobered again and he resumed his vigil over their hiding place. He could not see the goblins, but he could feel their presence. Very soon they would discover there were no more tracks to follow and would deduce their quarry were hiding in the trees because there was nowhere else for them to go.

Chapter Fourteen

Tamsyn

It did not take long for his worst fears to be realised.

His superior senses warned of their return. Against the serenity of the forest, their harsh language and their brackish natures were easy to detect. They were trampling over everything that lived, hacking away at living plants out of sheer spite as they sought their prey. They were coming back this way and, though Aeron was not as fluent in their speech as he would have liked, he understood their words clearly enough.

The goblins knew they were in the trees.

"We need to move," Aeron declared quickly, working his way across the long branches with Melia following closely. "They have guessed where we are."

"That was inevitable, I suppose," Melia replied as she followed him and watched his movements closely, remembering his instructions about repeating his every step. Elves knew more about stealth than Melia would ever learn in her entire lifetime.

"Watch out!" Aeron turned around sharply as his senses warned him of impending danger.

The arrow came out of nowhere and impaled her thigh.

Melia let out a cry of pain as the metal splinter tore through her flesh, upsetting her balance on the branch she was standing. Aeron watched in horror as she slipped of the perch and tumbled to the ground. He made a desperate effort to catch her but failed to reach her in time. She landed heavily in the centre of the goblin raiding party; the arrow still embedded in her thigh. There were at least ten of them but the two nearest her were archers with one of them almost certainly the architect of her injury.

Still on his perch, Aeron immediately armed his bow with two arrows. Positioning them carefully, he let them fly and felt some measure of satisfaction when both struck their mark as he leapt out of his hiding place to help the woman he loved.

The pain in her leg was beyond belief, but fear shunted it aside as she saw the goblins coming towards her. Rising to her feet far quicker than she thought herself able, in light of her injuries, she saw a goblin raising a weapon to her and could do little more than block the blow with her crossbow. The construction of her weapon was of steel and the heaviest wood known to the Eastern Sphere. It was her father's and it was already old when it was given to him. Hezare had claimed it could stop a blade and Melia prayed it wasn't an exaggeration.

It wasn't.

With far more determination to survive than the goblin had to kill her, Melia shoved the creature backwards and wielded the weapon like a club, smashing the crossbow's full span across its body. The goblin reeled backwards in pain. She wished more than anything she had a bolt to arm the thing, but her supply was exhausted after their flight at the riverbank. The other goblin barrelled through her, tackling her to the ground. With the pain in her leg, she was able to do little to stop him.

She winced when he struck her across the jaw hard, but it was not quite enough to disorientate her from retaliating. She struggled hard to dislodge him from the straddling position he had taken over her body and damn near succeeded, until the vile thing grabbed the arrow in her leg and shoved it in deeper. The white hot agony it produced was beyond belief and Melia screamed in pain.

Aeron heard her cry and slashed the dagger through the neck of the goblin closest to him. The other sneaking up behind him during the confusion soon found the elf prince glaring murderously at him. Aeron planted a foot in the goblin's chest and sent him flying backward before throwing his sword and impaling him against at tree. Black blood spurted forth from the wound, staining the sword's blade. Retrieving his weapon, he resumed the bloody task of killing anything standing between him and Melia. Goblins knew nothing of skill in battle. Their only strategy was to overwhelm by sheer numbers.

Fortunately, Aeron was lacking in neither.

Aeron had fought at Astaroth when Balfure used everything in his arsenal to keep them away from his Iron Citadel. After that battle, Aeron could make short work of these goblins if his fury was sufficiently provoked. Melia's scream did that and more. With dagger and sword, he fought without pause, swinging his blade with such force it more or less killed on the first blow. With two weapons in his hands, the battleground was soon covered with goblin corpses.

There would be more coming; he did not delude himself on this as he took the head from one of them. The creature's head spun in mid-air before hitting the ground hard with a loud squelch that would have made him shudder if he had cared enough to notice. He did not. His attention was focused on Melia who struggled to keep the goblin poised on top of her from bringing down its blade against her throat. Her face was contorted in pain as her assailant kept a firm grip upon the arrow in her leg and continued to twist viciously.

"AERON!" she screamed desperately for help, her strength faltering.

Aeron wasted no time in reaching her, now the way was clear. The goblin turned around, just in time to see his sword plunging through its back. Aeron shoved the creature off Melia and dropped to his knees next to her. Melia was on her back still, groaning in pain, her hand clutching her leg.

"I am here," he said, slipping his hand underneath her to help her up. He found himself on the receiving end of a heartfelt embrace.

"I almost was not," she said gratefully, tears in her eyes from pain and the relief at her survival. "Thank you."

"I promised you I would let nothing harm you," he said softly as their lips met in a soft kiss.

"Yes," she murmured, taking comfort from his mouth against hers. "I should have learned to believe you by now."

"Can you walk?" he asked softly, hating to disengage from her arms, but the urgency of the situation demanded it. Examining the wound briefly, he was grateful to see that, while it appeared painful, nothing vital had been severed.

"I think so," she nodded as he helped her to her feet. "Best to leave the arrow where it is," she suggested, looking at the sliver of wood protruding from her thigh. "I can manage until we reach the river."

"Are you certain?" Aeron asked, not at all happy about that.

Goblin arrows were known to be poisonous and the one lodged in Melia's thigh was causing her a great deal of pain, though she would not admit it. She was right, though. It would be unwise to remove the arrow now. If he did so, he would have to treat the wound immediately and they could ill afford to do that. Not when more goblins would be coming after them and Aeron's ability to fight them all was debatable. Even now, he could hear their distant voices and the soft thrum of their war drums echoing through the Gorge, a call for more of their kind to come aid in the hunt.

"Yes," she answered, slipping her arm around his shoulder for support. "I cannot hear them as well as you, but I know that they are coming."

Aeron shifted his eyes away from hers for a moment, having no heart to tell her that the goblins were nearer than she believed, when she was already trying so hard not to be a burden. If she knew how truly close they were, Aeron had no doubt that she would attempt to do something selfless and undoubtedly foolish to save his life.

"They are," he nodded grimly. "They are calling for reinforcements."

"I shall keep up as best as I can," Melia grunted, trying to force away the pain as she hobbled forward with his help. She did not wish their escape hindered by her injury, and grit her teeth to endure the white-hot agony that surged through her each time she made a tentative step forward with that cursed arrow stuck in her leg. If she removed it now, she would bleed out, unless he bound the wound immediately, and they did not have time for that.

"I will carry you," he offered.

"No!" Melia retorted hotly. "You need to keep your hands free in case they come upon us far sooner than we think." She kissed him lightly on the cheek. "Thank you for the thought."

"We will survive this," Aeron assured her as they left the dead bodies behind them. "I promise you."

"I expect to be killed by something far fouler than goblins," Melia replied bravely as they moved through the trees.

Climbing into their branches was beyond her now. There was no way she could maintain the poise or agility required to stay aloft, and so they were forced to take this course. Aeron tried not to think about what would happen if he could not get her out of these woods before the beating of those distant drums brought the swarm he knew was coming. The worst they would do to him was to kill him. The worst they would do to her was to keep her alive.

"I am glad you have some preference in the matter," he replied.

They kept a brisk pace, despite her injury, and Aeron tried to ignore the pain he saw in her eyes each time she took a step. She continued to reject his offer to carry her but, while she refused out of pride, he knew her argument to keep his hands free made sense. If they could reach the river, then perhaps they might survive this night, but as he heard the rushing water grow louder, he grew even more wary at their chances of reaching it alive.

He could feel them closing in even if he did not see them. Aeron felt his blood chill and he drew his sword even as he supported Melia's frame around his shoulder.

She saw him unsheathing his weapon and her eyes filled with sorrow at knowing that tonight, it could end here for them both.

"Prince, you need to leave me."

"No," Aeron answered promptly, anticipating some nonsense like this in the growing urgency of their situation.

"You must or you will die here with me," she implored.

"Mia," he paused long enough to look her in the eyes and say firmly, "do not tax my patience on this matter. I will not leave you. Clear that thought out of your mind this instant. It only wastes your energy."

"Why do you have to be so stubborn?" she grumbled in exasperation. "I do not wish you to die."

"And you think that my leaving you here to face those goblins will not kill me? Were I actually cowardly enough to do that, I would take my own life in shame."

"It is not cowardly to save oneself," Melia retorted. "Why must you be so difficult?"

"Because I love you and, like your entire race, your efforts to be noble are usually half-thought and made when high on emotion," Aeron replied, not really paying attention to her because the tree line was breaking apart for the embankment and the river beyond.

"If it were not my life you were trying to save, I would take offence at that," Melia frowned.

"You do not mean it," he remarked as his eyes searched the woods around him and found the shadows were too long for his liking. "You love me too much."

"Well," Melia glared at him through narrowed eyes, "you have me at a disadvantage, though I might ask you to remind me why that is again."

Aeron did not answer because the shadows began to move as he expected and the brief interlude withered away like ice in the sunlight. The goblins emerged, springing their ambush because the creatures knew that the river was their only means of escape.

Melia closed her eyes as she saw their numbers. There were too many to count and she knew there was no way either of them would survive the united assault of the forces rallied against them. The goblins sneered in triumph, their jagged and rotting teeth bared in expressions of exultant victory and menace as they closed in on the two. She released her hold on Aeron, putting her weight on her injured leg, for it did not seem to matter anymore. Taking his dagger as he held up his sword, Melia held her ground next to her Prince.

"I love you Prince," she whispered softly. "They will not take us easily."

Aeron met her eyes and tried to hide his grief and failed. "You were worth every moment, Melia. I love you!"

And that was all that they were allowed as they faced the enemy once more, preparing to fight to the death.

The goblins moved in for the kill cautiously, because an elf was nothing to be underestimated, even if they surrounded him in the dozens.

Aeron raised his weapon, preparing to kill the first goblin to attack, when a bright and powerful light flooded the clearing. Its brilliance was so strong even the prince and his lady, accustomed to daylight, flinched at its radiance. The effect upon the goblins was far more acute and the creatures screeched collectively in pain as the glare flooded their sensitive eyes.

The light was coming from an orb floating above their heads.

As stunned as he was by what he was seeing, the elf recognised salvation when it was upon him. Sheathing his sword, he wasted no time sweeping Melia into his arms before running towards the river, past the goblins trying desperately to shield their eyes from the overpowering glare. Some had started to scatter as their skin began to sizzle under the intensity of it.

Aeron saw none of this retreat, because he was running through the forest like a stag running from a hunter. The analogy was disconcertingly accurate, considering what would have become of them if the enemy had indeed captured them. He panted loudly as they passed through thinning forest and returned to the edge of the Yasnil.

Aeron's chest was pounding as he finally came to a pause and dropped to his knees with Melia still in his grasp. Only when he took a moment to catch his breath did he notice the wet streaks across her cheeks. The race to the river had jostled her injured leg and sent waves of agony through her. Melia had borne it in silence because they simply had to reach safety. When he put her down, she lay flat on her back, trembling with shock.

"Take this thing out of me!" she demanded, glaring at the arrow.

"Aye," he nodded and cast a final gaze at the wood and knew that they had a short time to do this. He did not know for how long the goblins would be frightened away, but he intended to take advantage of the time while they possessed it. Dropping down next to her, Aeron tore away the fabric of her breeches surrounding the shaft of the arrow. His stomach hollowed at the sight of the discoloured skin and the blood soaked material.

"What happened back there?" Melia asked as she looked away from what he was doing, trying to occupy her mind with something other than the impending pain she would soon be forced to endure.

"I don't know," Aeron answered honestly. "If I did not know better, I would say we were given a reprieve by a wizard."

"Then you would be right," a male voice suddenly spoke, emerging from the bushes. Aeron jumped to his feet to meet the new arrival with his sword.

Except found himself facing a friendly face.

"Tamsyn!"

Gaping at the wizard, Aeron realised that only a mage could have approached him so stealthily. "What are you doing here?"

For a moment Aeron thought his eyes were deceiving him. Was this a trick conjured up by a mind desperate for salvation? Yet as the mage approached, his black cloak draped over his dark red shirt, leather jerkins and breeches, Aeron knew it to be no else. In his hand, was the familiar staff of polished dark wood, ending with a crescent shaped carving on the tip. Tamsyn was covered in dust and bore the appearance of one who had been travelling in the wilderness for quite some time. When he greeted Aeron with a warm embrace, Aeron knew that this was no illusion.

"This is the last place I expected to find a familiar face," Tamsyn's pleasure at seeing them was obvious, but the surprise in eyes was even more evident. "What are you doing here, Aeron and..." he paused and stared at the watch guard, "Melia, wasn't it?"

"More or less," she nodded and offered him a small wave of greeting.

"Your help could not be better timed. Tamsyn. I thought we were doomed."

"Yes, I did happen to hear that rather touching moment," Tamsyn remarked with a little smile, having seen something of the attraction between the two during their adventure in the Frozen Mountains. He was not at all surprised to see it had since deepened. "But let us talk about how we both arrived in this place later. The young lady is hurt and we need to tend to her."

Aeron turned back to Melia, mortified he had forgotten about it in his relief to see Tamsyn. "I was about to remove the arrow. I fear that it might be poison-tipped."

"Poison tipped?" Melia stared at him with wide eyes. "What do you mean poisoned tipped?" She was accustomed to dealing with Berserkers. Goblins did not travel far enough west for her to encounter them at the Baffin.

"I did not want to worry you," Aeron admitted as he dropped to his knees next to her again, Tamsyn doing the same.

"It would worry me more if I was dead, Prince," she grumbled, hissing when Tamsyn made a quick examination of the wound.

"We had enough to worry about with the goblins," Aeron returned as she clutched his hand when Tamsyn touched the arrow shaft and the slight movement sent fresh slivers of pain running down her leg to the rest of her. "I wanted to spare you."

"Stop trying to shield me from everything. I think you know by now that I can handle most things."

"I am sorry to have missed the wedding," Tamsyn commented with amusement as he listened to the two argue over him.

"As always, your wit is singular," Aeron bit back. Still, he did feel compelled to clarify the nature of their relationship. "But we are *together*."

"I stand corrected," the mage said dryly as he concluded the examination of Melia's wound and reached for a pouch on his belt. "Your arguing has the strong stench of matrimonial bliss about it."

"No," Melia protested with another hiss of pain escaping her when Tamsyn pressed some herbs from the pouch against the raw wound. There was a momentary stinging that burned intensely for a few seconds and then subsided to a strange numbing sensation. "This is how we always speak to each other."

"Then it must be an interesting relationship," Tamsyn raised his eyes to hers and smiled.

"You have no idea," Aeron replied as he scanned the area around the river to ensure the goblins did not return while Tamsyn was performing his healing magic. "We thought you were travelling to gather acolytes for the Order. You have not been seen in Carleon for many months."

"I was," Tamsyn's concentration remained on his patient as he spoke. "I encountered some goblins and, during our battle, I learned that there was a wizard reputed to live in the Gahara. I came to seek him out," Tamsyn answered before adding, "This arrow must come out now. The poison is spreading and will kill her if I do not remove it."

Aeron agreed, having reached the same conclusion before Tamsyn had happened upon them earlier. He had only to look at Melia to see time was running out for her. There was a fine sheen of moisture on her skin and her pallor was grey. She was ill and growing worse by the minute.

Aeron wrapped her shoulder with his free arm to brace her for what was coming. "Melia," he said tenderly, staring into her face, "this will hurt."

"I know." She maintained her grip on his hand, trying to draw the strength he was offering her so readily. "Do what you must. Remove this accursed thing."

Aeron shifted his eyes back to Tamsyn and gave him permission to continue. The wizard said little, resting his hands on the shaft of the arrow, securing his hold. The world seemed to drain into that one moment, when Aeron waited for the arrow to be freed from Melia's body. He held his breath, trying to brace himself the same way she was preparing to endure the agonising pain that came with it. Even the most hardened warriors succumbed to the agony of such extractions.

Without warning, the wizard yanked the arrow out of Melia's leg.

The scream tearing through the air came easily from one who was so accustomed to hiding every weakness. Aeron flinched at hearing her cry of pain. Her fingers dug into his hand with such force, it nearly drew blood. Tears ran down her cheeks as she bit down hard, dizzy from the intensity of it. When it was over, Melia slumped weakly against Aeron as the ordeal sent her into a merciful faint.

"Mia!" Aeron cried as he caught her.

"She will be fine," Tamsyn assured him sympathetically. "It is best that she sleeps for awhile."

Tamsyn briefly regarded the bloody arrow in his hand, before tossing it away in disgust. While Melia remained unconscious, he proceeded to treat the injury by applying a fine powder to the raw wound to counter the poison in her body. Once that immediate action was completed, he turned to Aeron once more.

"Come, my friend," Tamsyn got to his feet. "Let us get to safer ground before the goblins return in greater numbers. I have only frightened them. They will return soon enough."

Aeron could well believe it and the scent of Melia's blood would draw them to her like flies to a bloated carcass.

Once they were ready to leave, Tamsyn led Aeron further along upriver, the trees flanking them as they moved to higher ground. The embankment was obstructed by large boulders the higher up they went, but Aeron was just grateful they were no longer pursued by the goblins. Despite Tamsyn's claims of rein-forcements, the elf knew the goblins were reluctant to confront a mage of Enphilim.

They walked for a good hour until his limbs grew weary from carrying her weight, though he did not mind at all. At some point, her faint became sleep and Aeron saw no reason to wake her. Unconscious, she would be spared the pain of her injury. She slept peacefully, with her head nestled against his shoulder and he marvelled at how childlike these mortals were when they were quiet like this. Sleeping, he could see the person she was without any of the reservations that kept her so guarded. He wanted to spend every morning, for the rest of her life, waking up to her face.

"I never thought I would see you look at a mortal that way," Tamsyn teased gently when he caught the prince studying the sleeping woman in his arms.

While there was no derision in Tamsyn's gaze, Aeron felt embarrassed at being caught indulging in such a personal moment when they were still in dangerous territory. He was a son of Halion, taught all his life to hide his emotions and always project an image of control and command. Even if he would never be king, Halion demanded all his sons carry themselves with the dignity of royal personage. With the Circle, Aeron learned to be himself, but he was always, at the heart of him, someone who kept his feelings and his counsel to himself.

"She is the woman I love," he muttered in response. "It matters not that she is human."

"Then you will live a good life together for however long it lasts," Tamsyn winced inwardly because it sounded like a taunt instead of a blessing.

"I am aware of that," Aeron snapped, wondering if *everyone* had an opinion on how impossible their relationship would be. "I have been told that a number of times already."

"And you chose not to heed their advice?" Tamsyn wondered how the elf's father would have reacted to such news.

"How can I?" Aeron retorted with some measure of irritation. "I love her. You know how it is with elves."

Tamsyn knew perfectly well how it was and thought immediately of his murky history with Arianne's mother, Queen Lylea. Of course, he took the coward's way out while Aeron was risking everything for the woman he loved. Tamsyn admired him for that.

"I do not mean to insult you, Aeron," Tamsyn said kindly, seeing now the distress in Aeron's face at the inevitable fate of his relationship with Melia. "I was merely surprised. Your father cannot have been happy with this."

"He was not," Aeron admitted. "He tried to tell me that I bring unnecessary pain upon myself."

"I suppose he would know."

"What?" Aeron stared at the mage. "How would he know?"

Tamsyn cursed inwardly, not having intended to blurt out Halion's secret, though he was rather surprised the prince did not know. It was not a secret really, but he supposed there were very few elves left who still remembered the Primordial Wars. "Forgive me, Aeron. It is not my tale to tell."

"I think it is a little too late for that," Aeron insisted, intrigued that he and his father might have some common ground. "Tell me, *please*."

Tamsyn frowned and hoped this revelation did not do more harm than good. "Your mother is not your father's first wife. Before he came to Halas from the north, Halion was married to an elf maid of Sanhael."

Aeron stared at Tamsyn in shock.

It should not have surprised him, because in the light of knowing, suddenly everything he had observed about his parents made perfect sense. Like the pieces of a jigsaw, Aeron saw the whole picture at last and it explained much about his parents. Knowing his father had a mate before Syanne explained the distance Aeron saw between them. He always suspected Halion was not bonded to his mother, but now he understood why. Of course, why his mother would choose to be bonded to someone who did not love her was puzzling.

"Why would my mother marry him, then?" Aeron had to ask. To Halion it would make no difference, but if his mother was not bonded, she could have been with someone else. She could have been happy.

"You must understand what it was like after the end of the Primordial Wars," Tamsyn explained. "The elves were scattered.

So many had died and the land was scarred. Your mother was alone. Like Halion, all her family was killed in the war. The match might have suited her and it was a chance to leave the ruin of Sanhael behind and start something new with Halion. Perhaps she thought her love would be enough."

It was not, Aeron thought bitterly. He had seen it all his life. "I know what I face by loving Melia, Tamsyn. I am willing to pay the price for a lifetime with her."

"Then I wish you both the best," Tamsyn said sincerely, though he did not envy the elf's fate once time had had its way with the couple.

Chapter Fifteen

Revelation

Melia woke with a start.

As a watch guard, she was accustomed to sleeping lightly and being aware of her surroundings at all times. To open her eyes and find herself in a place she did not recognise immediately sent fear though her heart. Her first impulse was to seek out her weapon, but when she clutched the space beside her, it was gone. It dawned on her she did not remember where she had put it because she had passed out. Attempting to stand, the pain that coursed through her at the slightest movement ended the effort with a loud groan.

"Let that be a lesson to you to not do that again," Tamsyn warned through the amber glow of flame before her.

It was then Melia remembered Tamsyn had come to their rescue and it was he whom she found herself facing across the fire. Lifting the blanket resting over her, she observed her leg to be bandaged and realised she owed her treatment to this mage who had appeared out of nowhere to save both her and Aeron from the goblins.

"You will have no argument from me," she sighed as she studied her surroundings. "Thank you," she gestured to the dressing on her leg.

"You're welcome."

They were obviously in a cavern of some sort, she decided as she ran her gaze over its span. Judging by its size, it was not very large and, from where she lay, she could see the opening into it. Beyond them, the stars twinkled in the night sky and Melia wondered just how long she had been asleep. It was night when she passed out, but she felt so rested it did not feel like only a few hours had passed.

"How long have I been asleep?" Her eyes searched for Aeron.

"Almost a day. The pain was too much for you after I removed the arrow. You fainted."

Melia balked at the suggestion. Fainting was the work of genteel females accustomed to soft living, not a watch guard of the king.

"I do *not* faint," she said stubbornly.

"Considering the agony you endured when I pulled that arrow out of your leg, there is no shame in it."

"I do not faint," she repeated herself, immovable on this point.

Tamsyn let out a heavy sigh that indicated he was not going to argue the issue. "In that case, you selected an opportune moment to fall asleep."

Melia frowned and said nothing, deciding to choose the safer option of studying her immediate surroundings instead of fencing with him on this matter. The cave was small but was littered with enough belongings and evidence of past fires to show it had been occupied for some time.

"Where is Aeron?" she finally asked. While Aeron trusted the mage completely, Melia did not know Tamsyn. When he had appeared to save them, as fortuitous as it was, Melia could not help being suspicious that a mage was in Gahara at the same time she was conducting her own search for one of his Order.

"He is merely ensuring that my spell of protection is doing its work. The goblins cannot reach us in here." He could understand her concern at waking up in a strange place and her lover nowhere in sight.

Melia nodded, recalling the same spell used during Arianne's quest to hide the cave where Antion's sword was kept. Imbued with the same magic used to conceal elven cities behind the Veil, they were tucked away safely from any threats for the rest of the night.

"That is good to know," Melia eased into her sleeping place once more, glad to hear Aeron was well, although she wished he were here.

According to Tamsyn, she had been unconscious (not fainted) for almost a day, and yet it felt as if she had been away from her love for much longer. While the desire to see him was intense, Melia could not help feeling a little embarrassed she was longing for her prince like a lovesick maiden.

"He scarcely left your side," Tamsyn guessed what was in her head. "Not even to sleep, even though I assured him you would be safe."

"He can be stubborn," Melia smiled affectionately before remembering herself. Despite Tamsyn saving her life and appeared trustworthy, her private emotions were her own and she had no desire to discuss them. "He forgets I am a watch guard and am quite capable of fending for myself, even if at this moment I find myself at somewhat of a disadvantage."

"He loves you beyond measure," Tamsyn reminded. "It is hard to be impartial when one's heart is as lost as his."

Melia swallowed thickly and allowed herself a small confession at that remark. "His feelings are not unique, though I think he does not fully appreciate what it is to love a mortal."

"He is a thousand years old," the wizard responded with an edge to his voice that could possibly be reproach. "I think he is perfectly aware of what he risks by giving you his heart. The question remains —do you know what it is to love an elf?"

Melia stared at him hard. "My hesitation is for his sake."

"Is it really?"

"What do you mean?" Suspicion crept into her voice as she made that demand. Of course it was for his sake, what other could there be?

"Perhaps a little of it is for yourself," he replied as he continued to smoke his pipe. "After all, it cannot be easy to love someone who will never age, who will remain as beautiful as the first time you beheld him while you, yourself, grow old and withered. There is no shame in admitting you fear your feelings for him might deteriorate into envy or your love might twist into hatred and jealousy because he does not decay as you do."

Melia opened her mouth to protest but she could not. She could not because there was truth to his words. Amongst all her reservations about Aeron were about such ugly possibilities, though she liked to think she was better than that. Still, she could not deny it never crossed her thoughts, even if he made her heart soar each time she saw him. It was one of so many reasons she feared a future with Aeron.

She loved him deeply. There was no denying it. What she did not know was if she was strong enough to be his wife. Then again, she wasn't even sure she was strong enough to give him up.

"You do not answer," Tamsyn noted, understanding her silence all too well. "It is none of my concern, however."

Melia wanted to respond. Hearing her fears put so starkly made her realize how petty it was, how paltry the doubts seemed in the face of how she felt. For the first time, she felt the uneasiness drain from her, because hearing a stranger's unbiased opinion was liberating and having it presented to her so bluntly made her understand love was not meant to be easy, not between a human and elf or between a human and human. Whatever the combination, there would always be some difficulties attached.

"For someone whose business none of this is, you have much to say on the matter."

"Thank you," Tamsyn remarked as he stirred the meal that had been simmering on the fire and had filled the cave with a pleasant aroma. "It is difficult being so astute in one's indifference when one is dealing with a friend."

His eyes met hers playfully and Melia could not help but agree. "Yes, it is."

"Now then," he stared at her as he filled the small bowl in his hand with some warm broth. "Tell me about your dreams."

"My dreams?" Melia exclaimed, startled by the sudden shift in subject matter. She cursed herself at being unable to remain silent in her slumber. He had probably overheard her cries while she was tormented by the usual demons in her sleep. "Why?"

"They seemed to be plaguing you while you slept. Your prince did not tell me a great deal, but I sensed they were connected to what brings you to Gahara and what you saw at Tor Iolan."

Melia's eyes widened in surprise that he knew of the visit and debated whether or not she ought to trust him. Aeron did without question. He was a part of Dare's Circle and that alone should have been reason enough for her.

"If I answer your questions, will you answer mine?" she countered.

Tamsyn nodded with a faint smile, "I will."

"How do you know that we were at Tor Iolan?"

"I asked first," the wizard replied, reminding her of their bargain.

Melia drew a deep breath before she spoke. It was difficult enough taking Aeron into her confidence without her having to reveal something so personal to a stranger she had met only once before. However, this stranger's identity made it easier to trust him with her innermost secrets. Furthermore, she was certain his presence here was no coincidence, and that he might have some part to play in the search for her mother and the Mage who had Ninuie in his power.

"Ever since I was a child, I have dreamt about my mother," Melia began reluctantly, capturing Tamsyn's undivided attention as she explained her unique heritage and its effect upon her nightly slumbers. Melia spared him nothing, explaining her visions at Tor Iolan and the terrible images that had brought her to the edge of the world with Aeron at her side. Tamsyn listened without comment. The only movement he made during her narrative was to present her with the bowl of broth he'd poured earlier.

"Now it is your turn," Melia declared once she had finished speaking, feeling as if a great weight had been lifted from her chest by her revelations. "It is time for you to keep your promise."

"Then it appears that I have returned just in time," Aeron announced himself as he appeared at the mouth of the cave.

"As always, Prince, your timing is impeccable," Melia said playfully, unable to hide her happiness at seeing him.

"I am glad to see you are well," he replied warmly as he dropped to his knees at her side and greeted her with a gentle kiss. "How do you feel?"

"Like I have been set upon by a goblin's arrow," she joked but, seeing the concern in his eyes, added further, "but I am better than I was."

"You must be," he said, sitting down next to her and facing Tamsyn, "if you were able to make Tamsyn reveal his secrets." He grinned at his old friend.

"She is a shrewd woman," Tamsyn chuckled. "She gave me no choice but to comply if I wished to hear her tale."

"And now that you have?" Aeron raised a brow in his direction. "Will you tell us what brought you here other than chasing news of another mage? I know you well enough to know that there is more to it than that. You do not chase rumours lightly."

"A promise is a promise," Tamsyn agreed, displaying some reluctance to reveal his own secrets, but a bargain was struck.

"You are right, Aeron. I do know something of this mage you are seeking. He was a part of my order during the Primordial Wars. I thought he was killed by Balfure."

"You actually knew him?" Aeron asked.

"Yes, though I was not certain of it until Melia gave me a description of him. He was one of the wisest of our order. His name was Edwyn. When Arianne made inquiries on your behalf, I too wanted to know what had become of the river daughters, and so I carried out my own search."

"I have searched for years," Melia declared, unable to believe that the wizard was able to accomplish in months what it had taken years for her to learn. "I found nothing."

"Don't feel too terribly, my dear," Tamsyn said sympathetically. "My sources of information included Berserkers. Now that they are no longer in Balfure's service, some of them are willing to talk if given enough incentive."

Melia and Aeron exchanged glances at that, wondering what possible enticement could Tamsyn have used to gain a Berserker's cooperation. Nevertheless, neither interrupted his narrative.

"They spoke of a mage at Tor Iolan who vanished at the beginning of the Aeth War, supposedly heading to the east. After that, it was not difficult to find my way to Gahara and learn the goblins also feared a mage living in those mountains. I had only been here a few days when I heard your cry for help," he concluded.

"So you came here to do what?" Aeron asked. "You surely cannot believe that he can be saved after what he's done to Melia's mother and others like her."

Tamsyn sighed sadly. "I hope that he can be saved. I mean to at least try. He always felt things too deeply, became too passionate about things, to the exclusion of all others. I believe there may be something left in him that can be reasoned with."

It was difficult for Melia to feel compassionately towards the mage who might have turned her mother into a monster, but she tried to keep her words tempered when she spoke. "I do not think it is possible, mage. He has done something unthinkable. He has twisted the river daughters into some aberration of life, an aberration he cannot control and fears unleashing upon the world. I do not think he can be saved."

Tamsyn's voice became sombre, understanding her scepticism even if he did not share it. "He was always something of a dreamer and he wanted to create a form of life deserving of Cera's great creation. Something beautiful and perfect, something incapable of being lured by temptation or greed."

"But the war we fight within ourselves to maintain the balance is what gives us our soul," Aeron argued. "If we lose the ability to choose between right and wrong, we no longer have free will. It is the choices that give our soul substance."

"I do not argue with you on this, Aeron, but to him, it was a dream he was determined to fulfil. He believed perfection came from an amalgamation of the best of both men and elf, to create a form of life that was beyond corruption."

"I cannot believe one who would be party to the kidnapping and despoilment of the Water Wife's river daughters could be anything but evil. It takes a great deal of free will to twist a thing of beauty into a creature of absolute darkness," Aeron said, staring at him.

"You may think so, but sometimes absolute darkness comes about because one has set out with good intentions and is forced to make compromises along the way. It is easy to keep making them until you are so far from where you wanted to be there is no way back." His voice became sad and distant as he spoke about someone who obviously meant a great deal to him.

"Tamsyn," Aeron said kindly, "I know this mage is your friend, but you must recognise the danger he poses. If we find him, he may not be happy to see you. He has spent a great deal of time in hiding and may not wish to be found."

"Did you know we would be coming?" Melia cut in abruptly, because the appearances of this cave seemed to indicate that Tamsyn had been here for some time. Had he been awaiting their arrival? If so, how did he know they would be coming?

"That is a question I would like answered as well," Aeron retorted. "Tamsyn, you know that I trust you with my life, but I do not think it was merely coincidence that allowed you to come to our rescue. Tell me, my friend, what is this really about?"

"I did not know it would be you two that would arrive specifically, but I had a sense that I should wait, that an important part of my quest would appear soon enough if I held my ground. Sometimes wizards are forced to rely upon their instincts as elves do, and mine told me that I could not complete my journey because I was not to walk the path alone."

"Do you know where he is?" Melia looked at him.

"Yes, I do, but I will not lead you to him without having your word that you will not move to strike him down until I have a chance to plead my case."

Both Melia and Aeron stiffened simultaneously at the suggestion, but it was the prince who voiced his displeasure first. "Mage, that is an exceedingly difficult promise to make. You said yourself, he has committed some heinous acts. Are you certain that he is capable of being reasoned with?"

"I have to try," the wizard said earnestly.

Aeron fell silent and Melia wondered what was running through his mind. Inwardly, she considered it extremely dangerous to grant the wizard his request. In the heat of battle, especially with a powerful mage, circumstances might not allow them the opportunity to hold back when the time came. Unfortunately, she knew her prince, and within him ran rivers of compassion far longer and more powerful than the great Yantra River itself. It was in his nature to see the good in everyone.

She loved him for this, but it was uniquely elven luxury to be so yielding in such matters.

"We will do as you ask," Aeron finally answered, and gave Melia a sharp look, demanding her adherence to his wishes in this matter. "But I will risk none of our lives if the situation calls for us to fight. Your mage is no longer the person he once was. Good intentions aside, he may seek to kill us all to conceal the magnitude of what he has done."

Tamsyn nodded slowly, agreeing to Aeron's terms. Despite his reluctance to believe that Edwyn was beyond redemption, wisdom demanded he faced the possibility. The prince's demands were not unreasonable. The elf was being prudent, so that none of them lost their lives if Edwyn was truly beyond all help.

Tamsyn met Aeron's eyes and answered softly, "If it comes to that, then I will stand by you and draw a sword to him myself."

* * *

Melia's injury saw to it the company could not leave their cavernous sanctuary for at least two days, despite her protestations otherwise.

When it became clear her claim of being fit to travel was falling on deaf ears, Melia surrendered to her situation, despite her frustration. Aeron remained at her side, ensuring she wanted for nothing while showing infinite patience in the face of her stormy disposition. While he understood her exasperation now she was so close to her goal, he also knew rushing in prematurely would get them all killed.

Besides, it was not simply the mage they had to worry about, they had to think about the monsters the wizard created using the river daughters.

Finally, after two days of rest, they resumed their journey to the Gahara Plateau whose presence was no longer on the horizon but achingly close. The journey there would take no more than a day on foot and they set off at the break of dawn, hoping to take shelter in the foothills of the mountain by the time the sun had set that evening.

While it was good to know that Tamsyn's enchantment would protect them from any goblins, Aeron was still filled with a deep sense of uneasiness. There was danger all around them and none more potent than the darkness he sensed coming from the mountain.

Not since Syphia and Balfure had Aeron felt such powerful shadowing.

"Prince," Melia noted as she walked alongside him, seeing the subtle shift in his body as they approached the looming mountain. He was uneasy, Melia thought to herself, wondering what could shake someone as brave and unswerving as he.

"Yes, Mia?" he glanced at her briefly before he resumed his vigil on the uneven line of the mountain before them.

Melia smiled, finding she liked his little nickname for her. "Are you alright?"

"Yes, yes," he nodded, still distracted. "Danger draws close to us. I feel it against my skin like a cold hand."

"Then let a warm one give you strength," she replied gently and took his hand in hers and clutched it tightly.

Aeron felt her touch and whatever loomed in the distance was forgotten for a moment. He gazed upon her, touching first the hand holding his and then the face looking at him with such affection.

"When we are done here, assuming that we survive, I will be returning to Eden Halas."

Despite what passed between Halion and his youngest son, Aeron knew he would have to go home at least one more time before quitting his childhood sanctuary for good.

"I thought you did not wish to return home," Melia stared at him.

"I have unfinished business there which requires me to make my appearance in my father's court. I owe it to Halion to say what must be said, face to face."

What Tamsyn had told him about his parents made him reconsider his view of his father and, for once, Aeron felt the need to resolve things between him and Halion before the rift between them became permanent.

Melia did not ask him to explain because she knew she was the reason he'd departed Halas so prematurely.

"What will you tell him?"

"That I am leaving his court permanently and I will be taking some of his people with me. I know of more than a handful of elves at Eden Halas who will want to come with me. I will not do so without first gaining his blessing. It is the proper thing to do."

Melia could respect that. She sensed there was more the prince was not telling her, but she left him his secrets because the relationship between Aeron and his father was already a complicated one even without her interference.

"It will be strange calling you the Lord of Eden Ardhen," Melia said playfully. "I have become so used to calling you Prince."

"It would be easier if you were called the Lady of Eden Ardhen," he returned, reminding her of the offer made at Tor Iolan.

"Prince…" she started to say, trying to think of a reason to delay her answer. She still was uncertain this was the wisest course.

"Marry me and be at my side. I know it will be hard toil, but I swear it will be worth it. We can build something together, something that will outlast us. Mia, I love you. I will never stop loving you and what time there is for you in the world, I want to spend it at your side."

"Prince, I told you I cannot give you an answer now. There is too much that is uncertain," she said, trying not to hurt him. "Please, let us wait until this quest is done. I do love you, but my heart is torn at this moment. I must know who I am before I can pledge my future to you. Do you understand?"

He did not, but Aeron was not about to force her to make a choice she was unprepared for.

"I will not speak of this again until we are finished here," he said quietly, unable to hide the disappointment in his voice as he pulled his hand out of her reach and strode some paces ahead.

Melia watched his back retreat further ahead, hating herself for hurting him after he had opened his heart to her and revealed his innermost dreams and desires for his future. She knew he did not make such revelations lightly and she rebuked herself for not being more sensitive to his feelings.

Tamsyn, who walked behind the two lovers, remained silent and watched.

Chapter Sixteen

Gahara Plateau

They were coming.

He had known it for some time now but, until their presence stirred the goblins in the Gorge like a nest of insects catching the scent of prey, he had not realized how close they truly were. Too much of his power was fixed on one purpose and very little of it could be spared for anything else, resulting in his miscalculation. His prescience was limited to his immediate surroundings though, in the beginning, he was able to watch a far wider field than what he was now able.

They were coming, yet there was little he could do to stop them.

Fear of discovery was no longer a consideration. No one was harsher over the years than himself. Nothing an outsider could say to him would equal the venom of his own self-loathing. His life's work was twisted into an abomination of horror and his victims were avenged by his total servitude to them. His entire existence was set on ensuring they would never leave the mountain and, to that end, he allowed them to consume his own life force.

There was no escape for any of them.

* * *

The foothills of the Gahara Plateau were very much like the rest of the landscape, abandoned. Tamsyn claimed not even the goblins dared traverse this terrain and remained at a respectful distance, even though there was no visible sign of what frightened them so. Not that Aeron needed to see it. Menace reeked from every crack in the mountain and, as they descended into the caverns beneath the great range of rock, it was almost palpable.

Tamsyn lit their way with the magic of his staff as he navigated twisting passages in the dark. They journeyed down the steep incline, into caverns once inhabited by the goblins, but now vacant. The lack of sun made the elf uncomfortable, but he hid it well, his senses seeking out danger even though at present the walls felt as if they were closing in on him.

He had not spoken to Melia other than to make a few obligatory remarks about their situation, her welfare, or the path they were taking to the mountain. Even though he despised himself for it, he seethed inwardly at Melia's refusal to give him an answer to his proposal. He supposed she could not be blamed for her reluctance. She had not his years of experience to draw from and her past was very different from his. To Melia, their situation seemed unworkable and, while he understood the obstacles they faced, he didn't share it.

His thoughts slipped away from Melia when they entered the mouth of a larger cavern. Before they even reached it, the glow coming through the tunnel leading into it was bright, like there was a sun on the other side of the wall. It eclipsed the glow of Tamsyn's staff and, when they stepped through, they were confronted by a flood of light so bright it made all three of them flinch. Once their vision cleared, however, there was nothing to do but gape in wonder at what they had stumbled upon.

A city lay before them. A magnificent monument to grandeur was carved out from rock and inlaid with marble. Not since the great dwarf city of Iridia had Aeron seen such astonishingly crafted splendour. Just as he had been in Kyou's home, Aeron admired the skill and dedication it took to build this place. He knew this was undoubtedly the work of dwarves, but had no idea they'd built a city so far away from the Western Sphere.

There were courtyards and squares, pavilions and fountains, great columns holding up ceilings so high Aeron marvelled at the diminutive race's ability to carve them. Polished marble covered the floor and it seemed to stretch across the entire city, prompting Aeron to wonder how they brought such materials to the mountain so far away from the centre of civilisation. Beneath the Gahara, the city remained unspoiled, save for the dust gathered from years of being forgotten.

It did not take long for them to see what created the brightness of daylight in the cavern. The ceilings were covered with the facets of millions of gemstones embedded in the rock. There was a king's fortune to be mined, but it had been left in place to provide the city with the illusion of day. Any source of light would be reflected on the many stones and provide the city with all the illumination it needed. Even now, the glow from Tamsyn's staff was reflected on thousands of polished facets.

"I did not know the dwarves built a city here," Aeron declared, his voice low and hushed with awe.

"This was one of their first cities," Tamsyn replied. "This is Tal-Shahar."

"This is Tal-Shahar?" Aeron glanced at Tamsyn, then continued to stare.

Following their arrival into the world, fulfilling Cera's plan of the Sacred Three, the dwarves left Iridia to explore the mountains of the Avalyne. It was believed they established a great kingdom in the Burning Plains and one of their first cities was Tal-Shahar.

"Indeed," Tamsyn nodded, similarly struck by the magnificence of the place. "They built this city two thousand years ago, before they left Iridia to explore the rest of Avalyne. As time went on, many wanted to return home to Iridia and, of course, Balfure's return ensured they could never really be safe, so they left and returned to the Starfall Mountains. Even with their departure, the goblins could never enter the city because of the light. It is the jewels they lust for so much that also keep them out."

"Good," Melia retorted, her eyes fixed on the glittering ceiling as she admired the ancient craftsmanship with wondrous awe. "It is too beautiful to be taken apart."

Aeron wondered if his father knew of this city and supposed that Halion would have given little thought to races that came after the elves, once he retreated into the Veil to begin building Eden Halas. This time, however, Aeron understood his father's reasons for animosity. He'd lost his entire family during the Primordial Wars and, now it appeared, also the love of his life. To learn the world was being cleansed for Cera to bring new races into existence must have been an affront to all he'd lost.

"Where are the krisadors?" Aeron asked suddenly, realising their entry into the city had taken place with a surprising lack of incident. He knew the creatures claimed the mountain but, since their party entered the plateau, they had seen no signs of any of the beasts. At first Aeron thought the krisadors might be staying away because of Tamsyn's presence, but now he started to think there might be a more sinister reason at work.

"There," Tamsyn said grimly, pointing ahead of them.

They were moving past a number of great columns framing the city's main square when Tamsyn's declaration made them all freeze in their tracks, staring in stunned horror.

No, it was not the krisadors keeping the goblins from reclaiming this mountain. It could not be, when the company was faced with the sight of all the creatures lying against the ancient marble floor—dead.

Their bones were bleached by time. Complete skeletons were lying in scattered collections throughout the cavern, as if some great force swept through the enormous city and felled them where they stood. What killed them was swift, giving the creatures neither time to escape nor a chance to fight back. There was no violence marking their bones. It was like staring at a menagerie of skeletons and, seeing such mighty creatures, killed with apparent ease, sent a shiver of fear through Aeron and Melia.

"What power could do this?" Aeron turned to Tamsyn, expecting the wizard to have some kind of an answer.

Tamsyn had no answer to give him, but his eyes revealed much.

Aeron saw he was just as horrified by what they had found, though not necessarily surprised. His expression shifted from shock to sorrow, possibly at the realization the mage he was trying to redeem may have caused this destruction. It was quite something to see death on such a scale, even if it was of creatures that had no value and were by nature vicious pack hunters. Still, seeing beasts as powerful as krisadors reduced to piles of bones chilled even the strongest of hearts.

"Edwyn," the wizard whispered softly.

Aeron stared at him sharply. When Tamsyn had fought the Nameless in Iridia, the battle nearly cost Tamsyn and Dare their lives. Tamsyn's power was great, but even Aeron did not think him capable of single-handedly vanquishing a nest full of krisadors with such totality their bones now lay in piles like an uncovered graveyard. It was beyond Aeron's comprehension that what he was seeing before him was the work of *one* man. And if it was the work of one man, how in the name of the Celestials could they hope to stop him?

"Do the mages have this kind of power?" Melia asked the question that Aeron could not.

"Not usually," Tamsyn answered, shaking his head as if he were in a daze. "But Edwyn has been dabbling in forces he should not be, and who knows how it may have affected him?

You saw what Balfure was able to do once he harnessed the power of the Aeth."

Melia shuddered. She knew. They all did. Sweeping her gaze across the skeletal remains of the krisadors she saw that, even in death, they looked fearsome. She could not even begin to imagine their chances if they had been called to fight the number that made up this nest, but neither did she condone this total annihilation.

"Then I do not like our chances," she commented, meeting Aeron's gaze.

"Do you really think you can convince him to return to the Order?" Aeron asked Tamsyn, who did not answer immediately. His mind seemed to be elsewhere and Aeron guessed that he was trying to decide if his friend could be salvaged.

"Tamsyn, before we go any further, are you absolutely certain he can be reasoned with?"

For the first time, the wizard's certainty was absent from his eyes. Aeron saw a man who was stunned by what he had seen and was no longer certain of anything. Perhaps in some corner of his mind, he clung to the hope that Edwyn might come to his senses but the evidence of what lay before them destroyed that belief. Now he was as rudderless as the companions relying on him to be their guide.

"I do not know," Tamsyn answered honestly.

Aeron let out a deep breath, trying to decide what he wished to do. It was no longer about simply finding Melia's mother, but rather keeping this menace from leaving these borders to wreak havoc upon the rest of Avalyne. A force that could destroy an entire cavern full of krisadors could do much damage beyond this mountain. Avalyne was just beginning to recover from the ravages of the Aeth War; it was too soon to find themselves pitted against the forces of a mage gone mad.

"I would prefer we were not alone in this endeavour," Aeron spoke after awhile. "Unfortunately, this is not to be. This menace must be stopped here and now. It cannot be allowed to leave this mountain. Do you understand?" He stared at Tamsyn hard.

"Yes," the wizard nodded in grim understanding. "I do."

Aeron turned to Melia, his expression softening as his gaze met hers once more. Forgotten was their earlier quarrel. It seemed trivial when their time together was dwindling fast, since it was very likely that neither of them would survive the battle with the mage. Yet, they still had to try. He looked into her eyes and saw that she understood what was being asked of her. Melia raised her head high and reminded him all over again why it was he loved her so.

"This was not my plan," he whispered softly as his hand reached for her cheek. "I wanted a lifetime with you."

She held it against her face, savouring the feel of his upturned palm against her skin. She shifted her head slightly and planted a small kiss on his hand. "I know."

"It must end here. You know that."

"Yes," she nodded. "Whatever we must do, I will be by your side."

Aeron smiled at her lovingly and whispered, "I love you more than my life. You would have made a wonderful queen for my kingdom in Ardhen."

"You would have made me happy," she answered in turn.

They kissed each other gently, taking a moment to themselves because it was all they had left to them. Neither expected to survive the battle with a mage who could do this, but dying was permissible if they could take him with them. They were both, at heart, idealists who believed in sacrificing themselves for the greater good, no matter how jaded each might sometimes profess to be.

"It is time, old friend," Aeron said firmly as he and Melia left behind their tender moment and returned to the business at hand. "Take us to the mage and let us finish this."

* * *

The Mage chose not to run.

It would have been so easy if flight alone was enough to solve his dilemma, but escape was never an option. He felt the determination of the new arrivals to end the threat of him because they believed him responsible for the destruction of the krisador nest in this mountain. A part of him wished he had the power to wreak such havoc, because it would have made things a great deal simpler.

So much would have been different if he possessed the strength. What power was bestowed to him by Enphilim was devoured by his creations. He was being siphoned off slowly and surely, feeling his grace and life draining from his body until nothing would remain but a husk. He would have died long before that.

And despite his doom, it was still not enough.

His creations were too powerful for him. All he had managed to do since bringing them here was to prevent their awakening into the world, and that had taken almost every ounce of strength he had to accomplish. He could not stop their ravenous hunger and they craved constantly. When they first arrived, the feeding had been good.

He'd had more than enough power at his disposal to ensure he and his charges were able to slip past the krisadors and find sanctuary in one of the forgotten rooms of the abandoned city. He had believed that the krisadors would never allow intrusion into their domain, so he would be safe from Balfure's forces, should they choose to pursue him. He never realised that, in making the decision, he was dooming all the krisadors in the mountain to death.

After all, his creations needed to feed.

Slowly but surely they drained the krisadors, who had no inkling of what was happening to them and thus had no way to combat it until it was too late. They continued as they always did, puzzled by their lack of energy but unable to reason out what was happening to them. They continued this way until one day they simply did not even have the strength to walk or to leave their nests to nourish themselves. They died where they had lain down in fatigue, aware some malaise had overtaken them, but not possessing the understanding to know what that might have been.

With the passing of the krisadors, their tendrils of hunger stretched beyond the mountain, seeking life in any shape or form. For a time, his creations were satiated by the goblins on the foothills, until the vile creatures, realising something hungrier than them was on the hunt, fled. The goblins retreated beyond the reach of the creatures slowly killing them. After the departure of the goblins, the feeding became poor and, with each day, the intense hunger drove his creations to escape more violently than they ever before, demanding birth into the world.

He'd struggled for so many years to keep this from happening, but now he was finally beaten.

He lingered and waited because he sensed one amongst the travellers who had the strength to take his place, to restrain the evil struggling for freedom in a battle he could no longer fight. If he could hold on for just a little longer until they arrived, all would not be lost. There was a chance the world would never discover the abomination he had spawned in Tor Iolan.

He just needed to hold on for a little longer. . . .

* * *

Even before Tamsyn told them that they were nearing their destination, Aeron of Eden Halas felt it most acutely. They crossed the graveyard of dead krisadors, leaving behind the splendour of the main hall and moving deeper into the city. Instead of cavernous passages, they now travelled within corridors of white marble, polished and smooth despite the years of neglect.

It felt strangely disorienting, and Aeron was reminded why he disliked enclosed spaces so much. Elves thrived in the sunlight and the open air. This confinement took them away from the light of the world in which they thrived best. The threat looming all around him was so thick Aeron was in danger of choking on it. He tried to dispel it from his senses, but it refused to go away, clinging to him like stink to the skin.

"Prince?" Melia took his arm as she saw him falter a little. "What is it?"

"We are close." His gaze fixated on the doorway at the end of the corridor.

"He is right," Tamsyn agreed, staring at the doors whose wood was rotting from age. "Edwyn is there. I can feel him."

"Can he feel you?" Melia asked as she unsheathed Aeron's dagger from her belt. He'd given it to her to replace her cross-bow. She would have preferred her own weapon, but it was useless without a fresh supply of bolts and Melia wanted to be capable of defending herself.

"Yes," the wizard nodded grimly, not about to hide this fact since it would become apparent the moment they crossed the threshold of the door. "He has been awaiting us."

"Well," Aeron sighed heavily as he removed his bow from across his back and prepared himself to engage the enemy, "we should not disappoint him."

Fearlessly, the elf strode forward, leaving Melia and Tamsyn behind briefly before they hastened their pace to match his. Melia found herself walking alongside her prince, ready to face whatever dangers awaited her. He offered her a little smile as they reached the door, but no words were spoken because all they needed to say to each other had already been uttered.

Aeron pushed the door open, causing it to creak loudly as fragments of wood crumbled underneath his palm. Aeron examined the fragments on his palm and determined the wood to be diseased. In the past, Aeron had encountered trees struck with blight and they had withered like this. He wondered if Tamsyn's friend was responsible for this too. Unfortunately, there no little time to ponder the question as the open door beckoned them inside.

They had taken two steps into the room before all three froze in horror.

For a few seconds, no one dared to speak. They could only stare at the grisly tableau before them. The skeletons of so many krisadors had been horrifying enough to behold, but it paled in comparison to what they were faced with now. Melia's hand flew to her mouth, feeling the pit of her stomach churn with sick. Aeron was forced to look away, while Tamsyn could only stare, transfixed. He had seen this only once before. During the Primordial Wars, when he was forced to watch Syphia birthing one of her hellish spawns.

The large room was occupied with large translucent pods filled with a viscous grey fluid. Dark veins pulsing with blood and black fluid ran across their mottled surface and dug into the ground as if the pods had been grown from the earth. Large tendrils criss-crossed the walls, with moisture oozing from the joints, making the inside of the room feel hot and humid. The room felt like the inside of some dark behemoth's belly and the stench of rancid flesh wafted past them.

That was not even the worst of it.

The worst of it was that, within the pods, they could see the vague silhouette of a body trapped within the cocoon. Through a thin membrane of skin, they could see fingers clawing at the walls from the inside, the prisoner within attempting to escape.

"By Cera's Heavens," Melia uttered in a strangled gasp. She knew without doubt these poor creatures trapped in their cocoons were the missing river daughters and one of them was her mother.

In the centre of this vile hatchery was its creator.

The mage named Edwyn stared at them with watery eyes sitting in hollow sockets. His cheeks were so sunken that his face was little more than a skull with a thin covering of skin. His hair was grey and long, pooling around him where he sat cross-legged on the grimy floor. His robes of amber were so filthy dark they appeared almost red. The outstretched arms, held out reverently towards the cocoons surrounding him, were spindly with skin hanging from the bones. The veins that criss-crossed the caverns were coiled around his ankles, keeping him in place.

Melia thought of the mage she had seen in her dreams, the strong, handsome man of ebony skin appearing every bit the powerful wizard. To see him in this condition was almost as horrifying as everything else inside this room. For a moment, she almost felt pity for him, seeing him driven to this complete and utter ruin. Her sympathy withered when she remembered that inside one of those vile cocoons was her mother.

The mage turned towards them, his milky eyes searching their faces as if he looking for something, until his gaze settled on Tamsyn. His eyes lit up with recognition. His shoulders slackened in relief, as if he had been waiting for Tamsyn all this time, and he spoke with a weak and exhausted voice.

"Tamysn, you have come."

Chapter Seventeen

Edwyn

For more seconds than Aeron could keep count, no one spoke.

"I knew you would not sleep forever," the mage named Edwyn spoke, his ghost-like face attempting to smile. But, to those present, it looked instead like a grimace of pain. "I knew you would find your way back to me."

"I am so sorry, Edwyn," Tamsyn whispered as he approached his friend, trying to equate the proud, lively man he had known so long ago with this withered husk before him. "I took the coward's way out and left you behind all alone. I should not have abandoned you or my responsibilities. It was our duty to help the new races on their feet. I left you to carry that burden alone. I will never forgive myself for allowing you to come to this."

Aeron saw the anguish in Tamsyn's eyes and the elf thought he had never seemed more vulnerable than at that moment. Tamsyn had always carried himself with an air of dignity and assurance. When times were at their darkest, it was the wizard they looked to for comfort and guidance. How easy it was to forget that he loved and mourned as they did. His pain at this moment was so naked upon his face Aeron wanted to comfort his old friend, wanted to absolve him of the guilt he so obviously felt.

"I thought I could teach them, but it was not enough! I thought the elves would help, but they were so angry at us for bringing men and dwarves into the world, they wanted nothing but to retreat behind the Veil!" Edwyn cried out, attempting to justify himself like the child who was caught pulling the wings off a fly. "I thought if I created something better than either, they could bridge the gap. Help all the races reach unity."

He might as well have been Balfure, Tamsyn thought sadly, having heard a similar speech when the Aeth Lord attempted to justify his fealty to Maelog. He was always so convinced anything was permissible for the greater good.

"Cera already had a plan for the Sacred Three," Tamsyn answered, trying to remind Edwyn of their original mission in Avalyne. "Enphilim told us that. Now you have created something that has no place in that plan. Where do these creatures sit in Cera's design?"

The mage's eyes dropped to the ground, shame overcoming his face, because he knew his creations had no place and, worse yet, might destroy everything completely because of what they were.

"I did not mean to do this," he wept, trying to explain so they would understand. "They said they would help me! They said they understood what I was trying to do! I sought to use them as a means to an end, but did not realize that I was the one being used!"

As he spoke, his body seemed to tremble, as if taking his attention from one act to accomplish another was weakening him even further. He seemed so frail it was impossible to believe this being was a seraf of the Celestials Gods, sent to save Avalyne from Mael's darkness. How had that mission become so utterly corrupted?

"You made a bargain with Disciples!" Tamsyn rebuked sharply. "How could you do that? How could you possibly imagine they had anything but their own interests in mind! How could you be so naïve to allow yourself to be party to this abomination?"

"I was alone! I needed help!" Edwyn spat back, his voice threatening to break at any moment at Tamsyn's lack of understanding. "I thought if I used the river daughters, creatures of purity, without any stain of darkness upon them, that I could make my creation work."

"Your creation!" Melia burst out, having heard enough. "My mother is one of those you took! Which one is she? Which one of these things did you put her inside?"

"Your mother?" Edwyn turned to her shocked, as if it was the first time he noticed she was there at all. "Which one is your mother?"

"Ninuie!" Melia almost shouted in fury, unable to believe that somewhere in this disgusting collection of cocoons was her mother or, rather, what was left of her. Worse yet, this mage turned her into a monster without even knowing her name!

If seeing Tamsyn started to bring him undone, then hearing the name of one of his victims completed his despair. The mage sobbed loudly at the mention of Ninuie's name and for an instant Melia was at a loss to react. She looked to Aeron for help, but the elf was just as bewildered as she. The mage venting his tears of grief left them too stunned.

"You are the child," he managed to say through his weeping. "You were the child she spoke of."

"She spoke of me?" Melia took a step towards him, but Aeron caught her arm to ensure she did not approach the mage any further. Despite the man's remorse, Aeron still did not trust that the seraf was as benign as he appeared. Weakened he might be, but he was still connected to these women. There was no telling its effect upon the mage or how dangerous it made him.

"You and the man were all she *ever* spoke of," he explained, as if a daze. "In the beginning, she used to beg for release so she could be returned to you. As the years followed, she stopped making the plea, but I often heard her muttering your names. In the end, the names were all that were left of who she was."

Melia blinked and felt tears running down her cheeks. For so long, she'd thought she was dreaming, but now she knew it was Ninuie reaching out to her, trying to make a connection despite the distance. She looked away from the mage, not wishing him to see her anguish, and took comfort in Aeron's hand on her shoulder. She stared at the hatchery and saw that, within their cocoons, the river daughters were oblivious to their presence.

All they seemed aware of was the flesh that imprisoned them. Their hands were flailing sluggishly through the noisome fluid, like flies trapped in amber, unable to break free of the membrane that kept them out of the world.

"Which one is she?" Melia demanded, when she finally turned to Edwyn, her eyes red with tears.

"She will not know you," Edwyn replied, his voice oddly disconnected, as if he did not really see her and was addressing an apparition in his mind.

"Tell her!" Aeron barked.

Edwyn's eyes drifted across the floor of the chamber before coming to rest upon a cocoon at the far end of the chamber. Melia's breath caught when he paused and nodded. She withdrew from Aeron's comforting touch and she approached it. It was no different than any of the other cocoons gestating within the room. She could see the faint outline of a body inside it, struggling to escape the prison of flesh. A wave of nausea welled up in the pit of Melia's stomach upon seeing the figure's hand clawing at the sheathe, trying to rip through the membrane that held her trapped.

Despite her revulsion, Melia placed her hand against the slick wall and recoiled inwardly at its warmth. She was reminded of an egg sac of an insect and the comparison almost made her gag in disgust. Beneath the cocoon's thin membrane, she felt the gelatinous fluidity of its contents. The figure inside became very still, sensing her presence. Suddenly, a fist struck the flimsy walls of the membrane, trying to break through in order to catch Melia's hand. Melia leapt back and was overcome with shame at the realisation she'd shrunk back from her own mother.

Aeron was there to catch her when she backed into him. Melia whirled around and buried her face in his shoulder, sobbing. He could feel her body shuddering against his chest and wished more than anything he could take the hurt away. This was beyond his power to do. Instead, he felt angry for her. After searching so long, Melia's reward for all her efforts was to be confronted by this creature bearing little resemblance to the woman who gave her life.

For that agony alone, he would happily take his sword to the mage.

"Tamsyn," Aeron spoke to his friend, having seen enough by now. "This cannot go on. These poor souls deserve peace. They cannot be allowed to exist in this way."

The wizard drew a deep breath, meeting Aeron's eyes, and it was in that instant the elf saw how difficult this was for him. The mage Tamsyn had come in search of his friend, hoping to lead him to redemption, but it seemed Tamsyn had greatly underestimated Edwyn's descent into madness. The hope of bringing his friend back to them was withering before his eyes at the realisation Edwyn might be beyond all hope.

"Tamsyn," Aeron continued to speak. "I know you wish to save him, but the evil I sensed approaching this mountain does not come from him. It comes from these creatures. We cannot allow them to leave Gahara."

"No, we cannot," Tamsyn agreed, and faced his old friend once again. "Edwyn, these beings you created out of the Water Wife servants must be released from their torment. What has been done to them cannot be undone and their torture will continue so long as they live. Let them go, Edwyn. Let them go to Cera, as they deserve. We will leave this place together. You will never be alone again, I promise."

The vague expression on Edwyn's face seemed to clear at Tamsyn's suggestion and he stared hard at his brother. For a brief instant, Aeron felt a flicker of hope at the possibility that Tamsyn's heartfelt entreaty might have succeeded in convincing Edwyn to surrender without further conflict. Until it vanished when the Mage's eyes sharpened into points of flint and he stood up, his body stiffening with anger.

"You did not come here to help me!" Edwyn screamed, indignant with betrayal. "I thought you would take my place! I have been waiting so long for someone to find me, to help me! Now you wish me to abandon my duty?"

"What duty?" Tamsyn shouted back in bewilderment. "These women have been twisted into monstrous versions of themselves! You have destroyed them more completely than any being has ever destroyed another! Let them go! Let them know peace! It is the least you can give them!"

"I am not keeping them alive!" Edwyn screamed in fury. "They do not require that of me! They drain the life of anything they desire to feed upon. The only reason they have not stolen your lives is because I have exerted what little strength I have left to keep them from killing you like they killed the krisadors."

"Then what are you doing?" Aeron asked, his own confusion rising. "If you are not keeping them alive and they have no need of you to be nourished, why then have you remained here?"

"SO THEY CANNOT LEAVE!"

Breathing hard, Edwyn continued to rant. "What they are cannot be unleashed into the world! I know what I have created and I have tried to undo it, but the knowledge eludes me and so I remain here, keeping them and the world safe from each other."

"If they are so dangerous, why not simply destroy them? Give them the release from this twisted existence they deserve," Aeron demanded.

"Because he does not know if he is strong enough to kill them," Tamsyn answered softly, understanding at last why Edwyn had bound himself to his creations in this dark place at the edge of all things.

Edwyn, blinded by the passion of his work, had allied himself with the Disciples, who hunted the river daughters, one by one, and brought them to Tor Iolan. At the fortress of Balfure's evil, Edwyn had foolishly put into effect his desire to create a master race, free of corruption, unaware in his hubris he created abomination instead of purity. Too late did he realize his creations had become the most dangerous creatures in Avalyne and tried to correct his mistake by spiriting them away from Tor Iolan.

He brought them to the Gahara Plateau, hoping distance from the world would see him forgotten by the Aeth lord. Despite Balfure's destruction, Edwyn was unable to reverse what he had done to the river daughters and so they remained in their cocoons, butterflies that could never be allowed to emerge into the sunlight. He kept them trapped, but even Tamsyn could see he could manage no longer.

Edwyn wanted Tamsyn to take his place, but Tamsyn had no intention of prolonging the existence of these poor unfortunates. Aeron was correct. This had to end here.

"While they are trapped in this shell, they must be vulnerable," Aeron declared, ignoring Edwyn's tirade. He was concerned with more practical matters as he studied the hatchery like a warrior preparing for battle. In essence they were, although Edwyn and Tamsyn did not know it yet. There was only one course to take, and though it pained Aeron to do so, because these women were turned into instruments of destruction through no fault of their own, do it he must! "Perhaps that is the way to destroy them."

"Destroy them?" Melia stared at him incredulously. "That is my mother in there!"

"Mia," Aeron turned to her, knowing of no way to soften the blow of what he was about to say. "It wounds me more than anything to have to say this to you, but she is not your mother. Not anymore. She has not been Ninuie since this mage turned her into his creature. A river daughter would die rather than become this thing he made them. Do not let her suffer further degradation inside the shell of her ruined body. Let her go to Cera and find some measure of peace."

"I cannot!" she wailed, unable to face the choice he was presenting her. Fresh anguish surged through her as she stared at the cocoon and the thing wriggling inside it like a worm. This was once her mother, the woman Hezare had loved until his last breath.

She approached it stealthily once again and placed her hand on the membrane, ignoring Aeron's words of caution. Her heart wanted to shatter inside her chest when she saw the figure inside reacting to her, its sluggish limbs moving through the fluid. Melia pulled away in revulsion, unable to bear the thing's touch. Her hand flew to her mouth, mortified by her reaction.

Aeron was right. What was inside this shell was not her mother.

Aeron came to her when he saw the guilt at her revulsion. He hated himself for forcing upon her such a choice, but he also knew there was no alternative. Placing his hands on her shoulders, he rested his lips against her hair and spoke gently, ""I would rather die than hurt you, Mia, but you have to see what she has become. She would not wish to live this way; no one would."

Melia wiped her tears away and nodded slowly. "I will not see her suffer any more than she already has. Let it end for her, so at least she and my father can be reunited in the afterlife."

Pulling away from him, Melia unsheathed her dagger and strode towards the pod, deciding if this thing was to be done then it should be up to her to carry it out. Melia raised the dagger, preparing to plunge the blade deep into the membrane to end the suffering of the poor creature within it once and for all.

"NO!" Edwyn screamed defiantly when he saw her approach, and lashed out without warning.

Melia was swept off her feet and swatted aside like a rag doll. She hit the wall hard, all sense of the world fragmenting a moment as the disorientation swept over her. Pain flared in bright colours across her face before she crumpled onto the ground, her hands and knees hitting the hard floor beneath her. She thought she felt the snap of a rib but could not be sure, even if her side was aching in pain. She heard Aeron calling out her name through the ringing in her ears.

"Edwyn, what are you doing?" Tamsyn demanded, stunned by Edwyn's sudden attack. Then again, everything his friend was doing was so beyond what he knew of the man, he could take nothing for granted.

"I will not risk their freedom!" Edwyn declared hysterically. "I do not know if they can be killed, but I will not risk the foolishness of others to give them their means of escape!"

"They must be destroyed, Edwyn!" Tamsyn implored, quickly seeing the situation deteriorate with the attack upon Melia. Tamsyn was reaching the painful conclusion Edwyn was beyond reasoning, as Aeron feared. The long confinement alone, and the guilt he carried at what he had done to these women, had snapped Edwyn's fragile mind.

"NO!" Edwyn screamed again, becoming more irrational by the minute.

Tamsyn attempted to approach him, but the wizard was swept off his feet by the same power that assaulted Melia. His heart sank when he realised Edwyn was turning his powers on him and would protect these creatures until death. Aeron was right, he lamented in silence. In the end, Edwyn would give him no other choice but to fight.

Pushing himself up to his hand and knees, Tamsyn raised his head to see Edwyn glaring down at him, surrounded by his cocoons, his eyes wide and feral with madness. He was too late, he thought with anguish. He should have stayed with Edwyn, should have braved telling Lylea he was afraid, instead of hiding. There were so many regrets in his past, but none would ever cut as deeply as this one.

"Do not make me fight you, brother," Tamsyn pleaded, his voice filled with sorrow. "I do not wish to hurt you."

"All I wanted was for you to help me!" Edwyn screamed, and his voice bore the edge of desperation. He was incapable of listening to anything else. Frustration, disappointment and despair had trapped him in a perfect storm of rage and he lashed out with all the might he had left. "To take my place before my life ended! I wanted to make things right again and you have taken that away from me!"

Another surge of power ripped Tamsyn from the floor and pinned him to the wall. Pain radiated through him as he stared at Edwyn. The wizard uttered a groan of pain and knew if he did not retaliate soon, he would unable to at all. Edwyn's madness had made his magic wild and frenzied. It would exhaust him soon enough, but not before he caused Tamsyn considerable damage. As Edwyn approached, Tamsyn saw the mage's eyes were wide and his pupils dilated. He was no longer able to hear anything but his own cries of persecution.

Tamsyn lashed out with his own power, throwing Edwyn to the ground, face first. The crunching of bone filled the air with its sickening sound and Tamsyn quickly pulled himself to his feet, hoping to incapacitate Edwyn before the mage could recover.

Edwyn's instinct for survival was strong and he raised his eyes to Tamsyn when his brother was a few feet away, revealing a smear of blood running across his forehead. There was black fury in his eyes as he screamed and threw out his arm, pointing his fingers at the ceiling above Tamsyn's head. Tamsyn looked up in time to see the fissure appearing across the rock before great chunks of it broke free and tumbled towards him. He barely leapt out of its way to avoid being buried beneath it.

Enphilim, help me, Tamsyn thought as he saw the pile of rock that was nearly his grave. He could not keep holding back. Edwyn was not bound by such restraint and was preparing to launch another assault, but this time Tamsyn did not give him the opportunity to attack.

Broken pieces of ceiling floated off the ground and flew towards the disgraced mage. Edwyn froze the rock in mid-air and for a few seconds, the fragments remained trapped in the space between them, suspended over the floor as it struggled to decide in which direction it would go. Tamsyn could see the strain in Edwyn's face as he maintained the battle of will and magic, his jaw clenched and his teeth biting down in a grimace of furious determination.

Suddenly the rock exploded, unable to take the pressure placed upon it by both wizards. Fragments became flying projectiles forcing both men to turn but neither was able to shield themselves from the barrage. Sharp and jagged shards bit into their skin and drew blood. The rest crumbled to the floor in a cloud of dust. It was at this point that Tamsyn remembered Aeron and Melia.

Where were they? He thought frantically and searched for them, hoping they were sensible enough to take cover when two wizards were duelling. But he knew Aeron only too well. The archer would not sit back and allow his friend to fight alone and neither would his lady.

It did not take him long to realize why they had remained out of sight.

Aeron and Melia were dealing with a much greater problem.

Chapter Eighteen

Ninuie

When the battle between the two wizards erupted, Aeron was at Melia's side, ensuring that she was not injured severely after Edwyn lashed out at her. Fortunately, the watch guard suffered only minor bruises and scratches, nothing that would impede her ability to fight. While she was a little dazed, by the time he helped her to her feet, Melia was recovered enough to become aware of the pitched combat taking place between Edwyn and Tamsyn.

"The Mage has gone mad," Aeron declared, stating the obvious as he took stock of the battle so he could ascertain how they might help Tamsyn.

"He was mad before this," Melia retorted bitterly, feeling no sympathy for the man.

All she could feel was fury for what he had done to her mother, until her eyes shifted to the cocoons and saw what was happening to all of them. Hands were push against the membrane surrounding, trying to break through. Nails pierced the flimsy material, ripping it apart easily and causing fluid to slosh about in all directions, splattering other cocoons and spilling across the floor.

"By the Celestial Gods," Aeron whispered softly. "They are awakening."

Tearing through the shell that had kept her prisoner for so long, the first to emerge was Ninuie. She stood up from the ruins of her fleshy cage, naked and covered with slime. Outwardly, she remained unchanged from her original form, except it was slick with fluid. The amber hue of the resin masked the colour of her skin, with her long hair plastered to her face and neck.

She paid little attention to the two observers, more concerned with her own appearance. Examining her long, tapered fingers, she ran their tips across her face and seemed to be adjusting to the world she had just stepped into.

For an instant, she looked like any woman, and Melia clutched wildly to the hope that perhaps the mage was wrong. Perhaps what was done to the river daughter was not as irreversible as he feared. The person before her was no monster, merely a woman appearing confused by her surroundings. If she was not a danger to others, then perhaps Ninuie could still be reached. Melia knew this was a desperate hope, but she was hurtling towards a path she was doing everything she could to avoid.

"What are you doing?" Aeron demanded when he saw Melia take a step towards the creature.

Aeron had no such illusions about the nature of the beast before him. While it was wearing the skin of a woman, beneath it was anything but that. His elven senses could detect the terrible evil emanating from it, the rage unseen by Melia's eyes. She was blinded by hope and fear of what was needed to release Ninuie from her torment. Aeron could not blame her for believing the creature before her was redeemable, but he knew better. Even as she approached it, Aeron could see its eyes narrowing, regarding the watch guard, not as a person but as *prey*.

"Mia!" Aeron ordered out before she got any further. "Hold your ground."

Melia froze in her tracks, but she was not ready to believe that there was danger, not when she could see other cocoons beginning to stir with life. They were clawing at the walls of their shells, breaking out of them the way this one had.

"Aeron, it is alright," Melia cried out in turn. "She does not want to hurt me."

Aeron was not listening. The archer was already retrieving his arrows and loading his bow in readiness to shoot. His eye was fixed upon the creature staring at Melia with her dark gaze. When he ordered Melia to stop her approach, the river daughter turned to him instead. Aeron saw the malevolence in her eyes, as well as the black hatred for interfering with her prey's advance.

"Back towards me, Mia," Aeron insisted.

"But Aeron …"

"DO IT NOW!" he snapped.

Melia jumped at the sharpness of his voice as she stared at the woman, fighting the compulsion to continue onward. It was not the first time he'd raised his voice to her, but she knew he would not do so without good reason. Trusting his judgement, Melia began to retreat. The river daughter observed her withdrawal and took exception to it.

Whether it was instinct or premonition Melia did not know, but when the woman raised her arms towards her, Melia's survival instincts told her to run. It was advice given well, because black tendrils shot out of the creature's finger tips. Melia had little more than a split second before those spidery appendages were being hurled at her. Diving out of its way, the tendrils struck marble and dug into the rock like hooks. The white stone immediately fissured, breaking apart and then crumbled to dusty fragments before Melia's eyes.

Aeron wasted no time releasing the arrow he'd been waiting to fire. It flew the air with a faint whoosh towards the creature. The river daughter's head snapped up at its approach. Screeching an unearthly sound, her fingers jerked in the direction of the approaching arrow. Tendrils flew from the tips, intercepting the projectile before it reached her face. The dark coils wrapped themselves around the shaft like black snakes. In seconds, the polished shaft was soon crumbling to dust. The fletching withering into spindly strands as the quiver rusted and flaked, falling to the ground at her feet.

She raised her eyes to Aeron, only to see another arrow already racing towards her, and this one, she could not stop. It struck her in her forehead, tearing through flesh and bone in a blink of an eye. Dark blood spurted out from the wound as the force of the arrow's violation sent the quiver ripping out the back of her skull. Her body went slack and she dropped to the ground without any sound, the blood creating a pool of crimson beneath her.

"Aeron! Watch out!"

Aeron averted his gaze from the creature he had just slain to see another emerging from her pod to witness the death of her sister at his hands. Her eyes were blazing with fury as she screeched at him and, once again, those ghastly tendrils were moving swiftly towards her prey, only this time it was he who was her intended target. Aeron leapt out of the way, dodging what would almost have been certain death. He landed hard and saw Melia throwing her dagger at the woman, trying to give him time to escape her reach.

As he scrambled to his feet, he looked up to see Melia's dagger slicing through the body of the enemy. More and more of the creatures were beginning to tear through the walls of their prison now that the mage was no longer holding them back. He knew without doubt that, if they were allowed to emerge from their shells, Avalyne would be doomed. He and Melia had the advantage, for now, because their first steps into this world were clumsy and new. If they were able to band together and attack, they would be unstoppable.

Even now, he could see more fingers tearing through the flimsy membrane keeping them trapped, ripping away the cage securing them for so long. The mage, for all his madness, had understood the danger and sacrificed his life to keep them here. Aeron pitied the part of Edwyn sane enough to do that, even if it was nothing. They had one chance to end this menace before it escaped into the world and Aeron was not going to squander it.

Despite her injury, the creature Melia struck was still capable of retaliation and she lashed out with those life draining tendrils. Melia took refuge behind a stone column and watched the spidery threads of black continue onwards until they found another source of nourishment. Wrapping themselves around the cocoon of the creature previously slain, the ruptured pod immediately crusted over and then crumbled upon itself, going from rancid to dust in the space of seconds. The tendrils drained what life remained within it.

Darting out of her hiding place, Melia hurried to the prince's side.

"What do we do?" she asked anxiously. There was no longer any question in her mind these creatures had to be destroyed. Even if one of them was her mother, Melia understood they needed to act for the greater good.

The cocoons all around them were shuddering with life even as Tamsyn and Edwyn were locked in their life and death struggle. Aeron saw their fierce battle and knew better than to be caught in the crossfire of two duelling wizards. Besides, he and Melia had enough to deal with as the river daughters continued to strain against their pods. A section of ceiling collapsed with a thundering crash, thanks to the deadly magic being wielded by the two serafs, and buried one of the pods for good.

The river daughters paid little attention to any of this. They were only aware that their jailor was distracted, providing them with the opportunity to escape. If anything, the commotion was compelling them to struggle even harder against their prison, to rip through the membrane while he was busy elsewhere.

Aeron stared at their attempts to escape and tried to think what was to be done. So far, he and Melia were fortunate in their confrontations with them, but if more of them were to emerge, not even luck would be enough to save them. Judging by the malevolence of the first creature, it would not take long for them to acquire a taste for murder.

Fire, Aeron thought suddenly.

They needed fire. It was the only substance incapable of withering or decaying under the creature's power. Fire was a power unto itself and could not be tamed once unleashed. While it did not sit well with Aeron what he was required to do to use this as his weapon, he also knew his choices were limited. Scanning the walls of the room, he saw the torches still hitched to the wall, covered in dust and cold ash.

"Melia, the torches!" he shouted.

"You are going to burn them?" Melia gasped when she saw him hurrying to the nearest bracket. Pulling the brass lamp from its fixture against the wall, he examined the inside of it and saw it had enough oil inside to start a fire.

"There is no other way Mia," he touched her eyes as around them, more and more of creature clawed their way out of the pods. "I am sorry."

He fumbled for his satchel and produced the tinder box that had miraculously survived the journey through the river. Unable to delay any longer, he struck the flint and ignited the oil.

Melia thought of facing her mother as one of those creatures and knew he was right. They had no other choice. Taking a breath that seemed to make her whole chest ache, she said quickly, "Do what you must."

No sooner than she said the words, he flung the lamp as far as it would go and caused it to smash against a stone column. The glass shattered spectacularly, spraying oil over the sealed cocoons. The flames spread quickly across translucent flesh. Shrill screams filled the air as the unholy creatures within the pods found death in a blanket of fire.

One of the river daughters, already emerged from the pod, screeched in crazed fury as she whirled towards her sisters' killer. Rage drove her forward, making her forget her formidable powers as she moved on uncertain legs towards Aeron, her claws bared. Melia intercepted her slime-covered body with a powerful tackle, toppling them both to the ground. The creature, momentarily stunned, turned her dark eyes at Melia. Before the creature could attack, Melia grabbed a nearby rock and staved it against her skull. Once, twice, three times and the river daughter struggled no more.

"Get on with it!" Melia snapped at Aeron, wiping the splattered blood off her cheek. This was hard enough to do without them wasting time.

He didn't answer and ran along the walls of the room, sword drawn, ready to cut down anything lying between him and the other lamps. One after the other, he took advantage of the oil left in them and hurled them at the cocoons, setting the room ablaze. The flames spread across the pods like wildfire, causing some of them to explode once the heat became so intense the pressure needed release.

The river daughters climbing out of unsealed pods before he began his fiery assault were now aiming the full torrent of their vengeance at him. Snarling and hissing at Aeron like animals, they broke free of their slimy husks and started towards him. Melia got to her feet and ran to his side as they attempted to converge upon him, swinging her dagger and forcing them to scatter before they could use their dreaded powers to subdue her Prince.

One of the creatures broke away from the others and was moving to intercept him as he moved from lamp to lamp, anticipating his movements upon divining his plan. Aeron saw her approach and lit an arrow with one of the ignited torches before shooting it into her chest. She screeched with pain as her body glowed with the dancing tongues of flames.

From the corner of her eyes, Melia saw another river daughter closing in on Aeron and immediately moved to stop the creature before it could reach him.

The river daughter flung those terrible tendrils at her and Melia dropped to the smooth floor, pivoting on one knee as she swept the creature's leg from under her. The creature snarled indignantly as she landed hard against her knees but raised her head sharply at Melia, preparing for a renewed assault. Melia did not give her the chance to use those spidery tendrils again and slashed them away with her dagger. A high pitched scream followed and Melia let out a sigh of relief at the narrow escape.

"Mia!" Aeron suddenly shouted, staring at her in horror.

For a moment she stared back at him in puzzlement, wondering the cause of his panic. Until she felt the tendrils coiling around her and pinning her arms to her side. Unable to move, she felt its fetid breath on her neck, making her stomach curdle. Worse still, she could feel the insidious black spines digging into her skin, overwhelming her with a terrible feeling of fatigue. In desperation, Melia threw back her head, connecting with teeth and soft flesh before using every ounce of strength she possessed to tear herself free.

The tendrils ripped out of her arms with a sickening snap and both she and the river daughter scream in pain. Melia recovered first and she swung around to face her attacker. Taking advantage of its disorientation, she swung the dagger in a neat arc and took off the creature's head. It toppled off her neck, black blood spurting from ruined veins before the head hit the floor with a sickly thud.

When she turned back to Aeron, he was dispatching another creature by flinging a lamp at it and setting it ablaze. When their eyes made contact, she rewarded him with a smile of relief. His efforts to set the room on fire had worked and the pods were all engulfed in flame. The room was dancing with the illumination of tall tongues of fire and the smoke filling the air was making it difficult to breathe or see. They needed to leave this place and the river daughters to their fate.

Neither could take any pride in what they had done here, even if they knew their actions had saved Avalyne from a monstrous menace. The momentary pleasure Melia felt seeing he was in one piece quickly diminished by the realisation that one of those screams belonged to her mother.

Suddenly, the creature whose fingers she had taken appeared out of the smoke and flame, closing in on Aeron with surprising speed. Aeron wasted no time firing the last of his arrows at the creature but, despite being wounded, she deflected them easily. He started to retreat, but she closed the distance, swatting him away like a fly.

"PRINCE!" Melia screamed as she saw him fly through the air from the blow, landing hard on the floor not far away. Freshly healed ribs broke once again, forcing a groan of pain from his lips. The sound struck cold terror into her heart. All this time, she had been worried about outliving him and the idea he might be killed first never occurred to her.

Despite the white-hot agony flaring in his side, he raised his head at Melia's panicked cry to see the river daughter advancing on him. She seemed determined, not about to let him escape her again. Aeron forced himself to his feet, grimacing as he straightened up to defend himself. He'd lost his bow and his sword when the creature had flung him across the room and searched quickly for a weapon. He sighted his bow but it was on the other side of the room and he would have to go through the enemy to retrieve it.

"Aeron!" The watch guard shouted, catching his attention. "Catch!"

Aeron turned to see his sword being flung at him. He ran forward and caught it with one hand, ignoring the pain as he secured his grip around the hilt and swung it wide. The river daughter avoided the blow, ducking at the last minute. The wide swing left his flank exposed and, when he straightened up, she caught him by the throat, lifting him off his feet. Dark tendrils emerged from the bloody stumps of her fingers to pierce his chest through his leather jerkin.

The pain was unlike anything he'd ever felt. It felt like hot knives penetrating his skin, his muscle, and then bone. This was what it felt like to be run through, he thought fleetingly, as a cry escaped his lips. He tried desperately to raise his sword but his strength failed him. His life was being drained out of his body through the black tendrils. In a matter of seconds, he was overcome with such uncontrollable fatigue he could barely keep his grasp of the hilt. The creature held him above the floor, his feet dangling as she proceeded to crush his throat with her iron grip, a sneer of victory across her face.

Suddenly without warning, a burning arrow struck her full in the neck.

The arrow completely penetrated her neck, stopped only by its fletching. The arrow took away any chance she had to scream and she released him abruptly, staggering away as the tendrils withdrew from his chest. Sickly, gurgling noises followed her. A second arrow flew past him, this one striking her heart and killing her.

Melia lowered the bow that felt uncomfortable in her hands. She preferred her own crossbow and, no matter how well she might shoot with the one she now held, it did not feel right. When she saw Aeron was still on his hands and knees, she bolted towards him, skidding to the floor next to him. Even with his elven fortitude, Melia knew he was hurt and hurt badly. He appeared pale and was having trouble getting to his feet.

Yet as she proceeded towards him, something in the corner of her eye caught her attention and she saw a hand tearing through the membrane of the one cocoon they had missed.

The one belonging to Ninuie. Note: I thought Ninuie emerged first, and has already been slain in this battle...

Melia could not help but turn around and stare as it split open, its viscous, translucent fluid spreading out around it in a large pool. The river daughter stood up, like a terrible goddess rising out of the sea. Melia found herself rooted to the spot, unable to move, unable to breathe. She heard Aeron shouting at her distantly, but could give him no answer. Melia stared into the face of the creature before and felt a swell of anguish rise from the pit of her stomach to escape in a single, wrenching sob.

The face before her was one she recognized. She had seen it enough in the mirror.

Aeron forced himself to his feet, ignoring the toll the river daughter had taken upon him with her life-draining magic. All he knew was that he had to move or Melia, blinded by her feelings for her mother, would die. He staggered to his feet, using his sword to prop himself up so he could walk.

The creature who was Ninuie raised her hands and he was brought down like a sack of flour. Aeron was driven to his knees once more as a terrible weight dragged him to the ground.

"Mia," he managed to croak, "she is not your mother! Not anymore!"

If anything could snap her out of her momentary lapse, it was seeing Aeron fall and she faced her mother once again and pleaded desperately. "Stop it! You are killing him!"

The creature did not seem to register she had spoken at all and, driven to desperation, Melia tried one more time to reach her mother.

"Mother! Please do not hurt him! Please! If you ever loved me or Hezare! Please stop!"

Until then, the eyes of all river daughters were the soulless black of a shark. They had stared ahead, seeing nothing and feeling only rage and hatred. At the mention of Hezare's name, the creature once called Ninuie blinked and tilted her head, staring at Melia as if puzzled. For a few seconds, she did nothing, but continued to stare at Melia in unspoken contemplation.

Then, without warning, her hand reached for Melia's arm and clenched it tight.

Melia did not know what to think as she felt nails digging into her arm. The dark tendrils used to drain all creatures of their life force were nowhere in sight and Ninuie had all but forgotten Aeron. Instead, the river daughter held her firmly, leaning forward as if studying her. Did she remember? Melia wondered. Had Hezare's words awakened her memories?

Melia did not care as long as she left Aeron alone.

Ninuie opened her mouth to speak.

"Hezare."

* * *

Images exploded in her mind in blinding flashes that made her flinch.

She could feel Ninuie's grip tight around her arm, but her touch seemed distant, eclipsed by the swirling images appearing before her, like she was at the bottom of a pool, trying to look up into the sky. A moment ago, she was standing in the middle of a monstrous hatchery, pleading for the life of her prince because he was being drained by the creature who was once her mother.

Now, they were somewhere else.

Around them, the wood and its fragrance assaulted her lungs with its fresh scents of moist, living trees and loamy soil. Melia was disoriented because it was such a stark contrast from the heated air and the stench of noxious smoke in the room earlier. Her confusion ebbed away when she recognised the wilderness she had come to know so intimately as a watch guard.

The smell was powerful and the heat of the sun overhead was just as intoxicating. Melia would have been lost by its power if she had not known it wasn't real. She recognised the Yantra River running past the woods of Eden Halas because, after years of searching for Ninuie, she was familiar with the land.

Ninuie was standing next to her, clutching her arm with her claw-like grip, but her face was devoid of its earlier malevolence. Instead, she appeared confused and troubled. Melia saw the all too human emotion of anxiety. Ninuie's eyes were staring past her and Melia followed her gaze to the green grass just beyond the banks of the river.

A couple were lying beneath the shade of a tree. The tree was large, leafy and its branches spread outward like it was trying to catch the rain when the heavens opened up. The man and woman were stretched out beneath the canopy of green, against lush, carpet-thick grass, firmly in each other's embrace, enjoying each other with the carefree abandon of youth. They stared at each other with a love Melia had only recently come to share with her. It was rich and all-consuming.

The woman, with her sheeny dark hair and luminescent skin, surrendered completely to her lover, a handsome man with dusky skin that glistened with a fine sheen of perspiration from the sun's heat. With a start, Melia realized this was her father. For the first few seconds, she almost did not believe what her eyes were showing her. He looked so young and happy. There was no trace of the weathered and seasoned warrior he would become in his later years. Here, he appeared as if nothing could stop him from conquering the world singlehandedly.

Melia ached with sadness at having never known this man.

Of the woman, she had no memory. In what could well be the last moments of her life, she was allowed a glimpse into the past and this was the only memory she would have of Ninuie, as she was. Not the creature twisted by a mage's hubris, about to murder her own child.

Still, if she was to die, then Melia was grateful for this final glimpse into the past to see her parents together just once. They were so happy and she wondered if her mother wrestled with the dilemma of a having a mortal lover the way Aeron was now. She doubted it. Ninuie's smile of adoration told her nothing mattered but their time together.

The scene before her suddenly melted away, colours bled into undistinguishable swirl, like a bucket of water thrown against a chalk painting on the floor. Melia blinked to refocus, but when she opened her eyes, she knew she was looking at something different. The tree was gone, but in its place was a small house that sat by the banks of the Yantra with a window facing the Baffin in the distance. There were small blue flowers in the garden and the cottage reminded Melia of those she had seen in Barrenjuck Green.

Ninuie was smiling as she walked down the path leading away from the house and, stumbling after her, taking clumsy steps, was a child with dark hair and bronzed skin.

Melia felt her heart stop beating when she realised she was looking at herself. She was very young, not much more than a year old, but she was loved by the mother who watched over her carefully. These were Ninuie's memories, she realised, buried deep inside her until Melia's reminder had awakened them.

Blackness swept over her and the sunlight disappeared from the sky. It became cold, so very cold that Melia could feel the chill right through her skin. Tendrils of ice wrapped around her spine and made her tremble. She reached a state of mind where these rapid images no longer disoriented her.

There was darkness all around her. The atmosphere was pregnant with sinister intent and the trees surrounding her were no longer comforting but ominous. The thunder of paws could be heard in the distance, gaining momentum with each second. It grew from a faint, distant sound to a loud, pounding thunder, making Melia flinch.

Ninuie was running.

She was running on bare feet, her dress trailing behind her as she ran desperately through the tall grass, breathing hard, her face revealing her terror. Dark hair followed her as relentlessly as her unseen pursuers. The scene was visceral. Ninuie looked over her shoulder, trying to see if they were behind her, but there was nothing there. Yet she and Melia could hear them, could hear them closing in. The exposed root of a tree tripped her and the sudden stop after running so fast ensured she landed badly.

A cry of anguish escaped her lips as she tried to get to her feet but realised that her ankle was twisted. Dirt covered her face, as well as scratches and bruises, as she hobbled forward unsteadily. She was sobbing pitifully, frustrated by her injury and the growing realisation she was not going to escape. Melia wanted to help her, but she was only an observer to events that were already years in the past. Fate could not be altered, no matter how painful it was to watch.

"I went to find my sisters," the creature stunned her by speaking.

The river woman appeared lucid for once, her gaze still fixed on what was happening before them.

"I was going to tell them goodbye."

Melia did not speak because she knew why.

"I was going away with him, with my man," the creature explained as if she were in a daze. "I was going to follow him to his land, because I could not be without him. I knew it would not be forever, because the man would not last, not him or the daughter I gave him, but I loved him so, I would have gone anywhere to be with him."

"What happened?"

Ninuie turned her eyes to the scene once more and the running paws pounding in their ears soon evolved into the explosion of black emerging through the trees. Melia almost screamed herself when she saw them and imagined the horror Ninuie must have felt being hunted by them. Melia had never seen the things that ran her mother down, but she knew instantly what they were. The description Arianne gave her and the reputation of these beings left an indelible impression upon the mind.

Armoured from waist up, their fingers tapered into the claws of a wild beast, while their lower half was bare, exposing the powerful legs of their feline bodies. The tail was coiled with a poisoned tip and their human mouths revealed serrated teeth. Their eyes glowed red through the eyelets in their helmets and their breaths were snorts of vile grunts. These were Balfure's most loyal servants, supposedly Syphia's lesser children. These were the Disciples.

Their prey screamed at the sight of them and she was running again, despite the injury to her foot, though she was not as fast as she could be. The desperation in her eyes was coupled with anguish, especially when she knew that she could not escape. They spread out and surrounded the terrified woman easily, circling her in a ring of doom.

Melia's despair at being unable to help was equally devastating, because this was a story already written. She could change nothing.

One of the Disciples broke the ring and thundered towards the frightened woman, tossing something into the air. Melia had trapped enough animals in her time to know what it was. The net fell over Ninuie and sealed her doom as easily as it sealed her in its meshed confines.

"They drove me from the river," the creature resumed speaking. "They forced me away from my place of power. I was helpless in the Wood. They knew that."

"Mother," Melia whispered, finding it strange to say, but knew they had bridged an important gulf. "We can help you. We can find some way to return you to yourself."

"I had forgotten all of it. I forgot until you reminded me. I forgot my name and I forgot the man.

Melia did not know what to say to that.

"He is dead, is he not?" Ninuie asked.

"Yes," Melia nodded slowly.

"He died believing I abandoned him." Her eyes showed a world of sorrow.

"Yes," the watch guard answered because there was no avoiding it.

Ninuie was silent for a moment before her eyes rose to meet Melia's again. "I am myself here because of you, my daughter. You make me remember, but I feel the wizard's power growing within me. It makes me want to hurt you. It makes me want to destroy you. I will not be able to endure for long. You feel it, do you not?"

Melia was weeping, but she understood. "Yes, I do."

"I should never have left him," Ninuie lamented. "I lost him the moment I chose to leave our home, long before the Disciples took me, before the wizard destroyed me."

"There must be some way," Melia pleaded. "There must be another choice."

"No," Ninuie shook her head. "The time for my choices is past. All there is left is the end, and I must find it. I will remain myself as much as I can when we return, but you must do what is necessary."

"I cannot!" Melia wailed, "I cannot do that!"

"Please!" Ninuie begged her. "Send me to the man. Send me to Hezare."

* * *

Aeron felt as if he was dying.

In almost a thousand years of existence, he'd never felt as terrible as he did at this moment. His limbs felt like stone and each effort to move made him reconsider the entire notion as pain coursed through him. It would have been so easy to let go, to let the fatigue claim him and succumb to the inviting numbness sweeping over his body, but he could not. Not when he did not know how his Melia fared.

Opening his eyes, he saw her caught within the grip of the creature who was once her mother. Melia no longer struggled and both stared at each other, as if trapped with the same spell. Aeron suspected something was taking place between them, but he could not even begin to imagine what that might be. Conserving his strength as much as he could, he crawled across the debris-covered floor towards her.

The air was thick with smoke and he wondered if Tamsyn still lived. His question was answered when he saw Edwyn spinning in the air before the mage landed hard against the floor, not far away from him. Edwyn's energy seemed drained with that final assault and he moved no more. Aeron watched as Tamsyn stepped forward, his eyes wet with tears as he approached his friend. The elf hid his shock, for he had never seen Tamsyn weep for anyone. How terrible it must be to put down one's brother like a rabid animal. Aeron prayed he would never know such pain.

"Tamysn!" Aeron cried out, snapping the wizard out of his grief and back to their present situation.

"Aeron," Tamsyn crossed the floor quickly and bent down to help him to his feet. "Those creatures have tried to feed off your life force. You need to rest and recover your strength."

"I care not for that!" Aeron gasped. "Something is happening between Melia and that thing!"

Tamsyn glanced at the exchange between mother and daughter, trying to determine what was taking place. Placing his hand on Aeron's chest, he closed his eyes and used some of his own magic to help the prince recover. Not enough to heal him completely, but enough to ensure Aeron could move a little better. The elves had remarkable powers of recuperation and it required only a little jolt for Aeron's natural ability to exert itself.

When Aeron felt some measure of strength returning to him, he pushed away from the wizard to approach Melia. Each step forward came at a price and the prince knew once he submitted to his exhaustion, he would be quite immobile for some time. His hand clutched his sword firmly as he strode purposefully towards Melia, ignoring the pull of exhaustion upon his limbs.

"Careful, Aeron," Tamsyn warned as he hurried next to Aeron's side. "Their minds are linked. You may kill one, but harm both."

Aeron stared at him in frustration. "This cannot go on! Who knows what this link between them is doing to Melia?" Both the creature and Melia returned to life. The river daughter relinquished her grip on Melia's arm, causing the watch to stumble backwards. She was panting, as if trying to recover from an extraordinarily strong dizzy spell.

"Mia!" Aeron called out and started towards her, his teeth gritting against the pain.

Melia wanted to answer, but her mother's voice kept her from doing so. Ninuie stared at her, appearing as if she were still herself, but the grip was tenuous and the ability to hold back the tide of murderous hatred was waning fast. Even now, Melia could see the darkness creeping into her eyes again. They did not have much time.

"Do it," Ninuie begged, her voice strained as if she battled even through her words. "Do it now, before I harm you! I cannot endure any longer!"

"No," Melia started to sob, crying out against the unimaginable course she had to take. "Do not ask me this!"

"It must be done!" Ninuie pleaded. "Release me while you still can!"

Melia blinked her tears away, knowing Aeron was there and spat out the words as if she was expelling bile from her throat.

"Finish her, Prince. Finish her!"

Aeron did not understand what transpired between mother and daughter, but he recognised the anguish in Melia's voice and was willing to spare her what duty demanded of her. Taking a deep breath, he delivered the killing stroke, determined to make this quick and fast, for Melia's sake. The blade sliced through air in a neat arc before Aeron pulled it back expertly. The room fell silent and only the crackling of fire made any sound.

Ninuie's head came away from her neck and tumbled to the ground before her body went slack and followed it. Melia did not look. She refused to. Aeron sank to his knees as the last of his strength gave out and not even Tamsyn's temporary salve could help him overcome the effects of the river daughter's attacks. He cursed his inability to move, because Melia was weeping uncontrollably into her hands, breaking his heart with each sob. He wanted to comfort her, but he could not even crawl in this lamentable condition.

"Mia," Aeron croaked as he rested on all fours, aware that soon he would meet the ground.

She turned to him, her face filled with sorrow, but was moved into action when she realised how badly hurt he was by the battle. She dropped to the floor next to him, wrapping her arms around him in an embrace she never wanted to let go. As weak as he was, just feeling him against her was enough to sooth Melia's sorrow. He had been right all along. Ninuie needed to be at peace and now, thanks to him, she was.

"Thank you, Prince," she whispered as she held him in her arms. "I could not have done it."

"I would spare you that anguish, my love," Aeron whispered weakly. "I would never have let you bear that burden."

"I love you," Melia said softly, holding him even tighter.

"I love you, Mia," he answered with a weak smile. "Your mother's soul will find her way to Cera."

Melia nodded and hoped perhaps she would find Hezare there, too.

Chapter Nineteen

Returning Home

Elves were not prone to black sleep, so when awareness finally returned to Aeron three days later, he was gripped with a great sense of loss. His dreams had been unpleasant, with images of fingers clawing through grey sacs. When he woke up, he found himself in the cave he and Melia had sheltered in, after Tamsyn had come so fortuitously to their rescue. As he sat up, a feeling of uneasiness gripped him.

At least he knew his return to lucidity meant he was on the road to recovery after the battle with the river daughters. Though he felt tired still, there was none of the debilitating fatigue or the life-draining exhaustion that imperilled him during the fight.

Sitting up, Aeron saw Tamsyn staring at him from across the small cave. A fire was burning in the middle of the space and outside he saw the glittering starts of the night sky. Tamsyn's expression was sad and Aeron supposed it was most likely because the wizard still mourned the loss of his dear friend. Edwyn did not survive the battle and Tamsyn was devastated at the mage's end. Disgraced or not, Edwyn was his friend.

It took only a moment for it to dawn on Aeron that Tamsyn was not only sad for Edwyn but also for him. Sweeping his gaze across the cave, it took but an instant for Aeron to realise what was wrong. There was no sign of Melia or her belongings in the cave.

"Where is she?"

Tamsyn drew in a long breath and, even before he spoke, Aeron knew the answer.

"She is gone, Aeron."

"Gone," he whispered.

"She said you would understand," Tamsyn continued, but could tell by the fading light in his friend's eyes Aeron did not understand at all. Not one bit.

"She helped me bring you here and departed once she knew you would recover. I believe she was returning to the Baffin."

Aeron swallowed thickly, forcing down the bubble of frustration and anguish rising up his throat like bile. His mind screamed in betrayal and fury at her departure. He could not believe that, after all they had endured together, her faith in them was so lacking. Worse yet, she could not even trouble herself to face him, to give her farewell in person. Once again, he was forced to wonder how much of this she had planned before her departure.

After all, she refused his proposal, using the quest for her mother as an excuse to deny him. Had she ever planned on staying with him? Was everything she said a lie? Was it merely a carrot to dangle before him, to ensure he remained to help her find Ninuie? Aeron refused to believe Melia could be so calculated, but it was hard to think anything else when he woke to find her gone, again. He swore by his life she meant everything she said to him and yet she *still* left.

How could he believe anything else?

"Are you alright?" The question seemed redundant, but Tamsyn was compelled to ask.

"Yes," Aeron answered with a voice that did not feel quite like his own. Considering what was happening inside his heart,

Aeron acquitted himself rather well, showing little sign of grief or his anger as he stared into the fire.

The pain through him was beyond belief, but on some level he should have expected it. Hope had blinded him from the reality of the situation. What took place with her mother was further proof of why they should be apart, the unbridgeable differences between mortal and elf. Knowing this did not make it any easier for Aeron to bear and the emotion churning through him was not anguish or astonishment, but rather fury. Once again, she had made this decision for the both of them without consultation.

After Eden Halas, had he not learnt how accustomed she was to running whenever she was faced with something with which she could not cope?

"She wished you well," Tamsyn offered, knowing what words he offered the prince were no comfort. Aeron was doing his best to keep his emotions contained, but it was obvious he was hurt badly by his lady's actions. "She said you fought bravely and she will always love you, but you know the reasons why she had to depart."

Aeron did not speak.

He lay back down on his bedding and rolled away from the wizard. His eyes were glistening despite his best efforts to contain his sorrow and he wished to be spared the indignity of having *all* his emotions exposed to Tamsyn. With his back to the man, Aeron was grateful when the mage did not try to console him with words but left him alone to his silent tears.

* * *

Despite the emotional pain suffered at Melia's abrupt departure, Aeron recovered quickly and far sooner than Tamsyn would have predicted. In a number of days, they were ready to depart the Gahara Plateau.

Aeron invited Tamsyn to return to Eden Halas with him and, as the wizard had no present destination in mind, he accepted the invitation. Tamsyn decided it would be good to visit with Halion. The king was one of the few beings in Avalyne with as much longevity as he. Also, Tamsyn was reluctant to let the prince make the journey alone, despite the facade Aeron presented at being unaffected by Melia's absence.

While Tamsyn understood the reasons for Melia's departure, he did not condone it, not when it was bringing them both such heartache. He suspected much of her desire to leave stemmed from the guilt of being the one to order her mother's death. Even if Ninuie asked for her life to end, it was no easy thing for any child to see dead the parent she spent so much time trying to find.

Once they had begun the journey towards Eden Halas, Aeron spoke nothing further of Melia and seemed to purge all thoughts of her from his mind. Of course, Tamsyn knew this discard was only skin deep and the lady was never far from Aeron's heart. Nevertheless, he respected Aeron's wishes and made no attempt to broach the subject with the prince.

* * *

Halion's gratitude at seeing Aeron was evident when they returned to Eden Halas. Syanne's anger with her king had not abated as it had done during past quarrels. This time neither were yielding the point and the days after the prince's departure from Halas were tense ones for the court. It was clear to all present that Halion and his queen were not on good terms.

Aeron's return ended that tension, with Halion pleased his son did not carry through the threat of never seeing him again. While they did not immediately speak of the argument that drove him away from Halas during his last visit, both father and son seemed to regard each other with a new understanding.

Melia's name was not mentioned.

It was plain to see that some rift now separated the prince from the watch guard, because he did not speak her name and left it to Tamysn to explain of Melia's return to duty in the Baffin. At the feast to welcome Tamysn to Eden Halas, Aeron played the part required of him, but those who knew him saw the sadness in his eyes. Even Halion, who was normally able to maintain an impressive facade of indifference, could not hide his concern at Aeron's pain.

Aeron tried hard not to show the court his sombre mood, but he could not help it. He tried to display an impassive front to all, because a prince always kept his emotions hidden. Halion taught him that. On this occasion, it seemed to serve, because it kept anyone from asking him uncomfortable questions. He could see their eyes burning with curiosity at what had transpired between Melia and him.

Since she left him, Aeron had done nothing but rationalize her behaviour, trying to see their relationship from her point of view. He knew she feared he would leave her, the way her mother abandoned her father. Surely, he had proved he would never do such a thing? How much more did he have to earn her trust? He had bound himself to her and he knew that, until he passed into the next life, he would always yearn for her.

For better or for worse, Melia was a part of him now, and that was all there was to it.

In the meantime, he distracted himself with the plans he intended to put into motion in Eden Ardhen, things the two of them had discussed when he still believed she might marry him.

As expected, there were more than a few elves in Eden Halas, particularly those who fought at Astaroth, who were willing to listen to his ideas of reclaiming Eden Ardhen and building a new kind of elven city. His Eden Ardhen would not live entirely within the Veil. It would remain in the woods of Arden where men and dwarves could come. No longer would they live in isolation, as had been the practice of elvenkind since the Primordial Wars.

Elves were granted immortality to fight in the Primordial Wars because it was too difficult to keep growing new soldiers when the old ones who did not die on the battlefield withered with age. When the war ended, they should have used their immortality to become teachers and recorders of history for the younger races, as Cera had intended, but resentment had disrupted that plan. Thus the promise of the Sacred Three was never fulfilled.

Balfure's invasion had awakened a good number of elves to the world outside the Veil. Some had lived without ever leaving its confines and they were eager to explore what lay beyond. Aeron had been fortunate to travel with Dare across the Western Sphere. He wished to be a part of the world and knew many at home in Eden Halas who felt the same.

If his father knew the discussions Aeron was having with his people, the king did not mention it, although Aeron knew the time to discuss the matter was fast approaching. How Halion would take his efforts was as much a mystery as everything else about his father.

* * *

When Aeron returned to his room that night, he found Syanne waiting for him. Since his return, he had taken pains to avoid talking to his mother, because he knew she would want to discuss Melia, and Aeron was in no frame of mind to approach the subject with anyone, even her. He had successfully buried all thoughts of the watch guard deep inside his heart so that he would not feel the pain of it. Discussing the matter would only bring to ruin that careful construction.

Syanne was seated on the same bed she had tucked him into as a child when her son entered the room.

To her, he would always be the most precious of her sons, the sensitive, thoughtful one that took so much after the brother she lost instead of his father. Growing up as a girl in Sanhael, Syanne adored her older brother Aeron, who would lose his life at the hands of the Primordials. When her youngest son was born, Syanne stared into that tiny face and knew his name could be nothing else.

"You have been busy since your return," Syanne announced herself when he entered the room. "I thought I better make some time to see you alone before you embarked upon your new venture."

Aeron felt immediately guilty for evading her. "I would have seen you before leaving," he admitted, closing the door behind him before coming to sit next to her.

"Would you?" Syanne asked, knowing her son better than that. Melia was not the only one who knew how to run.

Aeron could not meet her gaze. This was precisely the reason why he had avoided her. Syanne could look into his soul no matter how deeply he thought he buried his feelings. That was the power of all mothers, he supposed: their ability to see past all the barriers because they alone had seen their children before any had been constructed.

She took his silence for an answer.

"I am sorry about Melia," Syanne said quietly.

Aeron stood up and walked away. "I do not wish to speak of her. She made her choice. She is gone."

"Son, whatever else you may think of what she has done, she loved you," Syanne said, trying to offer him comfort. "I truly believe she acted in the hopes of sparing you."

Aeron turned around and faced his mother, allowing himself to vent his rage for the first time. "Spare me?" he exclaimed. "Perhaps you are right, mother. Perhaps she did love me, but not enough. Not enough for her to see I could never love anyone after her, not enough to believe I would never abandon her or have faith we could have had a life together. I do love her and I will love her until the day I die, but I do *not* forgive her."

He expected her to offer rebuttal, but instead she gazed into his eyes and said firmly, "I think it is time you spoke to your father."

* * *

When Aeron sought his father out at Syanne's request, he believed it was to discuss his intentions of leaving Eden Halas with some of its citizens.

Stepping into his father's study, Aeron could not help but think of the last time he had been in this room, and felt immediately embarrassed by how harsh he had been with Halion. After all, Halion was trying to protect him by sending Melia away and, in retrospect, Aeron supposed he was not so misguided in the wake of what transpired in Tal-Shahar. Nevertheless, Halion being right did not make it any easier to face his father.

"Father," Aeron announced himself as he entered the room.

"You are up early," the king glanced at his son before lowering the scrolls he was perusing. "Then again, I suppose rallying some of my people to leave their homes requires an early start."

Aeron exhaled deeply. He should have known better than to conduct any business thinking Halion would be unaware of it. "I apologise. It was not my intention to offend you. I only wanted to see how many of our people might wish to join me before I brought it to you. "

Halion eased back into his chair and looked at his son with puzzlement. "Do you think that I am offended?"

"Well, yes," Aeron replied, not expecting any other reaction. He knew his father.

"My son," Halion sighed, as if resigning himself to never truly understanding his youngest son, "let us take a walk."

Aeron stared at his father in puzzlement as Halion stepped away from the desk, then followed him onto the balcony outside his study. It ran along much of the outer wall of the city, like streets running through Sandrine.

He wondered what it was Halion wished to say to him. For years, Aeron had thought he knew his father, until Tamsyn's revelation showed him he knew little at all about the elf, just the persona he chose to show the world.

When they were outside, with the sun on their faces and the morning air crisp in their lungs, Halion finally spoke. "You were always the one child I understood the least when you should have been the one I recognised the most. You were always so introspective. Face value was never good enough for you and you had such far-seeing eyes. You are just like your mother's brother and I should have remembered that. It's odd how time blunts the memory, especially when he was my best friend."

Aeron blinked. "He was?"

"Oh yes," Halion nodded with a faint smile, pleased to surprise his son on occasion. "We were inseparable, Aeron, Gavril and myself. Not unlike your Circle with Dare. For most of the Primordial Wars, we fought at each other's sides. Tamsyn was there too, and the other mages, but it was on each other we relied the most. We were young, hungry, and there was nothing we thought we could not do."

It was hard to imagine Halion travelling the hills as he had done with Dare, Kyou, Tamsyn and Celene. Then again, his father had left the ruins of his homeland to build a kingdom here in Halas. Not unlike what he was attempting to do now in Ardhen.

"Of course, war changes one's reality very quickly, and after the battle that saw Antion die and Syphia vanquished, he lay in my arms dying on the battlefield. With his last breath, he asked me to take care of his sister and I promised him I would. I would ensure that what was left of his family survived. She was young, frightened and alone. I promised him I would protect her, no matter what."

"Were you married then?" Aeron finally asked the question he had been dying to ask his father since Tamsyn had inadvertently told him the truth.

Halion was mildly surprised, but surmised quickly where Aeron would have learned this part of his past. "Yes, I was married. Her name was Isabeau. I fell in love with her the first time I laid eyes on her. I was nineteen years old and she was seventeen."

Considering his father's age, Aeron blinked in shock. Even by human standards, that was young to be bonded. Imagining his father as a teenager, making such a commitment, went against everything he knew about the rigid, aloof authoritarian. Yet even as Halion spoke of these matters, Aeron could see the sorrow in his father's eyes, the pain he now understood intimately.

"How did she die?"

"It does not matter how she died," Halion replied softly, his eyes growing distant. "She was lost to me and I wished to leave, to travel south and start a new life. Your mother chose to come with me, though I told her she did not need to do so. Yet, she loved me. Perhaps it was my sadness or my need for something familiar that allowed me to let her. I do care for your mother, but you know the difference now. You know what it feels like to be gutted and then try to give what's left of yourself to someone who is not the person you want."

Aeron did and, for the first time, he had clarity regarding his father's relationship with his mother. "She accepted this?"

"Yes. I did try to talk her out of it. For whatever reason, she loved me and wouldn't be deterred. Furthermore, I wanted to keep her safe. I wanted her protected from everything terrible there was. I think she believed she loved me enough for both of us, and that was, perhaps, our mistake. I care for your mother.

I will always cherish her, but she always understood it could never be how it was when I was with Isabeau."

Aeron let out a heavy sigh, and with it went all the walls holding in the pain and anguish in his heart. He stopped walking and leaned against the railing, breathless. Gripping the wood so hard his knuckles turned white, he uttered, "I do not know what to do, father. I have this ache inside me and it will not go away. I am wounded and I do not know how to heal myself."

Halion's hand rested gently on his back. "You do not heal, Aeron. This is what I tried to tell you, what I wished to spare you. You do not heal. You learn to manage. That is all that can be done. I do not know if the afterlife will reunite me with Isabeau, but it is the hope I cling to. Melia loved you, but she is mortal and she cannot understand how love is for us. When I told her to go, I did so in the hopes it was not too late for you, but I was wrong wasn't I?"

"You said you loved Isabeau from the moment you saw her. It was the same for me and Melia. It was always too late, I just never wanted to admit it, and now it is done. I am bonded to her, but she does not wish to be with me."

"I am sorry, son," Halion said with genuine sympathy. "I did not want this for you, but know there are other forms of love. Your mother and I have survived on our love for our children, for our people, and – to some degree – with our affection for each other. I think I have been so intent on protecting her, I forgot the heart needs more than safety. I thank you, my son, for reminding me of that."

Aeron nodded, turning to meet his father's gaze, realising that, at last, they understood each other.

"Father, I will be leaving and some of our people will be coming with me. If I am to *manage* as you advised, I cannot do it here."

"I know." Halion put a hand on Aeron's head and drew his son forward so that their foreheads touched briefly, a gesture Aeron had not received since he was a little boy. "I have heard the discontent of some of my people, particularly the younger ones who were born here, not in Sanhael. Dare brought us kicking and screaming into the world and perhaps we needed waking up. I think this idea of yours to rebuild Eden Ardhen is a good one. I have not spoken to Lylea, but I am certain she would like to see those woods returned to elven hands. You may even find some of her people may wish join you in the south."

"Thank you, father," Aeron said softly, deciding that he rather liked the man, almost as much as he loved the father.

Chapter Twenty

The Lord of Eden Ardhen

More than a hundred of his people joined him for the journey south. Once there, they would restore the enchantments around the ruined city of Eden Ardhen and remain within its protection while they began the exercise of cleansing the woods of Balfure's minions once and for all. Tor Arden still stood and Aeron was determined to bring it down for good.

His father was gracious enough to provide them with supplies needed until they established themselves and his new colonists were elves possessing an assorted mix of skills and vocations. There were soldiers who fought in the Aeth War, artisans and craftsmen who wished a new tapestry upon which to hone their skill. Some simply possessed an adventurer's spirit and wanted to see new lands.

During the weeks he remained in Halas making preparations, he found his relationship with Halion greatly improved. In their grief over lost mates, they shared an understanding of each other and discovered a relationship that allowed Aeron to know the man instead of the king.

What also pleased Aeron was Halion's attention to his queen, softening his manner towards her. It could never be the love the youthful Syanne had once craved, but it certainly satisfied the queen. Halion was even allowing his mother more freedom beyond the Veil, as there was talk of her journeying to Sandrine, with Syannon and the Forest Guard as escort, of course. Syanne was eager to see her new grandchild and Aeron knew for a fact that Dare and Arianne would be delighted to receive her.

In the meantime, he tried not to think about Melia.

Despite the occasional irrational desire to ride to the Baffin so he could find her and make her see sense, Aeron chose to abide by her wishes. If Melia could not give herself to him, then Aeron would not waste his time trying to convince her otherwise. He would let her go, because he loved her and because it was what she wanted. He knew what he risked when he gave his affections to a mortal and now he would have to suffer the price of that gamble.

Still, there were times when he caught himself looking towards the Baffin wondering if he was in her thoughts as often as she was in his.

* * *

Sending his people onwards to Ardhen ahead of him, Aeron's first port of call was to Sandrine.

He went there not only to retrieve his horse Idris, left at the Keep since he set off with Melia on their long journey by river. He also wanted to give Dare an account of what took place in the Gahara. The Disciples had tricked a mage into creating a terrible weapon for them against the enemy during the war. Had Edwyn been the only Mage so used? There were other wizards and holy men scattered across Avalyne and not all of them were of the Order of Enphilim. Some might have even received instruction from Balfure.

The kingdom needed to be on its guard in case any more of these dupes emerged from their hiding places with creations as vile as that of the river daughters.

"Are you certain they are all dead?" Arianne asked when Aeron concluded his tale at the king's table that night.

"I believe so. Though, I must confess, I was in no condition to see for myself after the battle was done. Tamsyn was certain the hatchery was ablaze when we fled and I trust his judgement."

"Well," Dare said, lowering his cup of wine after taking a sip. "I am glad you fought so bravely. It would not have bode well for Avalyne if those creatures escaped and were unleashed upon us."

"We did what was necessary," Aeron shrugged, not wishing to dwell too much on the subject because, inevitably, Melia would enter the conversation.

"You did what you always do," Arianne commended, reaching across the table to clasp his hand. "You fought with courage with no thought to yourself. I am glad that you were not permanently injured."

Arianne appeared as if she wanted to say more but pulled back, particularly when given a stern eye by Dare that Aeron caught despite the King's effort to keep it fleeting. With an inward sigh, he knew that the subject of Melia was going to be revisited after all.

"You give me too much credit," the elf said after a moment and then added, "I sense that there is something on your minds that neither of you have yet to bring to my attention. I will spare you the trouble of finding some way to broach the subject with me. What is it that you wish to say?"

Dare frowned at Arianne, as if trying to tell her to let the matter rest, but it seemed his wife had other ideas.

Arianne ignored him and said to Aeron, her voice sympathetic. "We have not asked you about Melia because we have seen her."

"You saw her?" Aeron exclaimed and immediately cursed himself for his telling reaction. "When?"

"She came here for her horse, Serinda," Arianne explained. "Melia told us what took place between you two. Aeron, I am so sorry."

Aeron swallowed hard, wishing his parting with Melia could have remained private between them. It felt like the entire world new his heart was broken. His jaw clenched as he composed himself to hide just how much it still hurt him. If it were anyone but Arianne and Dare before him, he might have succeeded in concealing his sorrow, but they knew him too well. To his chagrin, his pain lay exposed.

"It was her game," he spoke after a pause. "I knew what I risked when I chose to play."

"I do not believe it was a game to her," Arianne tried to speak in Melia's defence, but it was difficult to do so when Aeron's eyes were filled with such pain. "She loves you, Aeron, but her heart is still wounded from what happened in the mountain."

Dare remained silent, allowing Arianne to speak, but he did not feel comfortable about discussing so private a subject with the elf, even with the best intentions. In truth, he did not think well of Melia for simply leaving as she had.

"Aeron," Dare found his voice at last. "You do not have to speak of this if you do not wish it. We just want you to know we are here if you need us. You are dear to us both, but should you decide not to confide in us, we will understand."

"Dare…" Arianne started to say, but Dare cut her off abruptly.

"I have spoken, Rian. This is a private matter between Aeron and Melia. We will say nothing more."

Aeron cast Dare a grateful look even though the king was being treated to a stormy scowl from his wife. Aeron had the distinct impression Dare would sleeping on the floor of his chamber before the night's end. Still, he had no wish to spurn Arianne's desire to help, so he made some concession.

"Arianne, I know you wish to help, but this matter can only be resolved by Melia. She made her choice clear and, though it pains me more than I can say, I have to abide by her decision. I cannot hold her to me if she does not wish it."

"But she loves you!" Arianne cried out in frustration, hating to think it should end so tragically between two people who were so obviously meant to be together. Arianne was certain what difficulties between them could be resolved, if they only saw each other face to face.

"Rian!" Dare groaned in exasperation at his wife's stubbornness in this matter. "I am certain Aeron knows that."

"Arianne. I know you mean well, and you are right. I do not doubt that Melia feels something for me, but she does not trust me and, until that can be overcome, nothing between us is possible."

Arianne frowned, realizing Aeron was right. Trust was vital in any relationship, even one without the complications of Aeron's and Melia's. Arianne trusted Dare with her heart to never betray her. She could look into his eyes and know without doubt or hesitation he loved her and would never do anything to break her heart. Such certainty made everything else between them easy. Arianne was convinced Melia loved Aeron, but she could not give herself to him because of doubt. Still, Aeron was wrong about Melia being unable to trust him.

Arianne believed it was herself Melia did not trust.

* * *

"You elves are a peculiar lot," Kyou remarked as he observed closely the construction of Aeron's hall almost three months later.

The construction at Eden Ardhen was well underway, with the ancient trees playing host to the new homes built above ground. The architecture differed from Eden Halas, as the dwellings were built on decking surrounding the thick tree trunks and supported by struts beneath. Aeron's own keep –

he was averse to calling it a palace – was one of the largest. Each tree house was connected to others by thin bridges that crisscrossed over the forest floor.

Within the protection of the Veil, the elves were able to build their new home, while in the woods of Arden they were slowly driving out the Berserkers still remaining in Tor Ardhen. Aeron wanted his people to have a place to return after a day of cleansing the woods of evil. There was so much to do and the safety of the Veil allowed them to rest without fear of attack.

Judging by all the building he saw around him, Kyou believed it would not be long before Eden Ardhen was as enchanting to behold as Eden Taryn or even Eden Halas.

"How so?" Aeron glanced briefly at the dwarf while he and Larone studied the parchment spread across the table before them. A member of his father's Forest Guard, Larone had fought with Aeron at Astorath and was one of his most loyal lieutenants. He'd been only too happy to join Aeron when the suggestion to reclaim Eden Ardhen was made.

Kyou had arrived only a few days ago, claiming an elf would be unable to build anything that would stand the test of time unless a dwarf was there to help him. It had taken a bit of time before Aeron was able to convince his elves the dwarf meant no offense, that Kyou was just being Kyou. Besides, a Master Builder of Kyou's credentials was nothing to take lightly.

"All this trouble to build around the tree when you could build inside of it," Kyou grumbled, staring at the huge trees whose trunks were thick enough to house the entire colony. Instead, the elves had chosen to build their home around the massive trunks, an enterprise that seemed more trouble than it was worth.

"You dwarves would destroy anything," Aeron grumbled, wondering whether Kyou was being obtuse to amuse himself or really knew so little of elves after all this time in Aeron's company. As it stood, elves were known to harvest trees, but it was done with the greatest of economy and following a ritual of permission from the Celestial goddess Inafsia.

"It's just a tree," Kyou teased and saw Larone smiling because the former forest guard knew the dwarf often amused himself by baiting his new lord.

"Like you are just a dwarf, but you do not see us trying to chop you down," Aeron drawled, his eyes still fixed on the plans before him, "probably because the whining would drive us to distraction."

Kyou gave Aeron a look just as Larone started to chuckle.

"You can tell the crafters this is fine," Aeron straightened up as Larone rolled up the parchment and made a hasty retreat before the dwarf and his lord launched into one of their infamous arguments. This usually ended either with axe or sword being drawn.

Kyou was glad to see Aeron was showing some measure of contentment. Even though there was occasionally a glimmer of sadness in his eyes, for the most part Aeron appeared recovered from his heartbreak. Immersing himself in the business of building himself a new home in Ardhen was just the tonic he needed, it seemed.

"See what you have done?" Aeron turned to Kyou. "You have frightened away the captain of my guard."

"Elves scare easily," Kyou said smugly. "It's all that time you spend hiding in the bushes."

"Why are you here? I thought you came here to help. All you seem to be doing is complaining about everything that is ill to your liking."

"Well, I had to see the Lord of Eden Ardhen in his domain," the dwarf replied sweetly, reminding Aeron of all the times he had called Kyou Master Builder, an ostentatious and important title that ought not to be bandied about as a joke to annoy him. It was nice to be able to return the favour.

"You have ridden all this way just to call me that, haven't you?"

"Absolutely," Kyou grinned, not all ashamed to admit it.

Aeron's face suddenly drained of colour.

Kyou saw his jaw setting as if he were going into battle and supposed in some ways he was when the dwarf followed his gaze.

Melia was walking across the grass towards them. She was clad in the dress worn the night they dined together at Sandrine, her dark hair worn loose over her shoulders. In her hand she held a bundle of clothes and a crossbow.

When she stopped walking, Melia and Aeron stood before each other, staring. The space between them was only inches, but it still felt like a great chasm. Neither said a word as they took in the sight of each other. Aeron was a statue carved out of marble, his expression unfathomable. Melia's expression was equally cryptic. Time seemed to stretch into an eternity as neither said anything, and the waiting drove Kyou mad with impatience.

Even a dwarf's patience was finite.

"Well, if you're both just going to stand there, I'm going to leave! But before I go, let me be the first to say that it's about time you both grew up and get on with things!"

With that, the dwarf made a less than discreet exit, hoping that his parting words would spur one of them into resolving the matter that stood between them like a great sea. Aeron's gaze wavered slightly at Kyu's departure before his attention returned to Melia, boring into her mercilessly.

If his stare was a dagger, he would have drawn blood by now.

Melia dropped her belongings at his feet, hoping it would prompt him to speak. It did not. Instead, he continued to stare at her, his jaw clenched and the thoughts behind his eyes were a curtain drawn to her.

Finally upon realising he would not break his silence, Melia spoke and said the words she'd be longing to say for months.

"I am sorry."

For once, it was she who was begging. She was coming to him as supplicant. She had behaved badly and she knew it. Though he remained as impassive as stone, she saw his hurt and knew and there was no adequate apology to make up for months of pain. Still, she had to try.

Melia was here because she loved him and the time apart had only served to deepen it, making her realise she was helping neither of them by staying away. The revelation did not excuse her behaviour, however. She had shattered trust by her actions at Gahara and, this time, she needed to earn it back.

"It was cowardly and unfair to leave you as I did. I was wrong," she continued, never believing an apology could be so hard to make.

"I used my mother's death as an excuse for why we could not be together, when in truth I was afraid. I was afraid I would fail you. You said you loved me and you would never hurt me. I believed you all too well, but I did not know if I could be trusted to feel the same when the years aged my body. I did not wish to see my love for you become resentment because you would be spared all the things I will endure when I grow old."

Tears were running down her cheeks and she wiped them away quickly, looking for some assurance in his eyes that her pleas were not falling on deaf ears. She needed to know it was not too late, but he offered her no such indication. Thus all she could do was continue to plead her case.

"I returned to the Baffin, thinking I could go on without you, but my heart felt torn apart every morning I woke to find you not at my side. I have not been able to stop thinking about you or yearning for your touch. I am sorry I made you suffer, Prince. I am sorry I made a decision for both of us without thinking what it would do to you."

Aeron's silence remained and Melia found herself weeping before him. She wished he would speak. She did not care if he screamed at her. She just needed to hear him say *something*.

"Please," she begged, her voice broken and desperate, "Please say something."

"What would you have me say?"

"Tell me you understand or hate me, tell me how you feel. Anything!" she exclaimed.

"Understand what?" he demanded, the anger held back for months finally exploding. "Understand that you left me there, without a word of explanation? Not even to say farewell! After everything we endured together, you could find it so easy to simply leave?"

"I was confused and afraid," she stammered a weak explanation.

"THAT IS NO EXCUSE!" he fairly roared. "You broke my heart when you left! Do you know that? I thought I would die when I heard you were gone! And you are here now for what purpose, to play with my affections again? For me to give you my heart only to have you toss it aside at a moment's notice when you begin to doubt? I may be immortal, Melia, but I am not invulnerable! Even an elf's heart can only take so much."

"I know that! I am so sorry!" She wept harder, trying to convince him, unable to deny anything he said. "I have no right to expect anything of you, but know I love you and if we are bound for tragedy then it is something I swear to you on my life we will face together. I have disappointed you for the last time, Prince. I swear to you I am here to stay!"

All these months, he'd abandoned the hope she would ever be with him. There was not a day since that morning in Gahara when he had not longed for her. If it was not for the goal of rebuilding Eden Ardhen, there was every possibility he would have died from grief. Sorrow had such power over the heart of an elf. Nevertheless, he had forced himself to heed his father's advice, to manage. And, for most part, he had.

Now she was here again, begging him to trust her with his heart. What was he to do?

He glanced at the clothes and the crossbow at his feet and saw the significance of it. Those leathers and her weapon were her whole identity and she placed them at his feet, a symbol of sacrifice and penance for leaving him. He stared at them and then at her. Against her tears, he had no power. Her seeking him out, here, gave him hope.

Crossing the space between them, he pulled her to him roughly and embraced her hard, holding her so tight she might snap from the strength of his arms. He held her close, hating the fact he could not refuse her, even as he took in the scent of her hair in his nostrils, the softness of her body against his. How could he do anything but surrender to her when she had his heart and always would?

"I will hold you to that, Mia," he spoke firmly, as he threw off the last moorings to safety.

"You can hold me as long as you wish, Prince, for I do not intend to let you go," she pressed her lips to his in a kiss, showing him there would be no more walls between them.

For the first time, they were on equal ground, because she was surrendering her heart as completely as he had given her his.

When Aeron and Melia took breath again, the prince could not bring himself to let her go, not after waiting so long to feel her in his arms again.

"So, Lord of Eden Ardhen. What now?" she asked, her cheek pressed against his chest.

"Well, I am still quite angry with you. You will have some making up to do."

"I see," she laughed. "Well, I do recall a proposal being made. How about we start with that?"

"Oh, so *now* you want to wed?" Aeron snorted, though he was secretly elated she was finally going to be his wife. It was an affirmation of her belief in their future together. "I do not know if I want to marry you. You mortal women are a fickle lot."

"Fickle?" Melia exclaimed playfully. "You elves are stubborn!"

With a grin, he pulled her close once more and replied before kissing her again, "I am not the only one."

Coming in October 2016

THE FAIRER SEX
BOOK THREE IN THE AVALYNE SERIES

About the Author

Linda Thackeray works at a publishing company a stone's throw from the Sydney Opera House in Australia, but lives on the coast in a suburb called Woy Woy, which apparently means "big lagoon" with her one cat, Newt. She has been writing for as long as she can remember and has never really stopped, although she has not written seriously for at least a decade. She had an epiphany moment a few months ago that made her decide to take it up again and now she is dusting off all the work she has let languish to take stab at e-publishing.

Lightning Source UK Ltd.
Milton Keynes UK
UKHW011234091120
373077UK00006B/1017

9 781715 758219